Scott Bradfield's

D R E A M   O F   T H E   W O L F

"Haunted with intimations of otherness...Bradfield is an amanuensis of alternative lives."

—The New York Times Book Review

"Scott Bradfield's stories are ironic, funny, and at the same time filled with a haunting tension between the ordinary lives we lead and the darker dreams that lurk at the edge of our minds. He is the most original voice of the new generation of California writers."

—Brian Moore

"Alternately haunting, humorous and ironic. Through the eyes of [Bradfield's] troubled characters we experience the disturbing effects of urban culture on the contemporary consciousness."

—Milwaukee Journal

"From time to time, authors bubble up with particularly restless imaginations. Scott Bradfield...is conspicuously one of these. Bradfield is a writer with an admirable mastery over words. The language flows like a swift, smooth river, and he is particularly winning with images that tell more than they say."

—Hartford Courant

DREAM OF THE WOLF

DREAM OF

VINTAGE CONTEMPORARIES

VINTAGE BOOKS

A DIVISION OF RANDOM HOUSE, INC.

NEW YORK

THE WOLF

STORIES BY

SCOTT BRADFIELD

FIRST VINTAGE CONTEMPORARIES EDITION, FEBRUARY 1992

Copyright © 1983, 1984, 1988, 1989, 1990 by Scott Bradfield

Many of these stories originally appeared in *The Secret Life of Houses,* published in Great Britain by Unwin Hyman Limited, London, in 1988. Copyright © 1983, 1984, 1988 by Scott Bradfield.

The author gratefully acknowledges the following publications, in which some of the stories in this book originally appeared: *Ambit, Interzone, Omni, Other Edens II, Soho Square II, The Tampa Review, Tarot Tales,* and *Twilight Zone Magazine.*

Library of Congress Cataloging-in-Publication Data
Bradfield, Scott.
Dream of the wolf : stories / by Scott Bradfield. — 1st Vintage
contemporaries ed.
p.   cm. — (Vintage contemporaries)
"Originally published in hardcover by Alfred A. Knopf, Inc.,
New York, in 1990"—T.p. verso.
ISBN 0-679-73638-7
I. Title.
[PR6052.R2515D74   1992]
823'.914—dc20   91-50037
CIP

BOOK DESIGN BY PETER A. ANDERSEN

Manufactured in the United States of America
10   9   8   7   6   5   4   3   2   1

FOR SONNY MEHTA

CONTENTS

DREAM OF THE WOLF

THE DREAM OF
THE WOLF

*Without the dream one would have found no occasion
for a division of the world.* — NIETZSCHE

"Last night I dreamed I was *Canis lupus tundrarum,* the Alaskan
tundra wolf," Larry Chambers said, confronted by hot Cream
O' Wheat, one jelly donut, black coffee with sugar. "I was
surrounded by a vast white plain and sparse gray patches of
vegetation. I loped along at a brisk pace, quickening the hot
pulse of my blood. I felt extraordinarily swift, hungry, powerful. . . ." Larry gripped his donut; red jelly squirted across his
knuckles. "My jaws were enormous, my paws heavy and callused." He took a bite, chewed with his mouth open. "My pelt
was thick and white and warm. The cold breeze carried aromas
of fox, rabbit, caribou, rodent, fowl, mollusc. . . ."

"Caroline!" Sherryl Chambers reached for the damp dish-
cloth. "Eat over the table, *please.* Just look at this. You've
dripped cereal all over your new shoes."

Caroline gazed up intently at her father, her chin propped
against the table edge. Her fist gripped a grainy spoon.

"I heard a noise behind me and I turned." Larry warmed his palms against the white coffee cup. "The mouse hesitated—just for a moment—and then quickly I pounced, pinned him beneath my paw. His eyes were wide with panic, his tiny heart fluttered wildly. His fear blossomed in the air like pollen—"

"What did you do, Daddy? What did you do to the mouse?"

Larry observed the clock radio. *KRQQ helicopter watch for a Monday, March twenty-third,* the radio said. *An overturned tanker truck has traffic backed up all the way to the Civic Center. . . .*

"I ate him," Larry said. The time was eight-fifteen.

"Caroline. Finish your cereal before it gets cold."

"But Daddy's a wolf again, Mommy. He caught a mouse and he *ate* it."

"I'm practically certain it was the *tundrarum*," Larry said, and pulled on his sport coat.

"Please, Caroline. I won't ask you again."

"But I want the rest of Daddy's donut."

"Finish your cereal. *Then* we'll discuss Daddy's donut."

"I think I'll stop by the library again tonight." Larry got up from the table. His spoon remained gripped by the thickening cereal like a fossil in La Brea.

"Sure, honey. And pick up some milk on the way home, will you? *Try* and remember."

"I will," Larry said, "I'll try," recalling the brilliant white ice, the warm easy taste of the blood.

"And here—bend over." Sherryl moistened the tip of a napkin with her lips. "There's jelly all over your face."

"It's the blood, Daddy. It's the mouse's blood."

"Thanks," Larry said, and went into the living room.

Caroline watched the kitchen door swing shut. After a few moments she heard the front door open and close.

"Daddy forgot to kiss me goodbye," she said.

Sherryl spilled pots and pans into the sink. "Daddy's a little preoccupied this morning, dear."

Caroline thought for a moment. The bitten jelly donut sat in the middle of the table like a promise.

"Daddy ate a mouse," she said finally, and made a proud little flourish in the air with her spoon.

Canis lupus youngi, canis lupus crassodon, canis niger rufus, Larry thought, and boarded the RTD at Beverly and Fairfax. The wolf, he thought. The wolf of the dream, the wolf of the world. He showed the driver his pass. Wolves in Utah, Northern Mexico, Baffin Island, even Hollywood. Wolves secretly everywhere, Larry thought, and moved down the crowded aisle. Elderly women jostled fitfully in their seats like birds on a wire.

"Larry! Hey—Spaceman!"

Andrew Prytowsky waved his *Wall Street Journal.* "Sit here." He removed his briefcase from the window seat and placed it in his lap. "Rest that frazzled brain of yours. You may need it later."

"Thanks," Larry said, squeezed into the vacant seat and recalled an exotic afternoon nap. *Canis lupus chanco,* Tibetan spring, crepuscular hour. His pack downed a goat. Blood spattered the gray dust like droplets of quivering mercury.

"*That's* earnings, Larry. *That's* reliable income. *That's* retirement security, a summer cottage, a sporty new car." Andrew shook the American Exchange Index at him, as if reproving an unhousebroken puppy. "Fifteen points in two weeks, just like I promised. Did you hear me? *Fifteen* points. Consolidated Plastics Ink. Plastic bullets, the weapon of the future. Cheap, easy to manufacture, minimal production overhead. You could have cut yourself a piece of that, Larry. I certainly gave you every opportunity. But then *my* word's not good enough for you, is it? You've already got your savings account, your fixed interest, your automatic teller, your free promotional albums. You've got yourself a coffin—*that's* what you've got. Fixed interest is going to bury you. Listen to me, pal. I can help. Let's talk tax-free municipal bonds for just one second—"

Larry sighed and gazed out the smudged window. Outside the Natural History Museum sidewalk vendors sold hot dogs, lemonade and pretzels while behind them ancient bones surfaced occasionally from the bubbling tar pit.

". . . in the long run we're not just talking safety. We're talking variable income *and* easy liquidity." Prytowsky slapped Larry's chest with the rolled-up newspaper. "Get *with* it, Spaceman. What are you now? Late thirties, early forties? You want to spend the rest of your life with your head in the clouds? Or do you want to come back down to earth and enjoy a little of the *good* life? Your little girl—Carol, Karen, whatever. She may be four or five now, pal, but college is *tomorrow*. *Tomorrow*, Spaceman. And you want your little girl to go to college, don't you? Well, *don't* you? Of *course* you do! Of *course*!"

The traffic light turned green, the RTD's clutch connected with a sudden sledgehammer sound. Oily gray smoke swirled outside the window.

"And what about that devilish little wife of yours? Take it from me, Spaceman. A woman's eye is *always* looking out for those greener pastures. It's not their *fault,* Spaceman—it's just their *nature*. . . . Hey, *Larry*." The rolled-up newspaper jabbed Larry's side. "You even listening to me or what?"

"Sure," Larry said, and the bus entered Beverly Hills. Exorbitant hood ornaments flashed in the sun like grails. "Easy liquidity, interest variations. I'll think about it. I really will. It's just I have a lot on my mind right now, that's all. I mean, I'll get back to you on all this. I really will." *Canis lupus arabs, pallipes, baileyi, nubilis, monstrabilis,* he thought. The wolves of the dream, the wolves of the world.

"Still having those nutty dreams of yours, Spaceman? Your wife told my wife. You dream you're a dog or something?"

"A wolf. *Canis lupus*. It's not even the same subspecies as a dog."

"Oh." Andrew discarded his newspaper under his seat. "Sure."

"Wolves are far more intelligent than any dog. They're fiercer hunters, loyaler mates. Their social organization a-lone—"

"Yeah—right, Spaceman. I stand corrected. I'll bet in your dreams you really raise hell with those stupid dogs—hey, Larry, old pal?" Andrew said, and disboarded with his brief-case at Westwood Boulevard.

As the bus approached 27th Avenue Larry moved back through the crowd of passengers who stood and sat about with news-papers, magazines and detached expressions as they vacantly chewed Certs, peanuts from a bag, impassive bubble gum, like a herd of grazing buffalo while the wolf, the wolf of Larry's mind, roamed casually among them, searching out the weak, the sickly, the injured, the ones who always betrayed them-selves with brief and anxious glances—the elderly woman with the aluminum walker, the gawky adolescent with the bad com-plexion and crooked teeth. Wolves in Tibet, Montana, South America, Micronesia, Larry thought, disembarked at 25th Avenue and entered Tower Tire and Rubber Company. He showed his pass to the security guard, then rode the humming elevator to the twelfth floor. When Larry stepped into the foyer the secretaries, gathered around the receptionist's desk, ex-changed quick significant glances like secret memoranda. Larry heard them giggling as he disappeared into the maze of high white partitions that organized office cubicles like discrete cells in an ant farm.

Larry entered his office.

"Ready for Monday?" Marty Cabrillo asked.

Larry hung his coat on the rack, turned.

The marketing supervisor stood in front of Larry's alumi-num bookshelf, gazing aimlessly at the spines of large gray

Acco-Grip binders. "Frankly," Marty said, "I'd rather be in Shasta. How was your weekend?"

"Fine, just fine," Larry said, sat down at his desk and opened the top desk drawer.

"I thought I'd drop by and see if the Orange County sales figures were in yet. Didn't mean to barge in, you know."

"Certainly. Help yourself." Larry gestured equivocally with his right hand, rummaged in the desk drawer with his left.

"Ed Conklin called from Costa Mesa and said he still hasn't received the Goodyear flyers. I told him no problem—you'd get right back to him. All right?"

"Right." Larry slammed shut one drawer and pulled open another. "No problem. Here we are . . ." He removed a large faded-green hardcover book. One of the book's corners was bloated with dog-eared pages. Larry wiped off dust and bits of paper against his trousers. *The Wolves of North America: Part 1, Classification of Wolves.*

Marty propped one hand casually in his pocket. "I hope you don't take this the wrong way or anything, Larry . . . I mean, I'm not trying to pull rank on you or anything. But maybe you could try being just a little bit more careful around here the next few weeks or so. Think of it as a friendly warning, okay?"

Larry looked up from his book.

"It's not me, Larry." Marty placed his hand emphatically over his heart. "You know me, right? But district managers are starting to complain. Late orders, unitemized bills, stuff like that. *Harmless* stuff, really. Nothing I couldn't cover for you. But the guys upstairs aren't so patient—that's all I'm trying to say. I'm just trying to say it's my job, too. All right?"

Finally Larry located the *tundrarum*'s subspecies guide. *Type locality: Point Barrow, Alaska. Type Specimen: No. 16748, probably female, skull only, U.S. National Museum; collected by Lt. P. H. Ray . . .*

"But for God's sake don't take any of this personal or anything. It's not really serious. Everybody has their off days—it's just the way things go. People get, well, *distracted*."

"I knew it." Larry pointed at the page. "Just what I thought. Look—*tundrarum* is 'closely allied to *pambisileus*.' Exactly as I suspected. The dentition was a dead giveaway."

Marty fumbled for a cigarette from his shirt pocket, a Bic lighter from his slacks. "Well," he said, and took a long drag from his Kool. Then, after a moment, "You know, Larry, Beatrice and I have always been interested in this ecology stuff ourselves. You should visit our cabin in Shasta sometime. There's nothing like it—clean air, trees, privacy. We even joined the Sierra Club last year. . . . But look, I could talk about this stuff all day, but we've *both* got to get back to work, right?" Marty paused outside the cubicle. "We'll get together and talk about it over lunch sometime, okay? And maybe you could drop the sales figures by my office later? Before noon, maybe?"

That night Larry returned home after the dinner dishes had been washed. He glanced into Caroline's room. She was asleep. Stuffed wolves, cubs and one incongruous unicorn lay toppled around her on the bed like dominoes. He found Sherryl in the master bedroom, applying Insta-Curls to her hair and balancing a black rectangular apparatus in her lap.

Larry sat on the edge of the bed, glimpsed himself in the vanity mirror. He had forgotten to shave that morning. His eyes were dark, sunken, feral. (The lone wolf lopes across an empty plain. Late afternoon, clear blue sky. The pale crescent moon appears on the horizon like a specter. Other wolves howl in the distance.)

Larry turned to his wife. "I went all the way out to the UCLA Research Library, then found out the school's between quarters. The library closed at five."

"That's too bad, dear. Would you plug that in for me?"

Sherryl pulled a plastic cap over her head. Two coiled black wires attached the cap to the black rectangular box. Larry connected the plug to the wall socket and the black box began to hum. Gradually the plastic cap inflated. "Larry, I wish I knew how to phrase this a bit more delicately, but it's been on my mind a lot lately." Sherryl turned the page of a K Mart Sweepstakes Sale brochure. "You may not believe this, Larry, but there are actually people in this world who like to talk about some things besides *wolves* every once in a blue moon."

Larry turned again to his reflection. He had forgotten to finish Cabrillo's sales figures. Tomorrow, he assured himself. First thing.

"I remember when we had decent conversations. We went out occasionally. We went to movies, or even dancing. Do you remember the last time we went out together—I mean, just out of the *house*? It was that horrid PTA meeting last fall, with that dreadful woman—the hunchback with the butterfly glasses, you remember? Something about a rummage sale and new tether poles? Do you *know* how long ago that was? And frankly, Larry, I wouldn't call that much of a night *out*."

Larry ran his hand lightly along the smooth edge of the humming black box. "Look, honey. I know I get a little out of hand sometimes . . . I *know* that. Especially lately." He placed his hand on his forehead. A soft pressure seemed to be increasing inside his skull, like an inflating plastic cap. "I've been forgetful . . . and I realize I must seem a little nutty at times. . . ." The wolves, he thought, trying to strengthen himself. The call of the pack, the track of the moon, the hot quick pulse of the blood. But the wolves abruptly seemed very far away. "I know you don't understand. *I* don't really understand. . . . But these aren't just dreams. When I'm a wolf, I'm *real*. The places I see, the feelings I feel—they're *real*. As real as I am now, talking to you. As real as this bed." He grasped the king-size silk comforter. "I'm not making all this up. . . . And I'll *try* to be a little more thoughtful. We'll go out to dinner this weekend, I promise. But try putting up with me a little longer. Give me a little credit, that's all . . ."

Sherryl glanced up. She took the humming black box from his hand.

"Did you say something, hon?" She patted the plastic cap. "Hold on and I'll be finished in a minute." She turned another page of the brochure. Then, with a heavy red felt marker, she circled the sale price of Handi-Wipes.

Larry walked into the bathroom and brushed his gleaming white teeth.

"Last night I dreamed of the Pleistocene."

"Where is that, Daddy?"

"It's not a place, honey. It's a time. A long time ago."

"You mean dinosaurs, Daddy? Did you dream you were a *dinosaur?*"

"No, darling. The dinosaurs were all gone by then. I was *canis dirus,* I think. I'll check on it. The tundra was far colder and more desolate than before. The sky was filled with this weird, reddish glow I've never seen before, like the atmosphere of some alien planet. Ice was everywhere. Three of us remained in the pack. My mate had died the previous night beneath a shelf of ice while the rest of us huddled around to keep her warm. Dominant, I led the others across the white ice, my tail slightly erect. We were terribly cold, tired, hungry . . ."

"Weren't there any mice, Daddy? Or any snails?"

"No. We had traveled for days. We had discovered no spoor. Except one."

"Was it a deer, Daddy? Did you kill the deer and eat it?"

"No. It was Man's spoor. We were seeking an encampment of men." He turned. Sherryl was beating eggs into a bowl and watching David Hartman on the portable television. "Sherryl, that was the strangest part. I've read about it, anthropologists have suggested it—a prehistoric, communal bond between man and wolf. We weren't afraid. We sought shelter with them, food, companionship, allies in the hunt."

Larry watched his wife. After a moment she said, "That's nice, dear."

David Hartman said, "Later in this half hour we'll be meeting Lorna Backus to discuss her new hit album, and then take an idyllic trip up the coast to scenic New Hampshire, the Granite State, as part of our 'States of the Union' series. Please stay with us."

"I've always wanted to live in New Hampshire," Sherryl said.

Every day on his way home from work Larry stopped at the Fairfax branch library. Many of the books he needed he had to request through interlibrary loan. He read Lopez's *Of Wolves and Men*, Fox's *The Soul of the Wolf*, Mech's *The Wolf: The Ecology and Behavior of an Endangered Species*, Pimlott's *The World of the Wolf*, Mowat's *Never Cry Wolf*, Ewer's *The Carnivores*, and the pertinent articles and symposiums published in *American Zoologist*, *American Scientist*, *Journal of Zoology*, *Journal of Mammalogy* and *The Canadian Field Naturalist*. Sherryl pulled the blankets off the bed one day and three books came loose, thudding onto the floor. "I'd really appreciate it, Larry, if you could start picking up after yourself. It's bad enough with Caroline. And just look—this one's almost a month overdue." Larry returned them to the library that night, checked out three more, and xeroxed the "Canids" essay in *Grzimek's Animal Life Encyclopedia*.

On the way out the door he noticed a three-by-five file card tacked to the Community Billboard. *Spiritual Counseling, Dream Analysis, Budget Rates, Free Parking.* Her name was Anita Louise. She lived on the top floor of a faded Sunset Boulevard brownstone, and claimed to be circuitously related to Tina Louise, the former star of *Gilligan's Island*. Her living room was furnished with tattered green lawn chairs and orange-crate bookshelves. She required a personal item; Larry handed her his watch. She closed her eyes. "I can see the wolf now," she said. Her fingers smudged the watch's crystal face, wound the stem, tested the flexible metal band. "While he leads you through the forest of life, he warns you of the thorny paths. When the time comes, he will lead you into Paradise."

"The wolf doesn't guide me," Larry said. "I *am* the wolf. Sometimes *I* am the guide, the leader of my pack."

"The ways of the spirit world are often baffling to those unlearned in its ways," Anita told him. "I take Visa and MasterCard. I take personal checks, but I need to see at least two pieces of I.D."

Before he left, Larry reminded her about his watch.

"I don't know, Evelyn. I really just don't know. I mean, I *love* Larry and all, but you can't imagine how difficult life's been around here lately—especially the last few months." Sherryl held the telephone receiver with her left hand, a cold coffee cup with her right. She listened for a moment. "No, Evelyn, I don't think *you* understand. This isn't a hobby. It's not as if Larry was collecting stamps, or a *bowler* or something. I could understand that. *That* would be understandable. But all Larry talks about anymore is wolves. Wolves this and wolves that. Wolves at the dinner table, wolves in bed, wolves even when we're driving to the market. Wolves are everywhere, he keeps saying. And honestly, Evelyn, sometimes I almost believe him. I start looking over my shoulder. I hear a dog bark and I make sure the door's bolted. . . . Well, of *course* I try to be understanding. I'm trying to tell you that. But I have to worry about Caroline too, you know. . . . Well, listen for a minute and I'll tell you what happened yesterday. We're sitting at breakfast, you see, and Larry starts telling Caroline—a four-year-old girl, remember—how he's off in the woods somewhere, God only knows *where,* and he meets this female dog and, well, I can't go on. . . . No, I simply can't. It's too embarrassing. . . . No, Evelyn. You've completely missed the point. It's mating season, get it? And Larry starts going into explicit detail. . . . Well, maybe. But that's not even the worst part. . . . Hold *on* for one second and I'll tell you. They, well, I don't know how to phrase this delicately. They get *stuck.* . . . *No,* Evelyn. Honestly, some-times I don't think you're even listening to me. They get stuck *together.* Can you believe that? What am I supposed to say? Caroline's not going to outgrow a trauma like this, though. I can promise you that." Sherryl heard the kitchen door opening behind her. "Hold on, Evelyn," she said, and turned.

Caroline blocked the door open with her foot. "What are you talking about?" Her hand gripped the plastic Pez dispenser. Wylie Coyote's head was propped back by her thumb, and a small pink lozenge extruded from his throat.

"It's Evelyn, dear. We're just talking."

Caroline's lips were flushed and purple; purple stains speck-led her white dress. She thought for a moment, took the candy with her teeth and chewed. Finally she said, "I think somebody may have spilled grape juice on one of Daddy's wolf books."

Larry read Guy Endore's *The Werewolf of Paris,* Hesse's *Step-penwolf,* Rowland's *Animals With Human Faces,* Pollard's *Wolves and Werewolves,* Lane's *The Wild Boy of Aveyron,* Malson's *Wolf Children and the Problem of Human Nature.* Marty gave him the card of a Jungian in Topanga Canyon who sat Larry in a plush chair, said "archetype" a few times, informed him that *everyone* is fascinated with evil, sadism, pain ("It's perfectly normal, per-fectly *human*"), recommended Robert Eisler's *Man into Wolf,* charged seventy-five dollars and offered him a Valium prescription with refill. "But when I'm a wolf, I never know evil," Larry said as he was ushered out the door by a blond receptionist. "When I'm a wolf, I know only peace."

"I don't know, Larry. It just gives me the creeps," Sherryl said that night after Caroline was in bed. "It's *weird,* that's what it is. Bullying defenseless little mice and deer that never hurt anybody. Talking about killing, and blood, and ice—and particularly at *break fast.*"

Larry was awake until 2:00 a.m. watching *The Wolf Man* on Channel Five. Claude Raines said, "There's good and evil in every man's soul. In this case, the evil takes the shape of a wolf." No, Larry thought, and read Freud's *The Case of the Wolf-Man,* the first chapter of Mack's *Nightmares and Human Conflict.* No. Then he went to bed and dreamed of the wolves.

"The wolf spirit has always been considered very *wakan*," Hungry Bear said, his feet propped on his desk. He poked out his cigarette against the rim of the metal wastebasket, then prepared to light another. "Most tribes believe the wolf's howl portends bad things. The Lakota say, 'The man who dreams of the wolf is not really on his guard, but the man haughtily closes his eyes, for he is very much on his guard.' I don't know what that means, exactly, but I read it somewhere." Hungry Bear refilled his Dixie Cup with vin rosé. His grimy T-shirt was taut against his large stomach; a band of pale skin bordered his belt. He wore a plaid Irish derby atop his braided hair. "I try to do a good deal of reading," he said, and fumbled in his diminished pack of Salems.

"So do I," Larry said. "Maybe you could recommend—"

"I don't think the wolf was ever recognized as any sort of deity, but I could be wrong." Hungry Bear was watching the smoke unravel from his cigarette. "But still, you shouldn't be too worried. It's very common for animal spirits to possess a man. They use his body when he's asleep. When he awakes, he can't remember anything . . . oh, but wait. That's not quite right, is it? You said you *remember* your dreams? Well, again, I could be wrong. I guess you *could* remember. Sure, I don't see why not," Hungry Bear said, and poured more vin rosé.

"*I* inhabit the body of the *wolf*," Larry said, beginning to lose interest, and glanced around the cluttered office. The venetian blinds were cracked and dusty, the floors littered with tattered men's magazines, empty wine bottles and crumpled cigarette packs. After a moment he added, "I don't even know what I should call you. *Mister* Bear?"

"No, of course not." Hungry Bear waved away the notion, dispersing smoke. "Call me Jim. That's my real name. Jim Prideux. I took Hungry Bear for business purposes. If you remember, Hungry Bear was the brand name of a terrific canned chili. It was discontinued after the war, though, I'm afraid." He checked his shirt pocket. "Do you see a pack of cigarettes over there? Seems I'm running short."

"You're not Indian?" Larry asked.

"Sure. Of course I'm Indian. One-eighth pure Shoshone. My great-grandmother was a Shoshone princess. Well, maybe not a princess, exactly. But *her* father was an authentic medicine man. I've inherited the gift." Jim Prideux rummaged through the papers on his desk. "Are you sure you don't see them? I'm sure I bought a pack less than an hour ago."

"This is very nice," Sherryl said, and swallowed her last bite of red snapper. She touched her lips delicately with the napkin. "It's *so* nice to get out of the house for a change. You wouldn't know how much."

"Sure I would, darling," Andrew Prytowsky said, and poured more Chenin Blanc.

"No, I don't think you would, Andy. Your wife, Danielle, is *normal*. You wouldn't know what it's like living with someone as . . . well, as *unstable* as Larry's been acting lately."

"I'm sure it's been very difficult for you."

"Marty Cabrillo, Larry's boss at work, got Larry in touch with a doctor, a *good* doctor. Larry visits him *once* and then tells me he isn't going anymore. I say to Larry, don't you think he can help you? And Larry says no, he can't, he can't help him at all. He says the doctor is *stupid*. Can you believe that? I say to Larry, this man has a *Ph.D.* I don't think you can just call a man with a Ph.D. *stupid*. And so then Larry says *I* don't know what *I'm* talking about, either. Larry thinks he knows more than a man with a Ph.D. That's what Larry thinks."

"Here. Why don't you finish it?" Andrew put down the empty bottle and flagged the waiter with his upraised MasterCard.

"I'm sorry, Andy." Sherryl dabbed her eyes with the napkin. "It's just I'm so shook up lately. All I ever asked for was a normal life. That's not too much, is it? A nice home, a normal husband. Someone who could give me a little help and support. Is that too much to ask? Is it?"

"Of course not." Andrew signed the check. After the waiter left he said, "I'm glad we could do this."

Sherryl folded her napkin and replaced it on the table. "I'm glad you called. This was very nice."

"We'll do it again."

"Yes," Sherryl said. "We should."

Two weeks later Larry returned home from work and found the letter on the kitchen table.

Dear Larry,
I know you're going to take this the wrong way and I only hope you realize Caroline and I still care about you but I've thought about this a lot and even sought professional coun-

seling on one occasion and I think it's the only solution right now at this moment in our lives. Especially for Caroline who is at a very tender age. Please don't try calling because I told my mother not to tell you where we are for a while. Please realize I don't want to hurt you and this will probably be better for both of us in the long run, and I hope you make it through your difficulties and I'll think good thoughts for you often.

Sherryl

"You can't just keep moping around, Larry. Things'll get better, just you wait. I sense big improvements coming in your life. But first you've *got* to start being more careful around the office." Marty sat on the edge of Larry's desk. He pulled a string of magnetized paper clips in and out of a clear plastic dispenser. "Did I tell you Henderson asked about you yesterday? Asked about you *by name*. Now, I'm not trying to make you paranoid or anything, but if Henderson asked about you, then you can bet your socks the *rest* of the guys in Management have been tossing your name around. And Henderson's not a bad guy, Larry. I'm not suggesting that. But there's been a sincere . . . a sincere *concern* about your performance around here lately. And don't think I don't understand. Really, Larry, I'm very sensitive to your position. Beatrice and I came close to breaking up a couple times ourselves—and I don't know *what* I'd do without Betty and the kids. But you've got to keep your chin up, buddy. Plow straight ahead. And remember—I'm on *your* side."

At his desk, Larry made careful, persistent marks on a sheet of graph paper. The frequency of dreams had increased over the past few weeks: the line on the graph swooped upward. Often three, even four times a night he started awake in bed, clicked on the reading lamp and reached for a pen and notepad from the end table, quickly jotting down terrain and subspecies characteristics while the aromas of forest, desert and tundra were displaced by the close, stale odors of grimy bedsheets, leftover Swanson frozen dinner entrées, and Johnson's Chlorophyll-Scented Home Deodorizer.

"I'm really sincere about this, Larry. I can't keep covering for you. I need some assurances, I need to start seeing some real *effort* on your part. You're going to start seeing Dave Boudreau on the third floor. He's our employee stress counselor—but that doesn't mean he's like a shrink or anything, Larry. I know how you feel about *them*. Dave Boudreau's just a regular guy like you and me who happens to have a lot of experience with these sorts of problems. You and Sherryl, I mean. All right, Larry? Does that sound fair to you?"

"Sure, Marty," Larry said, "I appreciate your help, I really do," and peeled another sheet from the Thrifty pad. Abscissa, he thought: real time. Ordinate: dream time. At the top of the page he scribbled *Pleistocene*.

"I'm dreaming now more than ever," Larry told Dave Boudreau the following Thursday. "Sometimes half a dozen times each night. Look, I've kept a record—" Larry opened a large red loose-leaf binder, flipped through a sheaf of papers and unclamped a sheet of graph paper. "There, that's last Friday. Six times." He held the sheet of paper over the desk, pointing at it. "And Sunday—*seven* times. And that's not even the significant part. I haven't even got to *that* part yet."

Dave Boudreau sat behind his desk and rocked slightly in a swivel chair. He glanced politely at the statistical chart. Then his abstract gaze returned to Tahitian surf in a framed travel poster. He heard the binder clamp click again.

Larry pulled up his chair until the armrests knocked the edge of the desk. "Increasingly I dream of the Pleistocene, the Ice

Age. The Great Hunt, when man and wolf hunted together, bound by one pack, responsible to one community, seeking their common prey across the cold ice, beneath the cold sun. Is *that* something? Is that one hell of an archetype or what?"

Casually Boudreau opened the manila folder on his desk.

CHAMBERS, LAWRENCE
SUPPLIES AND SERVICES DEPARTMENT
BORN: 3-6-45   EYES: BLUE

"And don't get me wrong. I'm just kidding about that archetype stuff. That's not even close, that's not even in the same ballpark. These aren't memories, for chrissakes. When I dream of the wolf, I *am* the wolf. I've been wolves in New York, Montana and Beirut. It's as if time and space, dream and reality, have just *opened up*, joined me with everything, everything *real*. I'm living the *one life,* understand? The life of the hunter and the prey, the dream and the world, the blood and the spirit. It's really spectacular, don't you think? Have you ever heard anything like it?"

In the space reserved for Counselor's Comments Boudreau scribbled "wolf nut," and underlined it three times.

When Larry arrived at work the following Monday the security guard took his I.D. card and, after consulting his log, asked him to please wait one moment. The guard picked up his phone and asked the operator for Personnel Management. "This is station six. Mr. Lawrence Chambers has just arrived." The guard listened quietly to the voice at the other end. He snapped his pencil against the desk in four-four time.

Finally he put down the phone and said, "I'm sorry. I'll have to keep your card. Would you please follow me?"

They walked down the hall to Payroll. Larry was given his

final paycheck and, in a separate envelope, another check for employee minimum compensation.

By the time Larry returned home it was still only 10:00 a.m. He cleared the old newspapers from the stoop, unbound and opened the whitest, most recent one. He read for a few minutes, then refolded the paper and placed it with the others beside the fireplace. He picked up Harrington and Paquet's *Wolves of the World* and put it down again. He got up and walked to the kitchen. Dishes piled high in the sink, four full bags of trash. The few remaining dishes in the dishwasher were swirled with white mineral deposits. In the refrigerator he found a garlic bulb with long green shoots, an empty bottle of Worcestershire sauce and an egg. He drank stale apple juice from the plastic green pitcher, then continued making his rounds. In the bathroom: toothpaste, toothbrush, comb, water glass, eye drops, Mercurochrome, a stray bandage, Sherryl's pH-balanced Spring Mountain shampoo, his electric razor. All the clothes and toys were gone from Caroline's room. Over the bed the poster of a wolf gazed down at him, its eyes sharp, canny, primitively alert.

He tried to watch television. People won sailboats and trash compactors on game shows, cheated one another and plotted financial coups on soap operas. After a while he got up again and returned to the bathroom, opened the medicine cabinet. Johnson's Baby Aspirin, an old stiffened toothbrush, mouthwash, a bobby pin. High on the top shelf he found Sherryl's Seconal in a childproof bottle. He took two. Then he got into bed.

Sometime after dawn he dreamed again of the wolves, but this time the dream was fragmentary and detached. He viewed the wolves from very far away. From atop a high bluff, perhaps, or hidden behind some bushes like Jane Goodall. The wolves moved down into the gully and paused before a small stream, drinking. Two cubs splashed and chased one another through the puddles. The other wolves observed them dispassionately. The sun was going down. Larry woke up. It was just past 6:00 a.m.

He stayed indoors throughout the day. In the evening he might walk to the corner Liquor Mart to cash a check and purchase milk, scotch, Stouffer's frozen dinners. Sometimes, remembering Sherryl and Caroline, he turned the television up louder. It wasn't their physical presence he missed (he could hardly recall their faces anymore) but rather their noise: the clatter of dishes, the inconstant whir and jingle of mechanical toys. Soundless, the air seemed thinner, staler, more oppressive, as if he were sealed inside an airtight crystal vault. The silence invested everything—the walls, the furniture, the diminishing vial of Seconal, the large empty bedrooms, even the mindless chatter of the Flintstones on television. He drank his beer beside the front window and watched the dust swirl soundlessly in the soundless shafts of light, recalling the wolves and the soundless expanse of white ice where not only the noise but even the aromas and textures of the landscape seemed to be leaking from the dreamlike atmosphere, as if from the cracks in some domed underwater city. In the mornings, now, he hardly recalled his dreams at all anymore. Sporadic glimpses of wolf, prey, sky, moon, interspliced meaninglessly like the frames of some surrealist montage. He smoked three packs of cigarettes a day, just to give his hands something to do. The scotch and Seconal compelled him to take so many naps during the day that he couldn't sleep at night. Wolves, he thought. Wolves in Utah, Baffin Island, Tibet, even Hollywood. Wolves secretly everywhere . . . Eventually the dreams disappeared entirely. Sleep became a dark visionless place where nothing ever happened.

The Seconal, he thought one morning, and departed for the library. He squinted at the sunlight, staggered occasionally. People looked at him. A book entitled *Sleep* by Gay Gaer Luce and Julius Siegal confirmed his suspicions. Alcohol and barbiturates suppressed the dream stage of sleep. He returned home and poured the scotch down the sink, the remaining Seconal down the toilet. He lay in bed throughout the afternoon, night and following morning. He tossed and turned. He couldn't keep his eyes closed more than a minute. His heart palpitated disconcertingly. He tried to remember the wolf's image, and remembered only pictures in books. He tried to recall the prey's hot, steaming blood, and tasted only yesterday's Chicken McNuggets. He wanted the map of the sky, and found only the close, humid rectangle of the bedroom. He got up and went into the living room. It was night again. In order to dream, he must sleep. In order to regain the real, he must dispel the illusion: newspapers, furniture, unswept carpets, Sherryl's letter, Caroline's toys, easy liquidity, magazines and books. He realized then that evil was not the wolf, but rather the wolf's disavowal. Violence wasn't something in nature, but rather something in nature's systematic repression. Madness isn't the dream, but rather the world deprived of the dream, he thought, selected a stale pretzel from the bowl, chewed and gazed out the window at the dim, empty streets below, where occasional streetlamps illuminated silent, unoccupied cars parked along the curbs. The moon made a faint impression against the high screen of fog. A distant siren wailed, a dog barked and in their homes the population slept fitfully, often aided by Seconal and Valium, descending through soft penetrable stages of sleep, seeking that fugitive half-world in which they struggled to dream beneath the repressive shadows of the real.

A few weeks after signing Larry Chambers's termination notice, Marty Cabrillo took his wife to Shasta. "Two weeks alone," he promised her. "We'll leave the kids with your mother. Just the two of us, the trees, candlelight dinners again, just like I always said it would be." But Marty said nothing during the long drive. Beatrice put her arm around him and he shrugged at her. "Please," he said. "I can't get comfortable." At the cabin they sat out on the sun deck. Marty held paperbacks and turned the pages. Beatrice read *People* magazine. After only a few days they returned home. "I'm sorry, honey," Marty said to her. "I'll make it up to you. I promise."

"What's the matter with you lately?"

"Nothing. Just things on my mind."

"Work?"

"Sort of."

After a while Beatrice said, "Larry," folded her arms and gazed out the window at Ventura car lots.

The following Sunday Marty drove to Ralph's in Fairfax, loaded four bags of groceries into his Toyota station wagon and drove to Larry's house on Clifton Boulevard. The front yard was brown and overgrown. Aluminum garbage cans, streaked with rust, lay overturned in the alley. Dormant snails studded the front of the house, their slick intricate trails glistening in the sunlight. Marty knocked, rang the bell a few times. The door was ajar and he pushed it open. A pyramid of bundled newspapers blocked the door, permitting him just to squeeze through. In the living room, torn magazines and moldy dishes lay strewn across the sofa, chairs and floor. The telephone receiver was off the hook, wailing faintly like a distant, premonitory siren. At first the room seemed oddly disproportionate, as if the furniture had all been rearranged. Then he noticed Larry asleep on the middle of the floor, his head propped by a sofa cushion, his arm wrapped around a leg of the coffee table. "He must've lost eighty, ninety pounds," Marty told Beatrice later that night. "His clothes stank, he hadn't shaved or washed in I don't know how long. And all I could think looking at him there was it's all *my* fault. *I* was responsible. Me, Marty Cabrillo."

Marty followed the ambulance to St. John's, wishing they

would run the siren. "Dehydration," the doctor told him, while Marty paid the deposit on a private room. Larry lay in a stiff, geometric white bed, a glucose bottle hanging beside him, a white tube connected to his arm by white adhesive tape. Every so often the glucose bubbled. "We'll bring him along slow, have him eating solid food in a couple days. I think he'll be all right," the doctor said, and handed Marty another form to sign.

"It's all my fault," Marty said when Larry regained consciousness the following morning. "Look, I brought you some books to read. And the flowers—they're from Sherryl. Beatrice got in touch with her last night and she's on her way here right now. The worst is over, pal. The worst is all behind you."

Later Sherryl told him, "We missed you. Caroline missed you. *I* missed you. Oh, Larry. You just look so *aw*ful." Sherryl laid her head in Larry's lap and cried, hugging him. Silently Larry stroked her long blond hair. Sherryl had been staying with her sister in Burbank, working as a secretary at one of the studios. Her boss was a flushed, obese little man who put his hand on her knee while she took dictation, or snuck up behind her every once in a while and gave her a sharp pinch. "Loosen up, relax. Life's short," he told her. Caroline hated her new nursery school and cried nearly every day. Sherryl's sister had begun bringing the classified pages home, pointing out to her the best bets on her own apartment. Andy had promised to help out, but every time she called his office his secretary said he was still out of town on business. And then one of the Volvo's tires went flat, and in all the rush of moving she realized she had misplaced her triple-A card, and so she just started crying, right there on the side of the freeway, because it seemed as if nothing, nothing ever went right for her anymore.

"We need you, Larry," Sherryl said. "You need us. I'm sorry what happened, but I always loved you. It wasn't because I didn't love you. And Marty thinks he can get your old job back—"

Marty leaned forward, whispered something.

"He says he's certain. He's certain he can get it back. Did you hear, honey? Everything's going to be all right. We're all going to be happy again, just like before."

Sherryl brought Caroline home a month later.

"Is Daddy home?" Caroline asked.

"He's at work now, honey. But he'll be back soon. He's missed you."

Caroline waited to be unbuckled, climbed out of the car. The front yard was green and delicate, the house repainted yellow. The place seemed only dimly familiar, like the photograph Mommy showed her of where she lived when she was born.

"All your toys are in your room, sweetheart. Be good and play for a while. Mommy'll fix dinner."

Caroline's room had been repainted too. Over her bed hung a bright new Yosemite Sam poster. She opened the oak toy chest. The toys were boxed and neatly arranged, just like on shelves at the store. She went into the bedroom and looked at Daddy's bookcase. The large picture books were gone, along with their photographs of wolves and deer and rabbits and forests and men with rifles and hairy, misshapen primitive men. Bent paperbacks had replaced them. The covers depicted beautiful men and women, Nazi insignia, secret dossiers, demonic children, cowboys on horses, murder weapons.

She heard the front door open. "Hi, honey. Sorry I'm late. I ran into Andy Prytowsky on the bus—remember him? I introduced you at a party last year. Anyway, I told him I'd drop by his office tomorrow. I figure it's time we started some sort of college fund for Caroline. I'm pretty excited about it. Andy says he can work us a nice little tax break, too. Oh, and look what else. I bought us some wine. For later."

Caroline walked halfway down the hall. Mommy and Daddy stood at the door, kissing.

"There she is. There's my little girl."

Daddy picked her up high in the air. His face seemed strange and unfamiliar, like the front of the house.

"So how have you been, sweetheart?" Daddy put her down.

"I'll finish dinner," Sherryl said.

"Come and sit down." Daddy led her to the sofa. "Tell me what you've been up to. Did you have fun at Aunt Judy's?"

Caroline picked at a scab on her knee. "I guess."

"What do you want to do? I thought we'd go to a movie later. Would you like that?"

Caroline clasped her hands in her lap. Here is the church, and here is the steeple. When you open the doors you see all the people.

"What should we do right now? Do you want to play a game? Do you want me to read you one of your Dr. Seuss books?"

Caroline thought for a while. Daddy's large, rough hand ran through her hair, snagging it. Delicately, she pushed his hand away.

"I want to watch television," she said after a while.

Three nights each week Larry went to the YMCA with Marty. Sherryl began subscribing to *Sunset Magazine,* and over dinner they discussed a new home, or at least improvements on their present one. Finally Marty suggested they buy into his Shasta property. "Betty and I don't make it up there more than three or four times a year. The rest of the time it'd be all yours." Larry took out a second mortgage, paid Marty a lump sum and began sharing the monthly payments. The first few months they drove up nearly every weekend. Then Larry received a promotion which required him to make weekly trips to the Bakersfield office. "I'm really bushed from all this driving," he told Sherryl. "We'll try and make Shasta *next* weekend." Caroline started grade school in the fall. Sherryl joined an ERA support group and was gone two nights a week. Occasionally Larry spent the night in Bakersfield, and drove from there directly to work the next morning.

"All I told Conklin was I've got a merchandise deficit from his store three months in a row. It wasn't like I called him a thief or anything. I just wanted an explanation. I'm entitled to that much, don't you think? It's my job, right?"

"I'm sure he didn't mean it, Larry. He was probably just upset." Sherryl sat on the sofa, smoking a cigarette.

"I'm sure he *was* upset. I'm sure he *was*." Larry sat at the dining room table. The table was covered with inventories, company billing statements and large gray Acco-Grip binders. His briefcase sat open on the chair beside him. "And now *I'm* a little upset, all right? Is that all right with you?"

"I'm sure you are, Larry. I was just saying maybe he didn't mean it, that's all. That's all I said."

Larry put down his pencil. "No. I don't think that's all you said."

Sherryl looked at the *TV Guide* on the coffee table, considered picking it up. Then she thought she heard Caroline's bedroom door squeak open down the hall.

"What you said was I'm imagining things. Isn't *that* what you said?"

Sherryl crushed out her cigarette. "Larry, I really wish you'd stop snapping at *me* every time you're mad at somebody." She got up and went to the end of the hall. "Caroline? Aren't you supposed to be in bed?"

Caroline's door squeaked shut. Sherryl watched the parallelogram of light on the hall floor diminish to a fine yellow line. "And turn off those lights, young lady. You heard me. Right now," Sherryl said. In high school Billy Mason had a crush on me, she thought, but I wouldn't give him the time of day. That morning she had seen Billy's picture on the cover of *Software World* at the supermarket.

"What I mean is, Larry, is that you're not the *only* person who's had a bad day sometimes—"

Sherryl was turning to face him when the telephone rang.

"Sometimes *my* day hasn't been that hot either," she said, and retreated to the telephone, picked up the receiver. "Hello?"

"Hi. Hello," the voice said. "I was hoping, well, I mean I didn't want to disturb anybody, but I wondered if Mr. Chambers was in. Mr. *Larry* Chambers, I think? Have I got that right?"

"This is his wife. Who's this?"

"Who is it?" Larry asked, picking up his pencil and jotting a number on his notepad.

Sherryl gazed expressionlessly over Larry's head at the dining room window and, beyond, the 7-Eleven marquee. The voice on the phone filled her ears like radio static. "—I mean, I just had the article here a moment ago, let me see . . . Look, tell him Hungry Bear called, and by the time he calls back I'll find the article—wait, in fact here it is right here—no, sorry, *that's* not it. But still, tell him Jim called. Jim Prideux—" Sherryl looked around the kitchen. She had forgotten to clean up after dinner. The sink was filled with dirty dishes, the countertop littered with bread crumbs. Stray Cheerios from that morning's breakfast had attached themselves like barnacles to the Formica table. She pulled up a chair and sat down, feeling suddenly tired. There was a television movie she had been looking forward to all week, and now, by the time she finished her cleaning, the show would practically be half over. She felt like saying to hell with it, to hell with all of it. She just wanted to go to bed. To hell with Larry, Caroline, the dishes, the vacuuming—every damn bit of it. The voice buzzed inconstantly in her ear like a mosquito, something about wolves, Navajo deities, sacred totems, irrepressible dreams of wolves, he wasn't exactly sure ... Wolves wolves wolves, wolves everywhere, she thought, and strengthened her grip on the receiver. "Listen to me," she said. "Listen to me, Mr. Bear, or Mr. Prideux, or Mr. Whoever You Are. Listen to me for just one minute, and I'll say this as *nicely* as I can. Please don't call here anymore. Larry's not interested, *I'm* not interested. Frankly, Mr. Bear, I don't think *anybody's* interested. I don't think anybody's really interested at all."

In Sherryl's dream the men and wolves loped together across the white plain. Larry was there, and Caroline, and Andy and Evelyn and Marty and Beatrice. Sherryl recognized the mailman, the newspaper boy, supermarket employees, former boyfriends and lovers. Even her parents were there, keeping pace with wolves under the cold moonlight. Everybody was dressed as usual: The men wore slacks, ties, cuff links and starched shirts; the women skirts, blouses, jewelry and high heels. Caroline carried one of her toys, Andy his briefcase, Marty his racquetball racket and Larry one of his largest gray Acco-Grip binders. Sherryl raised a greasy spatula in her right hand, a tarnished coffeepot in her left. We forgot to schedule Caroline's dental appointment, she told Larry. When I was a child you treated me as if I was stupid, she told her father, but I wasn't stupid. The sky is filled with stars, she told Davey Stewart, her high school sweetheart. The Milky Way: the Wolf's Trail. But nobody responded, nobody even seemed to notice her. The bright air was laced with the spoor of caribou. She felt a sudden elbow in her back; she turned and awoke in a dark room, a stiff bed. I forgot the shopping today, she thought. There isn't any milk in the house, or any coffee.

Beside her in bed, the man slowly moved.

Sherryl sat up, her pupils gradually dilating. Eventually she discerned the motel room's clean, uncluttered angles. The thin and fragile dressing table, the water glasses wrapped in wax paper, the hot plate, the aluminum-foil hot cocoa packets.

"What's the matter, baby?" Andrew sat up beside her, his arm encircling her waist. "Nightmare? Tell me, sweetheart. You can tell lover." He kissed her neck, stroked her warm stomach.

"Please, Andy. Not now. Please." Sherryl climbed out of bed. Her clothes lay folded on a wooden chair.

"Sorry. Forget it." Andrew rolled over, adjusted his pillow and listened to the rustle of Sherryl's clothing.

Sherryl stood at the window, gazing out through the blinds. Stars and moon were occluded by a high haze of lamplight. She heard the distant hishing of street sweepers, and pulled on her blouse. Then she heard the rain begin, drumming hollowly against the cheap plywood door.

Andrew took his watch from the end table. The luminous dial said almost 2:00 a.m. "I'll call you," he said.

"No," she said. "I'll call you this time. I need a few days to think." She opened the door and stepped out into the rain. They always do that, she thought. *They* have to be the ones who call, *they* have to be the ones who say when you'll meet or where you'll go. She pulled her coat collar up over her new perm, gripped the iron banister and descended one step at a time on darkling high heels. Puddles were already gathering on the warped cement stairs. "It's as if we don't have any brains of our own," she imagined herself telling Evelyn. "And I'm sure that's just what they think. That we haven't got the brains we were born with. That we have to be told *everything*." By the time she climbed into the Volvo the rain had ceased, as abruptly as if someone had thrown a switch. Her coat was soaked through, and she laid it out on the backseat to dry.

At this hour, the streets were practically deserted. She drove past a succession of shops and restaurants: Bob's Big Boy, Li'l

Pickle Sandwiches, Al's Exotic Birds, Ralph's Market. Inside Long's Drugs empty aisles of hair supplies, pet food, household appliances and vitamin supplements were illuminated by pale, watery fluorescents, like the inside of an aquarium. "It's not as if we couldn't do just as well without them," she would continue, awaiting Evelyn's quick nods of agreement. "I certainly didn't need to get married. I could have done just as well on my own. It's not as if it's some *man's* secret how to get by in this world. It's just a matter of keeping your feet on the ground, being objective about things, not fooling yourself. That's all there is to it. That's the big secret."

As she turned onto Beverly Glen her high beams, sweeping through an alleyway, reflected off a pair of attentive red eyes. Being realistic, she thought, and heard the wolves emerge from alleyways, abandoned buildings, underground parking garages, their black callused paws pattering like rain against the damp streets. They loped alongside her car for short distances, trailed off to gobble stray snails and mice, paused to bite and scratch their fleas. She refused to look, driving on through the deserted city. The alternating traffic lights cast shifting patterns and colors across the glimmering asphalt, like rotating spotlights on aluminum Christmas trees. Wolves, men, lovers, cars, streets, cities, worlds, stars. The real and the unreal, the true and the untrue. Unless you're careful it all starts looking like a dream, it all seems pretty strange and impossible, she thought, while all across the city the wolves began to howl.

THE DARLING

Afterward Dolores Starr would lie on her bed with a sort of stunned and implicate amazement at the power of things, the power of that vast, soft universe of force contracting gently around her body like a hand. Dolores, she thought. Dolores, dolorous, dolorous star. She didn't feel hurt so much as bewildered and tired, as if she had awoken from a mere dream of struggle in some other, distant room filled with ballooning silence and white, intricate spaces. Usually by now Dad had returned to the kitchen to drink, but sometimes he took his gun from the clothes closet and waved it around for a while. "Maybe we both learned a little lesson today, didn't we, Miss Teen Princess, little Miss Queen of the World." Dad aimed his Walther P-38 at vanity mirror, cheesecloth curtains, Dolores's desktop crucifix. "Ker-*pow*!" Dad said. "Ker-pow, pow, *pow! That's* the only lesson most people ever learn, Miss Beautiful, Miss All the Boys Love Her. A bullet in the old brainpan, a crack on the head with a flat rock. Pow, bang. That's just about the only lasting truth *this* goddamn world's got to offer." Dad's gun was very heavy and very solid, and filled the entire apartment with its weight and stress. Dolores liked to hold the gun in her hands too; the entire universe of force seemed to withdraw a little when Dolores took it from the closet; she felt as if she had more air to breathe. Most of all, though, she liked the sudden sound of it, and the way Dad looked at her as if she were someone strange and wholly unfamiliar to him. Then, very slowly, Dad lowered his head onto the kitchen table as Dolores moved his Jim Beam to one side. Dad's brains and blood virtually ruined the checkered tablecloth Dolores had bought at K Mart just that summer, and upstairs Mrs. Morris struck the ceiling three times with her burnished mahogany cane. Mrs. Morris was eighty-seven years old and lived alone. Mrs. Morris lived on a pension, and had bad knees. Mrs. Morris had raised four children of her own and often said she deserved a decent night's sleep every once in a blue moon.

She went to San Francisco and lied about her age, sat at a long Formica table littered with cigarette trays and ashes and solicited marketing surveys. All the operators wore miniature telephone headsets and resembled the crew of some shoddy spaceship. "Have you graduated college within the last ten years?" Dolores asked people. "Do you ever purchase Hallmark greeting cards? Do you have any children? House pets? Servants? Have you seen the recent television commercial for New Improved Wheatley Wheat Snaps? Have you ever been to Vermont?" She felt like a real adult now, with her own studio apartment on Fulton Street, a super-saver bus pass, a California Federal checking account and even a Versatellar cash card with her own secret code number. She developed a taste for Virginia Slims, piña coladas and Daniel, her Group Module Assistance Coordinator. Daniel was thirty-seven and lived in Brisbane. "The abdominals—that's what goes first. The old midriff section. That's why I either run or swim every morning. That's why I do fifty gut crunchers every night." Daniel had marvelous abdominals, a '67 Karmann Ghia convertible and a bookshelf filled with books. Dolores read Steinbeck's *The Grapes of Wrath,* Durrell's *The Alexandria Quartet* and Tolstoy's *The Death of Ivan Ilych* while Daniel jogged relentlessly down the peninsula, over San Bruno Mountain, around Candlestick Park. Dolores loved the world of books, which were a lot like adulthood, she thought. Both seemed rather smoothly improbable, at once perfectly real and perfectly contrived, like the uniform plaid tweed skirt and red wool sweater she had worn to a Catholic girls' school when she was very small. That was before Grandma died, and Dad started drinking.

Books made people different, she thought. That's why Daniel was different. That's why Dolores felt different every day, after every book. It felt as if every book she read somehow altered her chemical constitution. She thought she would be very happy with Daniel and his books, until the day he hit her. He hit her in the kitchen while she was washing up. He hit her because she hadn't been home when he called. He hit her because she just tried to tell him she was home all night. He hit her because he saw how other men looked at her and how she looked back. He hit her because he couldn't reach into that other part of her where she recognized other men. He hit her because he was just like Dad, he'd been fooling her all the time, he never really read all those books on the shelf. His face was red and damp and he'd been drinking with his friends at the ballpark, and three months later he thought she forgot what he did, thought the entire incident had gone far away when he crashed through the rear screen door, steaming with briny sweat in his Nike tank top and green nylon jogging trunks, and Dolores handed him his tall, cold protein shake. He took it down with one long parched swallow, his Adam's apple bobbing. The protein shake contained nonpasteurized whole milk, two fertile eggs, eight ounces of liquid protein, wheat germ, vitamin B complex and B12 and three heaping tablespoons of blue crystal Drano. It didn't kill him right away, though. He fell to the floor and pounded it, gurgling deeply in his chest and throat (ironically, Dolores thought, like bad plumbing) and pulled the telephone off the coffee table; it chimed brokenly. His mouth and eyes were pale and dry, and a hard green pellet popped from his throat and ricocheted off the blank, uncomprehending gaze of the Sony Visionstar. In a panic, Dolores sought razors in the bathroom, serrated knives in the kitchen, but discovered only Gillette Good News and disposable plastic cutlery. Finally she struck him twice on the back of the head with his simulation ivory and brass league-leading single-average bowling trophy, spring 1982. His wallet held almost three hundred dollars cash, assorted credit and gas cards. She drove his Karmann Ghia convertible down Highway 5 to Los Angeles, and read Wilde's *The Picture of Dorian Gray* that night in the Van Nuys Motel 6. She liked *The Picture of Dorian Gray* very much.

She made large cash advances on all of Daniel's negotiable cards and opened a money-market liquid-assets account at the Sears Financial Network. She acquired a one-bedroom apartment in Fairfax, a clerical position at TRW and a "new look" from Franklin and Schaeffer in West L.A. Men often asked for her number and said complimentary things; men took her to expensive meals, nightclubs, sporting events. In her closet she gradually assembled entire wardrobes of memorabilia from the Dodgers, Raiders, Kings and Angels. Men were easy. They smiled, laughed, offered services, took checks. They were grateful for the smallest attentions. Dolores carried a .380 automatic Beretta in her purse. She liked men, but that didn't mean she was going to take any chances.

Still, she felt vaguely dissatisfied with life. Something important seemed to be missing, or perhaps even beyond her comprehension. It was as if she were always forgetting something. She wanted to be happy. "I guess it's because I never finished high school," she told Michael one day at work. Michael sat with her at the Employee Benefits desk in Personnel. "I guess I never figured out who I wanted to be, like maybe I've gone and wasted some special part of myself somewhere. Maybe because my mother left me when I was very small, I never felt very good about myself as a person. I know I go on lots of dates, but nobody seems to love me for who I really am."

At Michael's suggestion she enrolled in night extension courses at Los Angeles City College. Every Tuesday and Thursday evening after work she attended lectures in abnormal psychology and functional human anatomy. Dr. Peters, who taught functional human anatomy, looked just like Dad before he started drinking. He told her about the jugular, spine, meninges, bile duct. The body was just a delicate bubble, really, which could be broken open very easily; it made her nervous to contemplate twice each week her own physiochemical vulnerability. Infection, hemorrhages, renal failure, metastasis, stroke. Polio, eczema, muscular dystrophy, brain death. Every Friday in lab she dissected large cats and divulged complexes of lymph, nerve and muscle. Dolores much preferred Dr. Deakin in her other class, where she tried to put out of her mind the dead cats with their rictus mouths and smell of formaldehyde. Dr. Deakin was relatively young. He wore pressed and faded Levi's with white, tapered shirts and knit ties. He always punctuated his intense, Socratic monologues with profound, intriguing pauses. "What does it mean . . . this word 'abnormal'? And how do we know . . . when it truly applies?" He had an overgrown walrus mustache, and as he paced the lecture floor he gazed up into the high fluorescents as if entranced by gravid implications only he could see there, like some spiritual medium. "Don't I think . . . *I'm* normal? And anytime you contradict me . . . don't I think *you're* abnormal? Don't we all like to define *ourselves* . . . as the 'normal' ones?" Dolores quickly grew to love him. This was a man who understood the way the world worked; he could see far beyond himself into the eyes of other people, other people who hurt, cared, loved and cried. "I certainly understand the importance of your class, no kidding," she told him over a shared turkey-and-sprouts-on-rye at the corner Blimpies. "I have had to deal with many abnormal people in my life, and I am just beginning to realize that they were not abnormal at all, but really were just normal, actually."

Dr. Deakin kept an immaculate duplex in Los Feliz, filled with lush hanging ferns and gleaming french windows, and Dolores cut his throat with one of the long steel carving knives from the immaculate and well-kept Spanish-style kitchen. He had been perfectly gentle and polite. She hadn't felt angry, or even perfunctory. There was just something in men which seemed to demand it now. Something in their eyes. It was like the look of seduction, really. The blood was suddenly everywhere, and if there was one thing Dolores was firmly resolved against from that night forward, it was knives. She began making a few strategic handgun investments. A .38 Special, a 9mm Parabellum. Dense compact Remington cartridges in a tidy cardboard box. She joined the National Rifle Association. She subscribed to *Guns and Ammo.*

Men were easy, but women were different. Women, in fact, were much more different from Dolores than men. Their glances click-clicked like the lenses of cameras, their tongues snapped faintly at you in reproach. They didn't like you talking to any of their men, and all the men in the world, it seemed, were their men. Women kept secrets, and liked to pay men special attentions in private. Dolores didn't even like women, though she hoped it was a condition which would change with maturity. Women practiced retributions on grand scales, they wielded sharp blades in profound ritual ceremonies beneath the earth in intricate, vast caverns filled with smoky incense and swelling female voices. Dolores never had a mother, so she never knew. Women shared a secret world of ritual, violence and redemption Dolores could only guess at.

"You know you gotta be careful in L.A., don't you, Di?" Michael said, always bringing hot coffee in Styrofoam cups to her desk, candy bars, crackers. "You read the papers, don't you? A single woman's got to be careful in this city; you know why? Because otherwise she'll get murdered, that's why. This city's filled with a lot of very crazy characters, Dolores. For example, just the other day I was reading about a whole club of murderers that lived out in the desert. The women, you see, would go to bars and pick up men. Then they'd take them out to the desert and they'd be murdered by the whole gang. It started out as an Indian cult, but then the white people started getting involved too. Even the white women. They skinned one man completely alive before they murdered him. So, what are you up to later, Di? Feel like a movie, maybe? Or dinner?"

They ate Thai, saw John Wayne in *Red River* and *Rio Bravo*. Dolores particularly liked Angie Dickinson, one of *Rio Bravo*'s costars who would go on later to star in the hit television series *Police Woman*. Angie Dickinson knew a woman could appear feminine and sexy and still know how to take care of herself. Michael sat quietly beside her and didn't even reach for her hand; she could even see the movie flickering and inverted in his brown eyes. The movie theater was called the Vista and was located at the corner of Sunset and Hollywood. It was filled with misshapen shadows, stained and thinning velvet draperies, high abandoned balconies and enormous Egyptian-style statues, like some film festival in the Middle Kingdom. "This used to be a gay theater," Michael told her when they first sat down. He shifted uneasily in his seat. "I can still smell them," he said. "Fucking queers."

They bought ice cream next door and then drove to Griffith Park. Michael was silent, and Dolores felt a hard, cool pressure accumulating in her, like the thickness of gravity.

"What are you thinking?" Michael asked.

Every so often they passed the hunched figures of strange men in the shadows. Usually the strange men wore leather jackets; they had dark complexions and quick dark hands.

"I don't know. What are *you* thinking?"

Dolores unclasped her purse in her lap. Her right hand slid through the clutter of checkbooks, wadded Kleenex, random cosmetics and a dog-eared paperback copy of James M. Cain's *Mildred Pierce,* sensing the buried and unalterable weight of it there before she found it. It was always the same, she thought. Men who really loved you were filled with a sort of emptiness. Sometimes you wanted to fill that emptiness before it filled you. They pulled into a secluded parking lot in a grove of drooping jacarandas. Over the roof of the park the power lines hummed.

"It's not easy living alone in a town like L.A.," Michael told her. "I mean, it's not hard for someone like me, since I'm a highly independent person with a firm commitment to being exactly who I am. In fact, I can honestly say I have a very firm commitment to myself, which is not to sound egotistical or anything. It's just that I'm not one of those people, you know, who always needs someone telling them, like, this is who you are." Michael reached under the driver's seat. "Some people never understand," he said.

Michael withdrew his .357 Magnum Desert Eagle just as Dolores withdrew her .380 Beretta Model 84, which featured a thirteen-round staggered magazine and a reversible release. A crumpled ball of Kleenex, dislodged from the trigger by Dolores's thumb, tumbled into her lap. It was a full moon outside that night, making only a dim impression against the high screen of smog.

Michael looked at Dolores's gun; then he looked at her eyes. He looked at her gun again. Finally he said, "Don't you have trouble finding a good clean-burning handload for a piece like that?"

"I use Blue Dot," Dolores said. "I don't want to stress the barrel."

They were married in July, bought a condo in the Valley and an Airedale pup named Bud. "Bud's a pup who's going to have one solid family unit to depend on," Michael said, dispatched a blizzard of résumés and acquired an administrative position at Lockheed in Burbank. "You've got to believe in yourself if you're going to be happy in this life. Don't you, Bud? Don't you, fellah?" Michael scrubbed the Airedale's addled head between his fingers. The puppy gave a succinct yelp.

"Be careful," Dolores said. "You're hurting him."

They went everywhere and did everything together. Tuesday evenings a self-actualization workshop in Sherman Oaks, Saturday afternoons an advanced gun care and safety program at the Van Nuys Police Academy. They installed a burglar alarm in their home, a doghouse in the blossoming yard and their mutual gun collection behind glass-paneled display cases in the den. "It's like I have all the energy in the world now," Michael said, and decided to build an arboretum in the backyard. "It'll be like our summer home, a home away from home. We'll sit out there and drink iced tea all summer." Michael loved their yard. "Gardening is what I always needed," he told her, returning from the nursery with marigolds, Lincoln roses, peat moss. "It helps me make use of my more positive side, my life-affirming energy. I don't believe in anger anymore. I don't believe in hate. The world's got enough of those negative vibrations already without me making any more of them." He installed floodlights on a high wooden vined terrace, and often worked on the yard alone and late into the evenings.

Dolores, meanwhile, would lie awake in bed at night and imagine the fluttery and somewhat appalled conspiracies of women. "I'm not a thing or a self-oriented person anymore,"

Dolores told them. "I'm a goal-oriented person now." Deep in their immaculate caverns, the women murmured; they tried not to listen; they were deeply and mortally offended. "I know you think I've just given in to some man, but that's not true. Michael isn't just some man. Michael respects me as a person. Michael respects me for being exactly who I am. You can't understand if you don't know that feeling how wonderful and important that feeling is. It's not something I can just explain." Faint fibrillations, echoes, pulses. The women shared sonorous voices, impossible confidences, their hearts synchronously beating in the black caverns. Dolores didn't trust them; she wanted to get far away. Someday we'll have our own energy-sufficient cabin in the Pacific Northwest, she assured herself. We'll have trained Dobermans, electrified fences, canned goods. We'll have shortwave, and a proper armory which includes autoloading carbines and antiballistic missiles. Often she fell asleep before Michael came to bed, and when she awoke she could hear him already at work again in the backyard, striking the ground with spades, shovels, rakes; installing seeds, bulbs, determined little saplings. "I thought we might have a little vegetable garden right here," Michael told her. "Then we don't have to worry so much about pesticides." Dolores loved to stand at the large picture window and watch him work. Michael had long, fair-skinned hands which, finely etched with the brown dirt, resembled beautiful antique figurines recovered from some archaeological dig. "I'm a high-energy sort of person," he told her. "I never sleep much." Bud lay on the sunny grass and contemplated a hovering fly, his tiny body coiled like the spring of an HK P7. Weekends Dolores would sit on the faded-green lawn chair, drinking tall ice-cold drinks and smelling the moist upturned earth. Every few minutes Michael would look up from his work and smile at her. His tools lay about casually or leaned against the varnished pine fence like intimate friends at some large garden party, flaked with dirt like Michael's hands.

There are places outside the world of men and women, Dolores thought. It's possible to live there safely and protected, like children with strong, enduring parents.

Then, one Sunday while Michael was pricing planters at Builders' Emporium, Bud uprooted the foot of a buried postman among a bed of Michael's blossoming dahlias. His shoelace was untied, and seemed to signify something, though Dolores was too shaken to decide exactly what. "I felt impossibly alone," she told Bud later, cradling him in her arms, dripping his still body with her tears. "Everything I tried to believe was true about Michael was really just a lie. His honesty, fidelity, love —all lies. He never cared about me. He never wanted to share his life with me. He only wanted his own secret little world." In the basement she had discovered jars of formaldehyde, handcuffs, ropes and enormous gray cloth sacks. "He was never going to let me into that world. I was always going to be completely alone." Bud was warm and motionless in her arms. It was dark out, and a full moon glowed faintly through the overcast. Then Dolores lay Bud in the trench in Michael's arms. She crossed Michael's arms across Bud, to keep him warm in the long darkness. Michael was wearing his three-piece Bill Blass double-breasted tweed, the same suit he wore the day they were married. Then, gently and with deep regret, Dolores distributed the damp brown earth across them both. It was as if she were burying herself in the tidy garden, placing her own humble body into the deep, whispering world of complicit women. The women themselves, though, weren't very happy. Nobody liked her there anymore. They didn't want her with them. Only men liked Dolores. Men and other men.

She drew the curtains on the picture window, and every night she slept alone. The loneliness was immense and unsettling. She felt unpopulated black continents forming deep inside her body, jagged mossy peninsulas orbited by forlorn craggy islands and glimmering gray water. In the long evenings she sat beside the curtained picture window, motionless within a cone of light from the standing lamp like a display in some anthropological museum, feeling the hard relentless yearning of the planet underneath the yard, the secret articulations of graves and bodies. She never looked at the yard anymore, but only imagined it. Michael's abandoned tools just lay there gathering rust, their wooden handles cracked and splintering. The flower beds and vegetable garden would be overgrown with fast green weeds, the wheelbarrow overturned and covered with a thick gray impasto of cement. And Michael, of course, underneath all of it, still telling his lies, still lying to her all night and all day. She couldn't even hear the secret ceremonies of the women anymore. They had gone into deeper caverns where Dolores was no longer privileged. They were teaching her a little lesson. If she wanted to be Miss Little High and Mighty, if she wanted to be independent and on her own, then that's just what she'd have. Just herself; nobody else for her to feel any responsibility toward. Now all she could hear were the power lines buzzing on the high poles, the crickets wheezing, the dark planetary heart beating against the floors of her condo. Sometimes, particularly late at night after she had smoked too much marijuana and too many cigarettes, Michael would appear and attempt to comfort her in her darkest, loneliest hours. He would sit on the beige sofa, absently patting Bud's loose, volitionless head in his lap. "You weren't secure enough in your individuality to allow me to be myself," he told her. "When people love each other, they have to trust each other as well, Di. I think you know that."

Dolores never looked at him directly. She looked instead at the curtained window. She imagined bright spiders spinning their webs in the piles of moldering lumber Michael had purchased for the arboretum. "I don't think I have anything left to say to you anymore," she said.

Sometimes Michael moved to the faded-gray Barcalounger which Dolores had stitched together in places; sometimes the marijuana gave Dolores a vague sense of self-possession, as if she were in complete control of her own lungs, blood, heart. She could will her heart to slow down a bit; she could demand more oxygenation or less. Sometimes she felt as if she were sitting in another, blurred room far away from this one. Usually during these long waking dreams her mind returned to the same questions over and over again. She wondered if her mother was still alive somewhere. Would we recognize one another if we met unexpectedly on the street? she asked herself. Is there something chemical about the bond between a mother and her daughter, or are we just like any two strangers now? Maybe we'll become great friends by sheer chance someday. She will find my naïveté charming; she will teach me all about men. We'll go to movies together and take turns fixing dinner. We'll become devoted roommates, go to nightclubs, even dancing. In Europe women often go dancing together, and it doesn't necessarily mean they're lesbians or anything.

"You sit cooped up every night smoking grass," Michael told her, the collapsed puppy draped across his knees like a hearth blanket. "I think you've done enough feeling sorry for yourself to last a lifetime. I think it's time you took a little responsibility for your life, and stopped blaming everything on people you love." Michael picked up the container of Herco smokeless shotgun powder from the coffee table. The shotgun, cleaned and loaded, was peering out from underneath Dolores's easy chair. "You don't leave something like this sitting open all day long," he said. "It gets damp." He affixed the aluminum lid with a quick hollow snap. "Also, you better start looking in on the yard. The neighborhood cats have begun digging up Mrs. Winslow again. If I were you, I'd go out there right now and check on Mrs. Winslow."

Dolores took the unfinished joint from the ashtray in her lap and lit it with her Cricket. A seed popped, and a fragment of paper sparked and fluttered through the air. Without exhaling, Dolores asked, "Who was Mrs. Winslow?" Her eyes began to water.

Michael shrugged. In his lap, Bud's head rolled to one side, his large eyes dry and vacant like the eyes of some collapsed puppet. "Just some lady worked at the library," he said.

Then, one Friday evening in late summer, Dolores returned home from Von's to discover numerous police cars and ambulances parked in her driveway, their soft red and yellow emergency bulbs pulsing and spinning in the smoggy twilit air. They seemed vaguely sudden and incongruous, like emergency flares designating some roadside picnic. Dolores removed her groceries from the trunk, and a uniformed policeman at the door gazed at her with a sort of obdurate and official complacency. Loaves of bread, a sack of red Delicious apples, gallons of distilled water in large clear-plastic jugs. Even though she lived alone, she liked to be prepared; if there was one thing life had taught her, you never knew what might happen next. She didn't feel surprised so much as slightly bemused when she was confronted by charges of multiple homicide with Birds Eye frozen vegetables under one arm, nachos and various snack crackers under the other. The arresting officer, Detective Rowlandson, was very kind. He asked her if the cuffs were comfortable. He transferred her frozen foods into the care of one of the random officers who were milling awkwardly about the small living room. The uncurtained window revealed a red, apocalyptic sunset and numerous men in white cloth shirts and trousers digging at the yard. Wearing surgical masks and gloves, they wrapped the moldering figures in white sheets and transferred them to stretchers which were then carried to the open chambers of patient white ambulances. When Detective Rowlandson drove her down the hill in his Eldorado the streets were filled with curious neighbors—housewives in faded terry-cloth robes, children leaning against their Stingray bicycles. "Anything you say can and will be held against you in a court of law," Detective Rowlandson told her, trying to find a classical station on the radio. "I know," Dolores said, "and I think that's perfectly fair." She was turning to look at the young officer in the backseat. The young officer was gazing aimlessly out the window. He seemed a little bored, or even homesick. When they arrived at the station Detective Rowlandson interrogated her in his private office, with another pair of uniformed patrolmen at the door and a cassette tape recorder whirring on the desktop. "Maybe you'd like a little soda or something?" he asked. "Maybe your throat's getting a little parched?" They were all very kind, Dolores thought. Even when they don't really know what's going on, men really do try to do their best. Men really do care about the unapproachable world of women.

She was awarded a private cell and instant, irremediable celebrity. "I can't say I'm proud of what I've done," she told the media, which were assembled around her in a bright fluorescent room of flashing cameras and buzzing tape machines. The journalists sat poised on the edges of their aluminum chairs as if expecting some race to commence without a second's notice. "It's not like I'm stupid either, since I always did well in school whenever I bothered to apply myself, and Dr. Weinstein, who is one of the very kind doctors visiting me while I am incarcerated, says I performed exceptionally well on the Wechsler Adult Intelligence Scale. I guess I can only blame my poor upbringing, being as that my mother left me when I was very little, and as my father beat me when I was little and took advantage of me in many ways which are too delicate to be gotten into at this time and place. But anyway, I can't blame everything on my parents, since I am a grown-up woman who must take responsibility for herself, and so I would like to say that I am solely responsible for all those dead bodies buried in my

yard"—which initiated a blizzard of bursting flashbulbs—
"and of course for my good husband Michael's senseless and
untimely demise as well, and if I get sent to the electric chair I
will certainly deserve every minute of it since Michael was the
kindest, most loving husband the world has ever known, and
he was certainly the only man who ever actually tried to understand and care for me in a totally unselfish and caring man-
ner. Thank you very much."

Dolores's private cell was in the women's maximum-security
prison in Lancaster. She had a toilet, a washbasin and a prison-
issue towel, soap and toothbrush. She had a rough green khaki
blanket and bristly sheets. Every afternoon they took her out
alone to exercise in the courtyard. She walked calmly around
the painted white basketball tableau. She did sit-ups and leg
lifts, pausing occasionally to gaze up at the bright California
sky. The guards were all women. When she saw other inmates,
they were all women. They all had hard, coarse expressions.
Sometimes, far off down the distant cement corridors, Dolores
could hear a young woman crying. She sounded very young,
almost a child.

Dolores was entering her Russian novel phase. She read
Crime and Punishment, Anna Karenina and *War and Peace*. For
the first time in her life, Dolores felt at peace with herself and
her innermost being. *It's like I never had a chance before to actually understand what it was like to be totally on my own,* she
wrote on her pad of white paper, which was inspected every
evening by one of the uniformed guards. *Maybe if I had only had
a chance to get to know myself without other people around me all
the time making me feel like somebody I wasn't, I wouldn't have
killed all those nice people.* She contemplated writing her own
autobiography and publishing it under the title *Bad Love.* Her
cell was absolutely silent for hours at a time. In fact, Dolores

rarely saw any men at all. She felt denser, more compact, more real. It was as if her entire body were filling up with sand. She refused newspapers and magazines. She was a quiet, respectable hermit living alone in a deep cave. She was contemplating convoluted and transcendent things. *Some things you just can't explain,* she told her writing pad. *Sometimes too you can be just happy not explaining them either.*

"They've got you now, baby," Michael said, picking at the celery on her evening meal tray. "As they say in the movies—the jig is up."

"We'll see," Dolores said. She felt a vague glimmer of hope, one which filled her with impossible sadness.

A few days later Dr. Weinstein fell in love with her, and she knew all the peace she had finally grown accustomed to would not last. "Primitive man didn't draw pictures on his walls because he liked pretty *pictures,* for chrissakes," Dr. Weinstein told her during one of his visits, trying to act like he wasn't in love with her, like he was different from other men. "It's not like *Neanderthalus australopithecus* buried his dead out of fucking sympathy and compassion. How much sympathy and compassion do you think you'd get from a *Neanderthalus australopithecus?* Not too damn much, that's how much. Not too damn much at all." He showed her a picture of *Neanderthalus australopithecus* in a large library edition of *The Encyclopedia of Human Anthropology.* "You see that guy? You see those teeth, that brow? Why do you think he painted pictures on the wall? For the same reason he ate the still-bloody hearts of the rival tribesmen he killed, that's why. He was appropriating the soul and strength of significant others. Family, beasts, enemies. The sun and the fucking moon, that's what."

He carried a black leather briefcase. He wore a dark suit and glasses. At first he appeared only every few weeks or so and asked her to complete psychological profiles, write personal compositions and analyze photographs of men, women and children in family situations. Then he began arriving every afternoon just as the lunch trays were being collected by a trusty on a wobbly aluminum cart. Sometimes he talked for hours while Dolores sat on her cot, her hands folded between her knees, her blank gaze trained upon the concrete floor which she had scrubbed clean just that morning.

"We do it every day," Dr. Weinstein said. He held the briefcase in his lap with his left hand; his right hand gestured vacantly at the cold and empty air. "We appropriate the souls and strengths of other people. It's just that most of us don't have to kill them, babe. You know what I'm saying at you, Di? You don't mind if I call you Di, do you? I saw it on your Wechsler examination under preferred nicknames." He offered her cigarettes and she smoked them, inhaling the grainy, desultory smoke, watching it settle across the stone floors like morning mist in a swamp. "Love and aggression are the same thing in human society. They're both responses to the same biochemical hums and pops. You love or hate the other and you want to blast them. You want to break them down into their elements and swallow them. You want to make them one with yourself by devouring, feasting, obliterating. Then they're part of you, aren't they, babe? Then *you're* in complete control. It's a biochemical desire, but when you live in society, see, we learn to develop displacements for those desires. We learn to turn acts into symbolic intentions. You don't *do,* in other words, Di. You learn to seem *not* to do, if you know what I mean. But you really *do* do, secretly, but only in your mind. Only you, babe, you don't know how to do that. You think there's just your mind and the world, that the world's the only object your mind's got to act on. You have to learn to invent other objects. You have to learn to compensate for your desires by instituting certain ritual behaviors in your seriously addled and definitely very sociopathic psyche, Di—and I think I can say that much for certain. Definitely sociopathic. These are things you're supposed to learn—when you're raised properly. But you haven't been raised properly. You've got to be raised all over, right? You see what I'm saying, Di? You've got to be raised all over again."

Dr. Weinstein testified at her first court appearance, and the charges were dropped on grounds of insanity. "Let's say they were pretty firm grounds, Di. Let's say we had a fucking continent full of firm ground for that one," Dr. Weinstein told her in the government car that took them to a county holding cell after the hearing. Three days later Dolores was remanded to the custody of the state psychiatric clinic in Reseda and, three months after that, quietly transferred to Dr. Weinstein's private facilities in Napa County. It was a different place from prison, and Dolores didn't like it. The grounds were green and unenclosed, with a view of rolling hills patched with vineyards. Dolores was apportioned her own private room, wardrobe, library and lawn chair. The patients here were all very quiet and composed, and didn't look disturbed at all that Dolores could tell. Rachel, an attractive, fortyish redhead, told her, "When my husband closed down our savings account and ran off with his secretary to Buenos Aires, I guess I just couldn't cope." Rachel was wearing a polka-dot cotton summer dress and reading *Cosmopolitan*.

Dr. Weinstein was personally committed to raising Dolores all over again. Her diet was strictly regulated. Listlessly, she attended the clinic's mandatory Exercycle workouts. Her blood pressure was intently monitored, her saliva, feces and urine; two interns from UCLA Medical Center received a grant to monitor her endorphins. She was steeped in megavitamins and zinc; she suffered a high colonic. "Symbolic displacement," Dr. Weinstein told her after each morning's "contact therapy" interview in his office. "There are certain amine molecules manufactured in the adrenal gland which generate rage. There's good rage and there's bad rage, and your rage, Di, is very bad. These amines are then conditioned and modified by those massive discharges of the endocrine system concerned with reproduction. Reproduction is something your body anticipates around the clock; your body's always preparing you for reproduction, Di." He took her hand and commented on her long, strong fingers; then he brushed a vein with alcohol and inserted the needle. "It's at the confluence of rage and sex where we're trying to get," he said. "We're trying to draw a line between intentionality and action, pure rage and sudden sex. That's the line that's been eliminated in you, babe. We're going to replace it. We're going to draw it fast and hard." She received the injections three times a day, and Dr. Weinstein began taking her on what he liked to call "field studies." They drove to Marin County and purchased a new Volvo. They went shopping for clothes, curtains, sheets, dishes. Dolores had never really enjoyed shopping that much before, but now she craved it like potato chips; it took her away from herself; she could lose herself in the vast chattering communities of women. Afterward she and Dr. Weinstein would return to his private office at the clinic and watch television; often they attended movies and plays together. He pronounced her fit for the home-based phase of her therapy. They were married in August and set up housekeeping in a beautiful, isolated two-story country house in Sebastopol. Dolores worked mornings at the local day-care center while Dr. Weinstein was at the clinic. Then she had the rest of the day to watch television. She didn't like books anymore. Dr. Weinstein's Literary Guild selections gazed down mutely from the high mahogany bookshelves like zoological specimens cradled in formaldehyde jars.

She still thought of murdering him. Not every day, but periodically. At these times she felt herself inflating with a strange, unidentifiable sensation. Her heart began to pound; the backs of her hands began to itch. Her face grew flushed and hot, and she developed splitting migraines. She had never felt so intensely aware of the flux and convection of her own blood before. "You're learning, Di. You're learning to accept the limitations of your own body, your own mind." Dr. Weinstein sat in the stuffed chair beside the jetting blue flames of the gas fireplace. The latest issue of *The American Journal of Psychiatric Medicine* was propped open against his knee. "Fix us a cup of coffee, babe. Sit down and relax with me." Dolores went into the kitchen and saw the immaculate wooden cooking utensils hanging from the varnished redwood cabinets. Then she went out the back door and made the screen door slam. She drove their second car to the Emporium mall and had a Bloody Mary at Marie Calendar's. She was still filling up with the unidentifiable feelings. She tried to repress them, but she didn't know what she was repressing. Terrible anger and rage, she suspected. That was what Dr. Weinstein told her; that's what the daily injections were investing her with. She was frightened and disoriented. She sat down at a row of plastic stools near a wide mirrored fountain. Blue water streamed from the blowholes of glass dolphins. The fear grew more and more terrible as she watched the pulsing crowds and families. Teenage girls emblazoned with cosmetics. Young couples pushing dazed babies in carriages with tiny stuffed toys dangling from their fabric awnings. Packs of young men with faces flushed from marijuana. It wasn't fear anymore, it was panic. Dolores felt panicked but she couldn't move; she couldn't face the crowds of people; she couldn't face the acres of cars in the vast parking lots. She started to cry and cry. She had never cried in front of strangers before. When someone tried to touch her she pulled away and screamed at them. She didn't know what she screamed, but she knew she didn't want anybody near her. She just wanted to cry and cry, as if the entire world had ended and now only its unaccountable sadness was left, filling her and filling her like the hard colorless rage with which she desperately desired to murder Dr. Weinstein.

After these "episodes" Dolores would be sedated and kept

overnight at the clinic. In the morning, Dr. Weinstein would drive her home in the Volvo, usually playing Philip Glass on the car stereo. "It takes a while to adjust," he told her. "We're teaching your entire body how to behave all over again. We're teaching it how to feel and breathe." His right hand reached out and held hers in her lap. She felt enervated and thick with barbiturates. Outside, the entire landscape was blurred and indistinct. "We're teaching you how to love, babe. We're teaching you how to love without hurting anybody." Dolores began to feel extraordinarily lonely and weak. "And you know I love you, Di. You know that, don't you?"

She couldn't even remember the faces of any of her old lovers anymore. Their memory seemed to be draining easily from her like water from a tub. She could remember their names—Daniel, Dr. Deakin, Michael, Dad—but she couldn't remember anything about the quality of their presence, the fabric of their skin or voice or hair, the strength of their muscles or intestines. In the long summer afternoons she would just sit outside in the sculpted front garden, wearing her cashmere robe, black stockings and a silk teddy, beside an ice chest filled with margaritas on the wrought-iron lawn table next to the Valium prescription and her strewn cosmetics, and gaze aimlessly at the blue sky, green trees and topiary hedges. There was just a dark inchoate sadness now, formless and buzzing. "It's the recognition that you're alone, babe. It's the human condition, it just means you're sane, that's all. It means you're not swallowing people. It means you know who you are, and who they are, and that line where the twain shall not meet. You're developing a nice clean, bright soul now, like Billy's bright T-shirt in a television detergent commercial. You've got your own world inside now, babe. You're ready to live your own life." Dolores sipped her margarita and thought about *Neanderthal australopithecus*'s cave. Someone had expunged all the pale etchings of bison and mammoth from the rough basalt walls. There was nobody left in the cave at all anymore, not even the flickering fire or the smell of roasting meat. Dolores lit a cigarette and looked at the impossibly blue sky. For a moment she thought she might start crying, but then she didn't.

The following summer Dr. Weinstein pronounced her cured, and exactly one year after that she gave birth to a nine-pound baby boy. The baby had a full head of black matted hair when he was presented to her by the nurse; his eyes were squeezed shut with pain and screaming. She held him against her breasts and listened to his heart beating in her private room while Dr. Weinstein sat beside her, beaming like a streetlamp and holding her hand. After a few days of bloodless discussion, they named the baby Andrew, in honor of Dolores's dad.

SWEET LADIES, GOOD NIGHT, GOOD NIGHT

"Women only seem like nature when nature's not around. But women are more deliberate than that. A woman's love is completely artificial, just like her cosmetics. Woman's love has design and strategy in it, unlike man's. I think men have been getting bad press for a few thousand years now, or ever since some woman elicited poetry." Arnold Bromley was picking at his right ear with a twisted paper match and sitting at the counter in Coco's on MacArthur Boulevard. Empty saucers and a single coffee cup sat before him on the counter. One saucer was tracked with chocolate cake topping, the other with coffee and cream.

"Did you want more coffee?" the waitress asked. Her name was Michelle. Michelle was an undergraduate in premed at the university.

Arnold looked at her a minute. She was thin, pretty and immensely uninterested. "I guess I'll just have the check," he said.

Then Arnold drove to Estelle's place and found Estelle in bed with a man whose name, he learned later, was Bob Reilley. Estelle, as it turned out, had met Bob Reilley at a neighborhood Safeway approximately two days before.

"There's something I've been meaning to tell you," Estelle said. Bob Reilley had pulled a towel over himself and, out of courtesy, was putting out his recently ignited cigarette. "I don't think I've been entirely fair with you lately, Arnold," she said. "Frankly, I think you can find a woman who'll treat you a lot better than I do." Bob Reilley yawned distantly, gazing at his extinguished cigarette in the glass ashtray beside the bed.

Arnold let himself out the front door and pushed Estelle's keys through the mailbox grate. He got in his still-warm car and drove around for a few hours. This time, he stopped for coffee at Denny's.

He looked at the menu just long enough to give himself time to unwind. He already knew the menu by heart.

"Chocolate cake and coffee," he said after a while.

The tiny plastic nametag on the waitress's blouse said Mary-Anne.

"Sex is only more acute than love. But that doesn't mean love is any less real," Arnold said.

Her name was Jilly, and she worked at I. Magnin. She wore sheer skirts and nylons and bright, almost fluorescent makeup. She had beautiful legs.

"Love's the way we learn the world's immediacy, and so we need it more. Love holds things in context. Love's the melody, and sex just the individual chords in a song. That's why love's so much more important to us when we're alone. Sometimes I think I'd give up my entire life for love. Sometimes I think I already have. Would you like to stop here? Would you like an ice cream?" They were standing outside Häagen-Dazs in the enormous shopping mall. The mall was filled with couples, families and running children. The windows displayed elegant clothes, furniture, table settings and expensive toys. The air reverberated with golden light. Plastic stools and benches down the centers of each aisle were crowded with dazed, expressionless shoppers and their baggage. The shoppers seemed to be contemplating nothing. They seemed very enervated, and annoyed with themselves for feeling so tired.

"How about a chocolate chocolate-chip ice cream?" Arnold said. "Does that sound good? Did I tell you, Jilly? Did I tell you you have beautiful legs?"

Jilly had a boyfriend named Bob. "But you're a lot more interesting than Bob," Jilly said. "You're always saying interesting things. It's not easy for a person to feel very intelligent about themselves when Bob's around. All Bob ever talks about is his car. This is what he's going to do to his car. This is what he's bought for his car. It's like living with instant replay. It's like living with Bob's car. Sometimes it's like not living with anybody at all."

Jilly broke up with Bob, and Arnold knew he was on warning. From that day forward Arnold tried to be as interesting as possible. He took Jilly to movies, museums, sporting events, RV and boat shows, carnivals and circuses. He told her about politics, language, culture, literature, theater, war, domestic surveillance, wok cooking, the history of unions, homemade salad dressings and just about anything else he could make up. But then one night at her apartment he just wanted to watch television. He couldn't think of anything interesting to say and, for that one night, he didn't really feel like saying anything interesting, either.

Jilly broke up with Arnold the following weekend and went back to Bob. "I'm a one-man woman, Arnold," she said. "And I'm afraid Bob's that man. It's not that I don't still care about you a lot. It's just I think you'll be better off finding the sort of woman that's right for you, and I'm afraid that woman's just not me. Now here, I've packed all your things in this bag, so if you could take just a quick look around. I'm expecting Bob here any minute. If you see his truck, try to step on it, will you? You'll know it's Bob's truck if it says 'Bob Reilley's Plumbing Supplies' on the side."

* * *

Arnold purchased new shirts and after-shave. He purchased new shoes. He restyled his hair and purchased a blow dryer. He even purchased a new futon with a straw mat base, hand-painted sheets and matching pillowcases. When he got home and looked at himself in the mirror, he liked what he saw. He looked different and he smelled different. He looked like a man who knew what he wanted from life, and was prepared to go out and get it. He smelled like a man who wouldn't take no for an answer.

"I guess I've always been an other-directed sort of person," Lydia Sanchez said, eating mushroom linguini at Marie Calendar's in El Toro. "A lot of people are self-oriented sorts of persons, because they've never progressed beyond the nipple stage. That doesn't mean I'll let other people take advantage of me. And *that* doesn't mean I'm just thinking about myself because I won't let other people take advantage of me. When you let other people take advantage of you, you're doing them a severe disservice. You're not letting them learn what it's like to live in a real world where people don't let you take advantage of them all the time. I received an EST summer scholarship when I was eighteen years old. I was audited by scientologists and believe it was the most profound, unforgettable experience of my entire life. Now I like to think of myself as a sort of Rosicrucian Buddhist, and I'm presently attending night classes at Valley College to receive my B.A. in cultural anthropology. During the week I'm a receptionist for Dr. Brady, Credit Dentist. You know Dr. Brady, don't you? He has those awful commercials on TV. In reality, though, Dr. Brady happens to be a really nice man."

Arnold looked over both shoulders, trying to locate the waitress who had virtually disappeared with his order of gin and tonic. Marie Calendar's was filled with young, attractive and well-groomed couples, all very much like Arnold and Lydia, who shamelessly flirted not only with one another but with members of the many other attractive couples seated at tables around them.

As if in afterthought, Lydia said, "I really love eating at Marie Calendar's."

Arnold loved Lydia because she did to him in bed everything he could possibly hope for and didn't even wait for him to ask. They had many wonderful times together for almost ten days. Then, like rain, it happened. One night Arnold brought the makings for sandwiches over to Lydia's apartment and they watched television together. "You know, this is all anyone ever needs," Arnold told her, gesturing with his pastrami salad on French roll. "I mean, we've got decent food, we're in love and there's a good movie on TV. It's not like we need those things other people need to be happy. You know, like fancy restaurants, or going to big stage shows. You know, like *Cats* or something. It just goes to show you don't need a lot of money or anything just to be happy."

That night, after Arnold had gone home alone, he felt it break in the dark air. It wasn't a sound so much as a beat, like a sudden shift in temperature, or some seismic tremor deep underground. Arnold sat up in bed suddenly. He looked around his dark room at the lopsided bureau, the paperbacks on their shelves and the tiny Casio electronic alarm clock on the orange crate beside his bed. There was something reproachful about it. The time was 3:45 a.m.

Lydia stopped returning his calls. "Is your machine working all right?" Arnold asked her answering machine. "Or are you just not getting my messages?" Finally, early the following month, Arnold went to Hamburger Hamlet and had three quick gin and tonics on an empty stomach. The gin filled him with resolve, fortitude and self-confidence. "Call it arrogance if you want," Arnold told himself, getting back into his car. "That's fine by me. You've just got to be a little arrogant in this life if you're ever going to amount to anything." He parked out-side Lydia's office on Van Nuys Boulevard and waited for her to come out.

"I want you back in my life," Arnold said when she ap-peared. She was accompanied by two young women who wore dental assistant uniforms. They both smiled at each other over Lydia's shoulder, as if they had been anticipating Arnold's sud-den courage all along. "I want us to spend the rest of our lives together," Arnold said.

Lydia removed the bolus of pink gum from her mouth and placed it delicately on the back of a wooden bus bench. Her eyes were deep, black and remorseless. "No," Lydia said. "No, Ar-nold. I'm afraid I don't think that would be a very good idea at all."

His name was Bob, she told Arnold finally in a letter. Bob Reilley. She and Bob were very much in love. But that didn't mean she wasn't still concerned for Arnold's own happiness and peace of mind. She sincerely hoped that, someday, after they had both, as she put it, "straightened out their lives emotionally and had gotten to know themselves deep inside," they could be friends again. Perhaps, at some elaborate reconciliatory dinner, he could meet Bob face-to-face, and she could meet his new girl-friend, and they would all feel very, very happy things had turned out so very well for everyone after all.

Arnold began putting on weight. He drank Budweiser by the case, and spent all his free time in front of his cable television, dialing the remote control and watching baseball games. He be-gan checking books out of the library concerning low blood sugar and dietary disorders. Then, suddenly one morning, he noticed his hairline was receding. For the first time in his life he developed faint rashes of acne around his jaw and neck, par-ticularly after he shaved. He felt generally tired and listless. His apartment seemed to be growing tinier and more unkempt. The new hand-painted sheets on his futon even began to unravel. Every few weeks or so he went to the supermarket filled with predictable resolve. He purchased fresh vegetables, low-carbohydrate oils and salad dressings. When he returned home, however, he already lacked sufficient energy for mixing them together. Over succeeding days the carrots and celery shriveled and diminished in the refrigerator. They began to resemble shrunken heads and genitalia, or the archipelagoes of fantasy kingdoms in garish paperback books. Sometimes they mildewed and he threw them in the trash.

"Love's an illusion we can't always afford," he said at Sambo's. The half-eaten chocolate cake was turning stale on his plate. The waitress, whose name was Polly, brought him more decaf. "Sometimes love isn't love at all. Sometimes it's just the past. Sometimes it's just some moment we never really knew." Arnold grew silent for long periods of time, watching the steam unravel from his coffee. There always seemed to be something important he meant to say, but he couldn't recall exactly what that something might be.

"I live right down the street," Polly said when he brought his bill to the register. Polly had bright, flat white teeth. Polly was in the university drama department. "Why don't you give me a call sometime?" Polly said.

He took long walks now rather than drove. At work, many of the female employees began showing him obvious and elaborate concern.

"Something wrong? Something wrong at home, Arnold? Bad financial investments? Vitamin deficiency? Have you ever heard of Epstein-Barr virus syndrome? Do you know a lot of young men are diagnosed with Epstein-Barr virus syndrome these days? It's mainly dietary, Arnold. It means there's something seriously wrong with your diet." Sometimes one of the women's long, brightly lacquered hands would flash and lightly brush Arnold's warm forehead. When they came up close to him he could smell their moist perfume. A silk sleeve might brush his bare arm. He might catch a glimpse of cleavage.

"You need someone who'll take care of you," they said. "You need someone who loves you. Why don't you lie down for a minute, Arnold? Why don't you come over tonight and I'll fix you a nice, hot dinner?"

Arnold, suddenly out of breath, would walk quickly from the office and into the men's room. There, among the harsh fluorescents (which felt to his skin more like texture than light) he would gaze at his florid, spotty face in the bright mirror, and feel the heart pounding in his chest like something mechanical and estranged. His stomach and colon fluttered. That spring he began to develop a bleeding duodenal ulcer. Whenever he returned home, the message light on his answering machine was flashing.

"Hi, Arnold? This is Vicky. Do you remember me? Do you remember San Diego? I was just thinking about you. I mean, if you wanted to give me a call or anything, I'll be at home. Okay, Arnold? And if you don't want to give me a call, well, that's all right too. . . ."

Bob Reilley's plumbing supplies franchise was located in Tustin, and one smoggy, humid day in April Arnold drove out to his office carrying in his right-hand jacket pocket a Smith Model 686 .357 Magnum which he had purchased earlier that month at Grant's for Guns in Costa Mesa. The gun felt very heavy in his pocket. It was a clean, comfortable sort of weight, however. There was a lot of security in the weight of a .357 Magnum, Arnold Bromley thought.

"It's not like I haven't been through all this before," Bob Reilley said. "It's not like I don't understand exactly how you feel, or why you've aimed all your misdirected frustration at me."

Bob Reilley was leaning back in his padded leather swivel chair. His feet were propped up on the desk, and his hands folded behind his head. Bob Reilley had changed a lot since that evening more than two years ago when Arnold had discovered him in Estelle Constantine's bed. Bob Reilley had developed a very significant belly, flaky red hands and face and a large bald patch across which he had combed elaborate swirls of greasy, dyed-black hair. "I do sympathize with you, Arnold. I really do." Arnold thought that Bob Reilley was just about the most nondescript-looking man he had ever seen in his entire life.

Arnold took a seat in the unsprung sofa facing Bob Reilley's desk. The sofa was inadequately covered by a thinning corduroy blanket. Arnold had let himself in through the unlatched back door of the abandoned plumbing supplies office, where the long aisles were filled with dismantled shelves, refuse and long, intricate ropes of dust. Only one, semicharred fluorescent bulb flickered overhead. The door marked MANAGER had already been open when Arnold walked in and found Bob Reilley asleep at his desk.

Without removing his feet from the desk, Bob Reilley reached behind himself for one of two half-empty bottles of Jim Beam and a glass from the bookshelf. "It always hurts to know we're not the only one. It always hurts to learn love isn't something that's been waiting for us, but just something that happened to be around when we got there. Look, if it's any compensation, I've been through it myself, you know. I mean —excuse me. Would you like a drink?"

Arnold looked thoughtfully at the proferred Jim Beam. He held the gun in both hands, the handle leaning against his crossed right knee. "No, thank you," he said.

"Well, don't want to let it go to waste." Bob Reilley finished his glass and poured another, taller one. "As I was saying—I've been through it myself, Arnold. It's not like I'm some heartbreaker or something. It's not like I just run around Southern

California trying to make time with other men's women." Arnold wiped his nose with the back of his hand. Then, thoughtfully, he wiped the back of his hand against the thigh of his gray slacks. "Look, we're both single guys, right? Every woman we meet's just *bound* to belong to *some* damn guy or another, right? Women aren't like us, Arnie. They don't sit around brooding very long when things are over with some guy. They move on. So what are guys like you and I supposed to do? Keep our eyes on the orbits or something, like apartment hunters in New York? The race goes to the swift, Arnie. The quick and fleet of foot. Don't tell me you've never done it. Don't you start playing holier-than-thou with that stupid gun."

"This isn't personal," Arnold Bromley said, indicating his heavy gun with a breezy gesture. "This one's for abstractions. This one's for love."

"Oh my. Sorry, Arnie." Bob Reilley had spluttered Jim Beam all over the back of his arm. "Love. I get you. We're talking love now, are we?"

Bob Reilley wedged his glass between his thighs and poured it full again, splashing some into his lap. The abandoned offices echoed with the buzz and flutter of the broken fluorescent. Bob Reilley's voice seemed to increase suddenly in both volume and confidence. "That's what women are for, are they, Arnie? Love. Love and beauty, right? You tell me about it, Arnie. You see those fucking empty shelves out there? What do you think those empty shelves used to contain? Well, I'll tell you what they used to contain. They used to contain the most complete hardware maintenance equipment selection in the tricounty area. That's what love does to a guy. It takes a big successful business and turns it into nothing. There was one girl, Arnie, she broke up with me, right? For six months she phoned me ten or twelve times every night and called me a bastard for letting her break up with me. She showed up on my porch with a hand ax. I took it away and the police arrested me for assault.

Women send their boyfriends after me all the time. They want to teach me lessons because I didn't love them enough. They want to teach me lessons because I loved them too much. I've had my telephone number changed about a hundred times. Do you want to know how many women are out there, Arnie? How many women in the world there are who hate my guts? I haven't any idea, Arnie. I really don't. Women aren't action, Arnie. They're judgment. And I think judgment's a lot worse than action just about any day."

Bob Reilley took another long drink and wiped his mouth. "So what are you going to do with that gun, Arnie? Shoot me? Put a bullet in my head? I'm really scared. I go to bankruptcy court on Friday. I've been sued, assaulted, defamed, perjured, disavowed, and once, I was once almost even impaled. How do you think things'll turn out in bankruptcy court this Friday, Arnie? The judge's a woman. So's my lawyer. Women are everywhere, Arnie. It's not like the good old days. Today there are women in government and banking. There are women in distributorships, construction, and even controlling the entertainment industry. My broker was a woman. We went out two weeks or so. I lost seventy-three thousand dollars after that one was over, Arnie—seventy-three thousand. Then, in February, one of them burned down my house. It was a nice house. The insurance policy had lapsed. No, my insurance agent wasn't a woman. But my insurance agent's wife was. My insurance agent's wife was probably the biggest mistake of them all. Two nights in a Best Western in La Jolla. If I could go back in my life and change just one thing, it would probably be those two nights with my insurance agent's wife in La Jolla."

"You're right," Arnold said, holding the gun just as firmly. "Women aren't nature. Women are judgment. Women are language."

"It's like there's nothing we can do, Arnie. We're damned if we do and damned if we don't. It's like no matter what we do or how we behave, they'll still be able to say anything they want about why we did it. What's our behavior matter if they can just remake behavior's rules anytime they want?"

"It's a losing battle."

"It's like time."

"It's like we're always being betrayed by our own bodies."

"It's women, Arnie. It's not us. It's not you and I, pal." Bob Reilley got up from his desk. "We got to stand up for one another, right, Arnie? We got to stick together." He was walking slowly, confidently across the room. His right hand reached out for Arnold Bromley's gun. "It's ridiculous for *us* to be arguing, isn't it? It's language again. It's like we're playing right into their hands."

Arnold Bromley stood up too. "No, Bob. This isn't language. This is reality. And now, if you don't mind, I think I'll get back to language again." At that point, Arnold shot Bob Reilley six times in the back of the head as he made his break for the door.

In the storage aisle, the fluorescent extinguished with a sudden audible pop. Everything went completely black.

"Good night, sweetheart," Arnold said. "Good night, Bob."

UNMISTAKABLY
THE FINEST

Every time Sandra Mitchelson's daddy came home on the boat he brought her things. French chocolates, a stuffed elephant, a golden heart-shaped locket, a transistor radio, a hand-painted porcelain Japanese doll with rice paper parasol. In return Sandra helped him work in the backyard. The front yard was covered with gravel, the backyard with tall yellow weeds. "This will be our family area," Daddy said, knee-deep in the weeds. "We'll have a barbecue, a swing set, a birdbath, a trellis, maybe even someday a swimming pool." They already had a fishpond. The water was dark and smoky, rimmed with algae. Large gold- and lead-colored fish glimmered dully in the muck, slowly blinking their bulbous eyes like monsters surfacing from some nightmare. Sandra held Daddy's white cloth hat and watched him hit the ground with a shovel. He overturned convexes of damp black earth, severed worms and pulsing white slugs. Sandra liked the pungent, musty odor of the fertilizer, and rode on Daddy's back while he pushed the reseeder. They watered every morning, and soon tiny green shoots appeared. After Daddy disengaged the garden hose he filled his coarse, red hands with water from the tap, flung the water into the bright summer sky and told Sandra the sparkling droplets were diamonds. Sandra tried to catch them, but they slipped through her fingers. One day she sat down on the patio and cried. Daddy promptly took her to the store and bought her a tiny "Genuine" brand diamond set in a thin copper band. The next morning he went away on the boat.

The new grass died, the earth turned gray and broken. Mrs. Mitchelson said, "He wants a lawn? Then let him water it his own self, why doesn't he." She toasted her reflection in the twilit picture window. "Here's to your damn lawn. Here's to your damn family area." Bourbon and crushed ice spilled over the rim of her glass. In the afternoons Sandra sat alone on the living room floor and observed through the smudged picture window the gradual destruction of the yard. In the spring, weeds grew—strange enormous weeds as tall as Daddy, bristling with thorns and burrs and furred, twisted leaves. Scorched by the summer sun, the weeds cracked and fell, and when spring returned, the mat of dead weeds prevented new weeds from sprouting. Sandra asked when Daddy would be home. Mrs. Mitchelson said, "Never, if I have anything to do about it," and departed for the pawnshop with the heart-shaped locket, the transistor radio, the tiny "Genuine" diamond ring. "You want to know what all that junk was worth?" Mrs. Mitchelson shouted, looming over Sandra's bed at 3:00 a.m. Sandra sat up, blinked at the light, rubbed her eyes. Mrs. Mitchelson's eyes were red and wet and mottled with discount cosmetics. "Twenty bucks. That's how much he loves you. Your wonderful father. Your father who is so wonderful." Mrs. Mitchelson stormed out of the room, the front door slammed. Sandra rolled over and went back to sleep. That summer they sold the house.

In Bakersfield Mrs. Mitchelson worked at the Jolly Roger Fun and Games Lounge next door to the public library. Every day after school Sandra waited in the library and read magazines. She especially liked the large, slick magazines that contained numerous full-page advertisements. She enjoyed reading phrases such as "unmistakably the finest," "the affordability of excellence," "the passionate abandon of crushed velour." When the library closed at nine she sat outside on the bus bench and thought about the sharp, clear photographs. Fashions by Christian Dior, natural wood-grain furniture, Chinese porcelain, a castle in Spain, a microwave oven with digital timer, an automobile with a leopard crouched and snarling on the hood. The doors of the Jolly Roger swung open and closed, releasing intermittent bursts of smoke, laughter and jukebox music. Buses roared past. Sometimes one of Mrs. Mitchelson's friends drove them home. Nervous, unshaven men; their cars were usually littered with plumbing or automotive tools; cigarettes with long gray ashes dangled from their mouths. They ate pretzels and laughed with Mrs. Mitchelson in the living room while Sandra went quietly to bed.

They lived in Pasadena, Glendale, Hawthorne, Encino. Sandra finished high school in Burbank, acquired a receptionist's job in Beverly Hills. In Compton they took a one-bedroom apartment which included some cracked windowpanes and numerous discreet cockroaches. Weekdays, however, Sandra sat at an immaculate mahogany desk in the public relations firm of Zeitlin and Morgan. She answered telephone calls (often from television and film celebrities), organized the week's appointments in a large leatherbound black ledger, typed advertising copy and allowed clients into the security building by activating a hidden white buzzer.

Sandra was usually alone in the office. Mr. Zeitlin had retired to compose Bermuda postcards. Mr. Morgan—with his distinguished gray hair, taut polished cheekbones and jogging outfit—arrived each day around elevenish, then quickly departed with Elaine, the leggy secretary, for the afternoon luncheon appointment. Occasionally Mr. Morgan's son Matthew dropped by and asked for Elaine. "Off with the old man again, huh? When am I supposed to get *my* chance?" Sandra admired Matthew—his capped white teeth, his knit ties, his shirts by Pierre Cardin. He resembled a man of "casual elegance," sipping Chivas Regal on a sailboat, displaying Jordache emblems at garden parties. Matthew was an executive with the Jiffy-Quick Messenger Corporation of Southern California. His solid-gold tie clasp depicted the comical (but fleet-footed) Jiffy Man dashing unflappably to his appointed destination. "My Dad didn't just hand me the job, either," he assured Sandra. "I started off at the bottom, and absolutely refused any sort of preferential treatment. I even drove the delivery van one weekend, so nobody can say I didn't pay my dues. It literally took me months to get where I am today, and it was never any picnic, let me tell you. But I like to think that in the long run my employees will respect me for it."

At four o'clock Sandra pulled the plastic jacket over the IBM, replaced paper clips and memoranda in their appropriate drawers and locked the office. On her way to the bus stop she window-shopped along Rodeo Drive, observed silk crepe de chine slacks at Mille Chemises, solid-gold Piaget quartz crystal watches at Van Cleef and Arpels. She admired the white, unblemished features and long, cool necks of the mannequins; their postures were perfect, their expressions distant and unperturbed, as if they attended a fashionable cocktail party at the heart of some iceberg. Maseratis and Mercedeses were parked along the curbs, and elderly women in low-cut blouses walked poodles on stainless-steel leashes. Everything and everybody appeared immaculate and eternal, like Pompeiian artifacts preserved in lava. Sandra avoided her own reflection in the sunny window fronts—her pale white skin and shiny polyester skirt made her feel like a trespasser in a museum. She caught the 6:15 bus and generally arrived home just after dark.

Mrs. Mitchelson started awake at the sound of Sandra's key in the lock, sat bolt upright on the living room couch. "Who's that? What do you want?"

Sandra opened the hall closet, removed a hanger. "It's only me. Go back to sleep."

Mrs. Mitchelson's dry tongue worked soundlessly in her mouth; she cleared her throat. "Well," she said experimentally. "Well, I wish I *could* go back to sleep. I wish I *could* get a minute's peace around this place." She gripped the frayed arm of the couch with both hands and pushed herself to her feet. "But don't worry about me. Just because I gave birth to you. Just because I took care of you when *you* were sick and helpless." Mrs. Mitchelson took three short steps and landed in the faded rattan chair. The chair creaked sympathetically. "I'm not saying I was perfect. I'm not saying I didn't make my share of mistakes. But at least I *tried* to give you a good home—which is sure a hell of a lot more than your father ever did."

"Sit down, Mom. I'll get your dinner."

"Do you think it's easy for me? Do you? Getting older and weaker every day, so sick I can hardly breathe sometimes. Just sitting around this lousy apartment wondering how much longer I've got left in this miserable life."

"Please, Mom. Don't say things like that." Sandra folded the comforter and slipped it under the couch. "Do you want Tater Tots or french fries with your dinner?"

Mrs. Mitchelson's attention was diverted by the TV tray which stood beside her chair. The tray held a depleted gallon jug of Safeway brand bourbon, an uncapped liter bottle of Coca-Cola and an unwashed Bullwinkle glass. "Why not? Why shouldn't I say it? I hope I *do* die. I hope I die tomorrow—how do you like that?" Mrs. Mitchelson absently cleaned the glass with the sleeve of her blue flannel bathrobe. "You wouldn't miss me. You'd finally be free of me, just like your father." She filled Bullwinkle waist-high with bourbon, added a few stale drops for texture. "When I needed your father, where was he? Traipsing all over the world, *that's* where he was. *You* might as well be a thousand miles away too, for all the good you ever do *me*. . . . *Ah*." Mrs. Mitchelson put down the empty glass and snapped her dentures with satisfaction.

In the kitchenette Sandra turned on the stove and emptied a can of Spaghetti-O's into a saucepan. She could hear the neck of the Safeway jug clink again against the rim of the glass.

"When I remember when I was younger, all the opportunities I had. I had a lot of boyfriends. They took me to nice restaurants, bought me expensive presents. Then I met your father. I was so stupid stupid stupid. I threw everything away for that louse. *Now* look at me."

Bullwinkle looked at her.

The following summer Mrs. Mitchelson was admitted to City Hospital. "This is just what you've been waiting for, isn't it? Now I'll be out of your hair for good." Mrs. Mitchelson's voice was uncharacteristically restrained. Sometimes she almost whispered, leaning toward the side of the bed where Sandra sat. "But just you wait. Now you'll learn what it's like to be alone. You'll know the hell I went through when your father left me for some cheap Filipino whore." Mrs. Mitchelson's eyes were wide and clear and moist, like the eyes of Bullwinkle on the drinking glass. Sandra sat quietly with her mother behind the cracked plastic partitions, listened faintly to the moans and cries of neighboring patients, read paperback romances in which elegant women were kidnapped and fiercely seduced by pirates, rebel cavalry officers, terrifically endowed plantation slaves.

Mrs. Mitchelson's cirrhosis was complicated by undiagnosed leukemia, and she died unexpectedly just before dawn on a Monday morning. Sandra was fixing coffee in the kitchenette when the nurse called. Her mother had been wrong, she abruptly discovered. She did not feel alone, she did not feel betrayed. She did not, in fact, feel much of anything. She took the morning off from work, arranged disposition with the hospital crematorium and smoked a pack of Mrs. Mitchelson's menthol cigarettes.

The medical bills were formidable, and Sandra had less money than ever at the end of each month. Her window-shopping expeditions grew less frequent, and she began taking an earlier bus home. Without Mrs. Mitchelson to care for she rarely thought to fix dinner. She became pale and listless. Elaine said, "Why don't you lunch at Ramone's today? They've got an outdoor patio and it's a beautiful day." Instead, Sandra remained in the office alone, lunched on vended crackers, bagels and candy bars.

Then one night Sandra discovered Reverend Fanny Bright and the Worldwide Church of Prosperity. Reverend Fanny's sermons were broadcast live every Saturday evening from Macon, Georgia. Reverend Fanny told her followers, "You can't expect happiness to just come *knocking*. You must *pursue* riches, you must *pursue* happiness, you must *pursue* the power of Divine Creation. When you see something pretty you want to buy, how many times have you told yourself, 'I cannot afford this'? Is *that* what you think, children? Is *that* what you believe? Then you are *negating* the power of Divine Creation. You must convince yourself you can afford *anything*. You *can* afford it, you *will* purchase it, you *shall* possess it. You must impress your super-conscious with *affirmation*. The super-conscious is His workshop where, with the divine scissors of His power, He is constantly cutting out the events of your life. But first you must show Him the *patterns* of your desire, you must fill your *mind* with beautiful things." After each sermon Reverend Fanny pulled a chair up close to the audience and solicited tales of miraculous prosperity. Middle-aged men and women described flourishing investments, sudden cash gifts from strangers on the street, gratuitous office promotions. "All I want to tell you," one woman said, "is that I love you, Reverend Fanny. Prosperity has taught me how to love. Now I no longer feel so empty and alone."

Every month Sandra mailed the church a check for ten dollars. In reply she received a mimeographed request for further donations. The stationery was inscribed with the church motto: *If you do not wish to be denied riches, you must not deny riches to others.* Sandra closed out her savings account transferred the $2,386 to her previously minimal checking account and prepared herself for imminent prosperity. She purchased navy cashmere sweaters, suede pants, a silk crepe blouson dress fringed with lace, a deep-breasted brown satin coat, labels by Calvin Klein, Oscar de la Renta, Halston, Adolfo, Bill Blass, Ralph Lauren. She joined a health spa, subscribed to tanning treatments, visited prestigious beauty salons. Her checking balance dropped to $1,900, $1,350, $1,000. She did not question the beneficence of Divine Creation; instead she used her Visa card. Elaine said, "You're looking so much better, girl. Why don't we have a drink together after work? I'm meeting a couple of Tokyo software executives, they told me to bring a friend." Mr. Morgan granted Sandra a fifty-dollar raise and told her, "You really bring a lot of class to this office," on his way to a toothpaste manufacturer and lobster bisque.

Church doctrine was unequivocally validated. Sandra increased her monthly contribution to thirty dollars.

Then one night Sandra discovered her super-conscious in a dream. She ascended a long winding staircase. She was wearing her ankle-length "Cameo lace" nightgown from Vassarette, her Nazareno Gabrielli padded cashmere slippers. Her fingers ran lightly along a polished oak banister. The summit of stairs met a long off-white corridor lit by globed ceiling fixtures. The fixtures were white, opaque and sprinkled with the silhouettes of mummified insects. At the end of the corridor a solitary door stood slightly ajar. Bright yellow light from behind the door cast long, angular shadows down the length of the corridor. Sandra stepped quietly, afraid of disturbing anyone. As she approached the door she grew light-headed and her ears popped, as if she were descending in an airplane. The tarnished aluminum doorknob rattled at her touch. She pushed open the door.

The room was small, windowless, lit by a naked overhead bulb. Cobwebs scribbled the pale walls and cornices. The plaster was pitted and crumbling, mapped by an extensive network of cracks and crevices. The hardwood floors were sagging, whorled and discolored. A full-feature model A-20 integrated amplifier sat in the middle of the floor beside a matching AM-FM stereo digital-frequency synthesized tuner and cassette player. An identical system had been advertised in *Stereo Review,* and Sandra still recalled many of its vital statistics. A pair of three-way loudspeakers were stacked against the wall, with twelve-inch woofers, four-inch midrange drivers and one-inch dome tweeters housed in walnut-veneer cabinetry. A mass of electric cords were joined by a plastic adapter to a solitary wall outlet. A tiny green light activated on the amplifier's monochrome panel, an eight-track tape clacked faintly inside the tape player. The speakers suffused the room with white, cottony static.

Louis Armstrong began to sing, accompanied by bass, piano and drums.

> Baby, take me down to Duke's Place,
> Wildest box in town is Duke's Place,
> Love that piano sound at Duke's Place . . .

Sandra disliked jazz, pulled shut the door. The music diminished to a low, persistent bass that fluttered in the off-white corridor like a staggered pulse. The door's surface was Formica, with simulated wood grain. She tested the knob, the lock clicked distinctly. Then she woke up.

It was still dark when the music awoke Sandra on the living room couch. She reached sleepily for the portable television. The green, baleful screen stared vacantly back at her, containing only her dim reflection—a shrunken body attached to one enormous, elongated hand. Louis Armstrong continued to sing.

> Take your tootsies into Duke's Place,
> Life is in the swim at Duke's Place . . .

The bass thudded soundly in the floors, the walls, the cracked wooden frame of the couch.

Sandra turned on the lamp and saw the stereo components stacked against the far wall, partially hidden behind the TV tray. The amplifier's monochrome panel glittered intricately. I am a miracle magnet, Sandra thought, recalling one of Reverend Fanny's prescribed affirmations. Beautiful things are drawn irresistibly to me. I give thanks that every day and in every way I grow richer and richer.

On her way to work Sandra mailed the church a check for one hundred dollars.

That night she couldn't sleep. She lay on her back on the couch, her hands folded on her stomach. She closed her eyes and tried to visualize the off-white corridor, the half-open door. What did she want to find inside? A color TV, jewelry, kitchen appliances, a new car? What kind of car, what color? Would it fit inside the room? How, exactly, had the room looked? She remembered the pitted walls, the stained floors, the quality of light—but she couldn't put all the elements together at once. A Maserati, she decided firmly. Like the one Mr. Morgan drives. There, it's all decided. Now she was closing the door. Okay, the door is closed. Everything is very dark. Had she heard the living room floor creak just now? Yes, she was almost certain. Still, she kept her eyes closed a few more minutes.

She sat up and opened her eyes. The living room contained the portable TV, the aluminum TV tray, the new stereo, the broken wall clock, the dingy venetian blinds.

She closed her eyes and tried again. No matter how hard she concentrated she could not make the car appear. It was nearly dawn before she fell asleep and stood again on the winding staircase. The wooden stairs were firm and cold against her feet; they even creaked occasionally. The car, she wondered. Will the car be there, or something else? It doesn't matter, she told herself. She would accept what was given. She wasn't choosy; she wasn't greedy. She only wanted her fair share. She walked to the end of the corridor, pushed open the door. Books were stacked haphazardly around the small, otherwise empty room. Dozens and dozens of books, as if waiting to be shelved by some divine librarian. Sandra stood at the doorway, but she did not go inside. The room's strange powers might harm her, she thought—jolt her like electricity, singe her like fire. She pulled the door shut.

When she awoke the next morning, she examined her new books. They were accompanied by a bright orange and green brochure which described them as "The Greatest Books Ever Written." *Madame Bovary, The Scarlet Letter, Fathers and Sons, The Red and the Black, Jude the Obscure.* Each volume was bound in genuine leather and filled with numerous illustrations by "The World's Greatest Modern Artists." She imagined the spines upright and glistening on a brand-new bookshelf. A blond oak bookshelf, perhaps. With glass-paneled doors and gleaming gold fixtures . . . But any bookshelf will be fine, she reminded herself abruptly. Really, any kind at all. She wasn't in any kind of hurry. She didn't want to test the power, or challenge it unduly. She would accept what she was given.

Every night the dream recurred and the room presented her with beautiful things. A Schumacher "Pride of Kashmir" Indian rug, a hand-carved Japanese console with iridescent moiré lacquer wash, a hand-cut glass chandelier by Waterford, a Miró original, a Roe Kasian dining set, a Giancarlo Ripa white-shadow fox fur. The next time Matthew visited the office she was wearing Fernando Sanchez's latest, a sheer silk-taffeta dress anchored to a black lace bra. Her ruby earrings were the color of pigeon's blood. Matthew sat on the edge of her desk.

"You like Japanese food?"

Sandra stopped typing, looked up. Her lashes were Borghese, her mascara Lancôme. "I guess I don't know. I've never had it before."

"Never?" Matthew's face was puzzled, as if confronted by an enigma. "Tempura, teriyaki, Miso soup? You're in for a real treat. I know the best place in town. They've got shrimp the size of my fist." He showed her his fist for emphasis. "How does eight sound?"

"Eight?"

"All right. Eight-thirty—but try and be on time. I'll only honk twice. Here." He handed her the steno pad. "I'll need your address. Draw me a little map or something."

Matthew picked her up at nine and they drove directly to his apartment, a West Hollywood duplex. "Is the restaurant nearby?" Sandra asked. For the occasion she wore an obi—a broad black sash belt—with her cobalt-blue, raw-silk dress. "It just suddenly occurred to me," Matthew said. "They probably aren't open Thursdays. I'm almost certain, in fact. If you're hungry, see what's in the fridge." In bed Matthew was fastidious. His hands and mouth made routine, scheduled stops at each of her erogenous zones, like miniature trains on a track. Sandra, meanwhile, observed herself in the mirrored ceiling. "What's the matter with you?" he asked finally. "You didn't tell me you had problems with men." Matthew's body was sleek, firm, unblemished. His underwear was by Calvin Klein, his cologne by Ralph Lauren. Sandra said she just wanted him to hold her, and Matthew grew suddenly tense in her arms. He said he was short of cash at the moment—could she pay her own cab fare home? He *would* reimburse her.

Matthew stopped coming by the office. Whenever Sandra called his home she couldn't get past the girl at his answering service.

"Matthew Morgan residence—Mr. Morgan is out at the moment. Can I take a message?"

At this point Sandra usually heard the click of a second extension being lifted, and knew Matthew was listening when she asked, "Has he picked up his messages today?"

"One second and I'll check. . . . This is Sandra again, right?"

"Yes."

"Well, I'm afraid he still hasn't called in. But you can leave another message, if you like. . . ."

One day Sandra waited outside Matthew's office building until he emerged for lunch. "You know I really care about you," he said. "I just think it would be better if we didn't see each other again for a while. It's nothing the matter with you, babe. It's *me*. I just don't think I'm ready to make the kind of commitments you seem to expect from a man. You tend to be very possessive—which is *fine*, it's only *right* . . ." He paused to wave at his secretary, who tapped one foot impatiently at the curb. "Look, baby. Let's talk about this later in the week, okay?

We'll have lunch. And do you think I could borrow a twenty until then?" He palpated his vest pocket. "Seems I left my wallet in the office."

Matthew never called. Sandra waited at home, certain he would. She broke dates with Mr. Takata, the software executive, and Steven, her aerobics instructor. It was only a matter of time. Matthew would come around. She was a miracle magnet. She was one with the creative power. One night she received an Amana trash compactor, the next a Zenith Gemini 2000 color television. "You must not be afraid of total fulfillment," Reverend Fanny warned, her brows knit with sincerity. The glazed, speckless TV screen crackled with static electricity as Sandra reached to increase the volume. "You mustn't fear, you mustn't doubt, you mustn't lose faith. *Total* fulfillment requires *total* commitment. Have you, for instance, hoarded away a little nest egg, some rainy day money? Then you doubt the complete power of Divine Creation. Why put a time lock on your security savings when your love can be bullish on the stock exchange of heavenly devotion?"

That afternoon Sandra walked to the corner and mailed the church a check for $327.43, the balance of her account. Later the same night, Matthew called.

"Hello, Sandra?"

"Yes."

"Sandra, baby. It's me. Matthew. You remember me, don't you?"

"Of course I do."

"I know I should've called. But it's been really hectic in the messenger biz, you know?"

"I'm sure it has."

"You're not mad or anything, are you? I seem to sense a lot of hostility on your part. I know I owe you twenty and all—"

"No. I'm not mad. I'm glad you called. I was waiting for you to call."

"Good. Look, I was thinking. Let's have dinner tonight— all right with you? I'll pick you up a little after eight, we'll go find a nice quiet spot."

Matthew arrived at half past ten, and rang the doorbell.

"You think my car's safe parked outside? It's so late, I thought we could scrounge up a snack right here. You can show me around your apartment." Matthew entered the living room. "Hey, where'd all this great stuff come from?" He reached for the tape player—*Louis Armstrong's Greatest Hits*. Lengths of crumpled brown magnetic tape spilled onto the floor. "Seems you've got the tape caught on the heads. If you've got a screwdriver, I can probably fix it."

"I pushed a wrong button or something," Sandra explained quickly, took the tape from his hands and plugged it back into the player. "I'll have it fixed one of these days. I just like the way it looks. It really brightens up the room, don't you think?"

"What's down here? Is this the bedroom?"

Sandra followed Matthew through the door. He crouched in the corner of the bedroom, picked up and assessed one silver candelabrum. "This is worth a few bucks," he said.

"It's getting late. Aren't you tired?" Sandra asked, and began straightening the Wamsutta silk sheets.

"Where'd you get all this loot? My old man doesn't pay you this well just to answer telephones."

"My father sends me things. My father has a very important job in Asia. Now, please—put those things down. Get into bed."

"What a sweet deal. I think I'd like to meet this old man of yours someday."

Sandra pushed Matthew's hand away from her belt. She just wanted him to hold her, she said. This time, he obliged.

Sandra and Matthew were very happy together for a while. She enjoyed cooking his meals in the microwave, washing his clothes in the Maytag. Every morning she walked to Winchell's and brought him coffee and jelly donuts. Matthew took the next few weeks off from work. "I want to be with you more," he said, wiped a dollop of red jelly from his chin and peered over Sandra's shoulder at the new Panasonic Omnivision VHS video recorder with wireless remote. "I never saw that before. Did it just arrive this morning or something?"

Every evening Sandra stopped by the market on her way home. Matthew requested steak, swordfish, veal, king crab, champagne, Jack Daniel's Tennessee sour mash. She began computing her checking balance in negative numbers. When she arrived home Matthew was usually on the phone in the bedroom. "—yeah, Bernie. It's me, Matt. . . . I know I haven't been home—I don't see what it matters to you where I'm staying. I want you to put a grand on Blue Tone in the sixth. . . . Bernie, don't insult me. You know my old man's good for it."

Sandra collected soiled glasses and plates from the living room. On the burnished mahogany coffee table she noticed a tiny soft white mound of powder centered upon a small rectangular mirror. A gold-plated razor blade, attached to a fine-link silver chain, lay beside it. She took the dishes into the kitchen, started hot water in the sink, wiped a bit of fried egg off the lid of the trash compactor. Her mail was stacked on the countertop. A lengthy, itemized Visa statement. The landlord's second eviction notice. Urgent utility bills with bold red borders. My mind is centered in infinite wealth, Sandra reminded herself, and opened the last envelope. *Dear Friend,* the letter began. *Are you prepared to receive the wealth of Divine Creation? Then you must be prepared to dispense wealth to others. Wealth flows two ways, not one, thus maintaining universal harmony.* The letter was concluded by Reverend Fanny's mimeographed scrawl. Sandra removed her checkbook from the kitchen drawer, computed her balance on the Texas Instruments Scientific Calculator. Zeitlin and Morgan would pay her Wednesday. Perhaps she could deposit the paycheck in time for her outstanding checks to clear. Her balance, then, would be $23.97. She thought for a moment, turned off the sink faucet, dried her hands on a towel. I am a money magnet, she thought. Every dollar I spend comes back to me multiplied. I have all the time, energy and money I require to accomplish all of my desires.

She wrote the church a check for one thousand dollars. She licked and sealed the envelope, then heard the broiler door squeak open behind her. She turned.

"Porterhouse, huh? Great, baby. My favorite." Matthew slammed the broiler door shut. "Listen, I need to ask you a little favor—*por favor?* Just a couple hundred for a day or two. My accountant's got all my assets tied up in some sort of bonds or something. I don't really understand all the technical details. It'll take me a few days to get hold of some free cash. You know these accountants. They think it's their money, right?"

Matthew's smile was beautiful. His teeth actually sparkled, like the teeth in television commercials. Matthew and Sandra are very, very happy together, Sandra thought. Marriage, they both realize, is inevitable. They mean so much to each other. They will honeymoon in Brussels, where Matthew has important family. After a year they will return to the States where, with the aid of a personable nurse, Sandra will raise two beautiful adopted children, a girl and a boy. Matthew will eventually be recruited into politics. "We need you," his influential friends will say. "You're the only man who can beat Patterson." Matthew will win by a narrow margin, but his reelection four years later will come in a landslide. They will rent a Manhattan penthouse, and Matthew will commute to Washington.

"I can write you a check," Sandra said.

One morning before she left for work Sandra made a long-distance call to Macon, Georgia. "Worldwide Church of Prosperity," the receptionist said. "How can we help each other?"

Sandra asked to speak with Reverend Fanny, and the receptionist said, "Oh, I'm afraid that simply isn't possible. Regretfully, the Reverend's numerous personal and public commitments make it virtually impossible for her to speak privately with each and every one of her brethren. But should you, perhaps, be contemplating sizable donations—say, ten thousand or more, and all of it tax-deductible, of course—then I *might* be able to connect you with one of the Reverend's close advisers—"

"I *am* contemplating sizable donations," Sandra assured her. "I *am* grateful to the power of Divine Creation. My life is abundant with beautiful things. But at the moment I'm experiencing some problems of *cash flow*. . . ."

"Oh," the receptionist said.

"I'm sure it's just a temporary problem—but I was wondering if there weren't any special prayers or affirmations for someone in my situation. You know, prayers which might *focus* my miracles a little more. And please, don't think I'm trying to be greedy or anything—"

"Cash is not wealth," the receptionist said. "Money only travels in one direction. True wealth flows both ways. Now, if you would like to give me your address, I'll see to it you receive our free monthly newsletter."

On Friday Sandra received a series of overdraft charges from her bank, and a tense telephone call from the local Safeway manager. "I realize these things happen," the manager said. "Have to admit even I've bounced a few in my day. But how soon can I expect your check to clear?" Very soon, Sandra answered. She would deposit funds first thing tomorrow morning. She was so embarrassed. It wouldn't happen again.

"You'll get your damned money!" Mrs. Mitchelson used to shout, after the store's third call or so. "What's the matter with you people, anyway? Don't you realize I'm just a single woman, trying to raise a child? No—*you* listen for a minute. You men always expect us to listen to you—well, *you* listen for a change. I'll pay you when I'm good and ready, and not a minute sooner. Got *that*? And *another* thing. You've got the worst stinking produce section in the city, do you know that? Your apples are wormy, your lettuce is wilted, your vegetables are rotten. Do you hear me? *Rotten.* Instead of me paying you, you should pay *me* for all the lousy produce I bought from your store and then had to throw away. That's what *I* think." After Mrs. Mitchelson hung up the phone she would fix herself a drink and tell Sandra to go pack her suitcase. "We're going to stay with your Aunt Lois again for a while," Mrs. Mitchelson would say. "Then maybe we can find a new home where the bastards will let us live in peace."

After Sandra hung up the phone, as a sort of grudging memorial to her mother, she climbed a stool, reached the Safeway jug down from a high, dusty shelf and poured herself a drink. She carried her glass into the living room, which was crowded with mismatched and extravagant furniture, video and stereo components, unopened crates of records, Abrams art books and glassware, like the award display on some television game show. Matthew was playing Galactic Midway, an arcade pinball machine by Bally. Bells chimed, lights flashed, hidden levers pumped the next gleaming silver ball into position. Gripping the machine's sides Matthew nudged it from time to time. "Have a good day at work?" He pushed the reset button. On the scoreboard the digits clacked noisily around to zero.

"It was okay." Sandra cleared some stray pearls from the ottoman and sat down.

"Did I tell you the electric company called? Something about a last notice. I think I'd look into it if I were you. . . ."

On the coffee table the mound of soft white powder had

nearly doubled in size, like a miniature avalanche. Sandra sipped her drink and glanced around the room.

After a while she asked, "Where's my new VHS? My video recorder. The one I got this week."

The flippers clacked noisily. Then Matthew hit the machine with his fist. "Damn!"

"The VHS. I asked what happened to it."

"How the hell do I know?" Matthew pressed the reset button. "Do I look like the maid or something? It's around someplace. You probably haven't looked hard enough."

"I don't see it. It was in the living room this morning. It couldn't just get up and walk away."

"It'll turn up, you'll see. Everything turns up eventually," Matthew said, and pumped another ball into the game.

That night Sandra sat down and wrote a letter on her IBM Selectric.

Dear Reverend Fanny,
Please excuse the fact my check didn't clear. I had a very bad week last week. I tried to call and explain but the lady who answered the phone said you were very busy. I will try to make the check good at some date in the near future. I agree that if I expect to receive riches I must not deny riches to others, but I'm afraid my boyfriend Matthew whom I live with sold my Tiffany silverware set yesterday while I was at work in order to pay his gambling debts. Also he says he took my tape deck in to be repaired but I doubt that seriously. Also my electricity is being shut off tomorrow unless I pay them which I can't, and then what good will my new TV or any of my new kitchen appliances be good for? I would appreciate any help or advice on these matters you might like to impart to me. I wish I could send

you money like I usually do but I'll try to send you twice as much next time and hope you understand and forgive my present fiscal situation.

Yours faithfully,
Sandra Mitchelson

When Sandra fell asleep later that night she did not dream of the corridor. She dreamed instead of vast darkness, where silence filled everything like a heavy fluid. The fluid filled her mouth, throat, lungs. Breathing was impossible. I believe, she thought. I believe, I believe, I believe. She looked up and thought she detected, at the surface, a glimmer of white light. She tried to push herself up through the black weight but something gripped her ankle, something warm, pulsing, insistent. Like a tentacle, it moved up her leg. "Baby," the darkness said.

Sandra started upright in bed. The bedroom glowed with dim moonlight.

"Baby," Matthew said again. His arms wrapped themselves around her waist, his hands pulled her back into the weighted darkness.

On Monday, when Sandra returned home from work, she found Matthew in the bedroom, packing his Cricketeer wardrobe into the Samsonite. "I think I've done my part. I can honestly say I've done my share to try and make this relationship work." Underneath his packed clothes the tip of a silver candelabrum glinted dully. "But I'm the type of guy who demands a certain amount of honesty from a woman. Once she starts lying to me I know it's time to hit the road."

"I never lied," Sandra said. "I sent the electric company a check, just like I said. It must have gotten lost in the mail—"

"I'm not talking about that and you know it. I'm not talking about the fact that there aren't any lights or any food in the

house—or even that the television doesn't work. I'm not talking about what it's like living in the goddamn Stone Age. I'm
talking about simple honesty—something you obviously know
nothing about. I'm talking about the check you gave me for
Bernie, which wasn't worth the paper it was printed on. I'm
talking about my reputation in this town, which is now just
about shot because of you."

"I'll make it good," Sandra said. "It won't be any problem.
We can sell the television, the washing machine—"

"It's just a little too late for that, Sandra. Bernie went to my
old man for the dough. I'm free and clear. I've still got a job to
go back to, or don't you remember. You didn't expect me to
live *here* all my life, did you? In *Compton?*" Matthew latched
the suitcase and swung it off the bed.

"You have to stay. You can't leave," Sandra said over and
over again as she followed him down the hall and watched him
walk out the front door.

The telephone was disconnected, the water, eventually the gas.
Every night the vast, liquid darkness displaced Sandra's dream
of the miraculous corridor. Elaine said, "You look like hell,
girl. When was the last time you took a bath? There's a distinct
odor creeping into this office, and don't think Mr. Morgan
hasn't noticed." At the end of the week Sandra returned home
and found the front door sealed shut by the Sheriff's Department. The lock had been changed. She jimmied open the bedroom window, the one with the faulty latch.

Everything was gone. The brass bed, the pinball machine,
the Maytag, the Lenox crystal. Rectangles of dust marked the
former locations of impounded furniture. The room grew
dark, and Sandra went to the window, turned open the venetian blinds. Outside, it was dusk. She watched the phototropic
streetlamps glow and gradually brighten, casting pale, watery

red light through the blinds. Now she had nothing, and it didn't surprise her one bit. She was stupid, she never did anything right. Mrs. Mitchelson was right, Reverend Fanny was right, Matthew was right. Everybody was right, everybody except her. She was all alone; she was afraid of total commitment; she was dishonest—dishonest with herself. She was sick of being wrong all the time. Things must change; things were going to be different now. *I* am going to be different, she thought. From now on *I'm* going to be right, *I'm* going to make the right decisions.

She just needed one more chance. Finally she knew what it was she wanted, and that was the important thing. It was all very simple, really, like psychoanalysis on television. She wanted someone who cared about her, someone who would stay with her. Staring out the window at the streetlamp, Sandra leaned against the wall. Eventually she grew sleepy and closed her eyes.

She heard the door open behind her, the crack of its ruptured plastic seal.

Sandra opened her eyes. "Matthew?" She turned around. The door stood open, the living room remained empty. She walked to the door and looked out. The air was filled with blinding, devotional light. I am one with the creative power, Sandra reminded herself. I am not afraid. I believe, and I am not afraid. She stepped outside.

She stood again on the winding staircase. As she ascended she turned and caught a brief glimpse of the downstairs room. The light swirled and dust motes revolved slowly, like nebulas and constellations in some twilit planetarium. Large wooden packing crates were stacked everywhere, their lids nailed shut.

Sandra reached the summit of stairs. At the end of the corridor the door stood slightly ajar.

Quickly she crossed the length of the corridor, flung open the door and, without a second thought, stepped inside.

The overhead bulb flickered and extinguished with a sudden

pop. She was not afraid, she told herself. The place was very cold and very dark. Slowly her eyes adjusted. Tall yellow weeds surrounded her, rippling as an icy breeze blew past. The foundation of the fishpond was broken and upthrust; all the water had drained away, leaving a few green puddles of algae. The skeletons of the monstrous goldfish, partially devoured by stray cats, lay strewn about the yard like weird leaves. She got down on her knees. Burrs and thorns scratched her legs. Her hands groped among the weeds, discovered fragments of the Japanese porcelain doll. The tattered rice-paper parasol was damp and stained with mildew. She heard a noise and looked up.

A tall figure stood between her and the half-open door.

"Daddy?" Sandra asked.

Another sudden breeze blew past. The door slammed shut.

"Isn't that just what I should've expected." The dark figure approached, briefly stumbled. "*Damn*—I could break my leg on these lousy gopher holes. Just look what a holy mess your father made of this place. But who's the first person you hope to see? Your father, your wonderful father who never called, who never wrote, who never came to visit, who certainly never provided one nickel of support. Your wonderful father who never really gave a good goddamn whether either of us lived or died."

Sandra sat down on the damp ground, weeds brushing against her face. The porcelain fragments crumbled apart in her hands.

"Aren't you a little old to be playing in the dirt? Here, get up." Mrs. Mitchelson offered her hand. Sandra took it, pulled herself to her feet. "Try and grow up a little, will you? I can't keep my eyes on you every minute. Just *look* at this mess." Mrs. Mitchelson slapped the dirt from Sandra's knees.

They took one another's hand. Mrs. Mitchelson's hand was cold and dry and soft. Sandra squeezed it tightly against her stomach, afraid of the dark.

"Try and remember that sometimes I need a little help and

consideration too, you know. I can't do everything. I can only do the best I can, that's all. The best I can. Come on, now, and fix my dinner. It's been ages since I've had a decent meal in this dump."

Then, together in the deepening darkness, they made their way carefully across the ruined yard toward the shadows of the house.

GHOST GUESSED

Nor mouth had, no nor mind, expressed
What heart heard of, ghost guessed.

— GERARD MANLEY HOPKINS

"Didn't expect you home so soon," the ghost said, seated on Mother's prize rococo revival sofa, a late-Victorian design with mahogany frame and black horsehair upholstery. The ghost's features were vague, faintly phosphorescent, like mist in the beam of an outdoor film projector. "I knew those stale pills of Mother's wouldn't do the job. I told you we should use the gun. But you wouldn't listen to me—"

Kenneth Millar shut the front door, attached the chain, turned the bolt. He knelt, removed his Hush Puppies and placed them on the plastic mat, toes square against the wall.

"What did we *buy* a gun for if we weren't going to use it? You only had to pull the trigger once, one bullet, bang, that's all she wrote. Then you wouldn't have had time to chicken out, to get on the phone to every hospital in the county . . . Hey, where you going? I'm not finished talking to you!"

In the kitchen Kenneth filled a trembling Dixie Cup with Sparklettes. He still felt weak, somewhat dizzy, nauseous. He sat and braced his elbow against the kitchen table as he drank, swallowing against a sore throat. The lavage tube had blistered his trachea, the doctor told him, and prescribed antibiotics.

"I'm not letting you ignore me." The ghost stood in the hall. Sunlight from the kitchen window angled through his body, illuminating a soft blizzard of dust motes. "I knew you'd try that. It's just your style, just the cheap sort of trick you'd pull. Ignore me and maybe I'll go away. But I'm not going away, pal. You better get used to it."

Kenneth removed a dog-eared paperback from his jacket pocket. The book's open spine was thumb-soiled, the pages curiously stained in places. The book had been deposited beside his bed the night he was admitted to County Emergency. The inside front cover had been inscribed by its anonymous donor. *Only God's love will save you. Only God's love is really real.*

"Do me a favor. Before you start reading that crap, could you turn on the TV? I seem to be pretty helpless in regard to material objects. See?" The ghost reached his arm through the kitchen wall, waved his impalpable hand. "You realize I've been stuck in this lousy house all weekend with absolutely *nothing* to do?"

Kenneth opened his book to a random page. "In this world a few men find happiness. They are loved by God—"

"You're a champ, Kenny. You know that? A real champ."

"Most men never know that God is . . . that God *is*. They live like animals. They are those who live to die, and die to live again. . . ." The short, precise syllables buzzed senselessly in his sinuses like flies in a tin cup. After a while he gathered his courage and looked into the hall again. The hall was empty. He took his book into the bedroom and quickly shut his door. He was afraid of making a sound. His colon twitched like a tiny snare drum. He must be imagining things, he assured himself. A stale residue of Seconal, perhaps. Authentic supernatural events were reputedly accompanied by frigid temperatures, crashing plates, conventional shrieks of alarm. All Kenneth felt was a bit of melancholy solipsism, like the night he waited alone at a downtown bus stop.

The house was quiet, and Kenneth quieter still. Might as well not tempt things. He went to the rolltop desk, quietly removed from its bottom drawer a polished walnut case with stainless-steel clasps and opened it in his lap. As a child Kenneth had asked his mother for a set of army men. The army men were sold in large fishnet sacks that hung in the window of the local toy store. They came in a number of theatrical poses, firing rifles from a crouch, hurling grenades, charging with upraised bayonets. In the afternoons, restricted to the front porch until Mother returned home, Kenneth sat and watched the neighborhood children play in the abandoned lot across the street. They balanced their plastic army men atop rocks, logs, bushes, and then, backing off a few paces, hurled small stones and sound effects at them. *Pih-chew! Pih-chew-chew-chew!* One Christmas morning Mother presented him with a small oblong box, wrapped in austere yellow paper like a festive toy coffin. She sat him in the pale living room and, with much stern ceremony, permitted him to open the card first. *Merry Christmas, Love, Mother.* "Now you can open your gift." Kenneth peeled away the limpid yellow tissue, unhinged the tiny cardboard coffin, disinterred the layer of soft white cotton and, beneath, the heavy lead soldier. The soldier stood at attention with fixed arms. His painted uniform and features were chipped and dull. "I'll bet there's not another boy in town who has a soldier like that," Mother informed him. "It was manufactured by William Britain in the early nineteen hundreds. They were the first hollow-cast military miniatures in the smaller size. This one is a French hussar. The detail work for the period is, I am told, remarkable. That hanging at his side is a sabertache, see? Now you must be very careful. It's probably best not to remove the plastic wrapper." Over succeeding birthdays, holidays, graduations and other dismal events, Kenneth accumulated more of the toy soldiers in his desultory walnut case. King's African Rifles, Boer, Royal Sussex Regiment, USA, Montenegrin Officer, Australian, West Indian Regiment. Each item was sealed in a tiny plastic bag, a placenta for an artifact. Unable to impute to the objects any imaginative activity, Kenneth instead learned to adopt their forlorn, attentive expressions and, on rainy afternoons, stood the soldiers on his desk and stared at their faces through the yellowing plastic, conspiring with them in inanimate silence as they awaited together the tread of Mother's car on the graveled driveway.

Kenneth closed the case and returned it to its drawer. He sat very still, listening for noise from the living room but hearing only the thermostat's hollow click. After a while he checked the gratuitous lock on the bedroom door and crept furtively into bed.

Kenneth was awakened the next morning by the blare of the television. "—and you could win—A NEW CAR!" Appropriate audience response (applause, cheers, spontaneous squeals) shook through the thin walls of his bedroom and faintly rattled the loose ends of wallpaper. He put on his robe and slippers and went into the living room, squinting at the noise.

"Morning, champ." The ghost was gazing vacantly at the flickering screen. "You shoulda seen it. This dumb Puerto Rican broad didn't even know the price of a bar of soap—" His features were sharper today, more clearly defined. After a few addled moments Kenneth recognized the features as his own. Soft unwashed black hair, a goatee. Anxious, bloodshot eyes. A pale, waxy complexion.

"Could you turn that down a bit?" Kenneth asked.

"Look, I can even change channels." The ghost reached for the selector, dialed. Static pulsed on the screen.

"But can you turn it down?"

"What?"

The telephone rang amid the resumed hysteria of the audience. Kenneth took the receiver and cupped his hand over the mouthpiece.

"I said, *turn it down*."

"I can't hear you." The ghost reached and decreased the volume. "This damn set is too loud. What did you say?"

Kenneth turned his back on the sofa. "Hello?"

"Hello? Kenny? What's all that shouting going on? What's happening over there? Are you all right?"

"Just the television, Aunt Agnes."

"What are you doing watching television at this time of day? You should be out in your mother's garden, getting some color. And where have you been all weekend? Do you know I called twice on Saturday, *three* times Sunday?"

"You must have just missed me, Aunt Agnes. Yes, the garden. Yes, yes, I will. I know she would. Of course, you're right. I know I should have called. I'll try and remember." Kenneth glanced idly over his shoulder as he herded Aunt Agnes's questions. The ghost held one hand high in the air. He was giving Aunt Agnes the finger.

Kenneth hung up the phone, returned to his bedroom and dressed. On his way out the front door the ghost said, "Hey, you're gonna miss the best part. Everybody gets a chance to spin this big wheel, see? And the winner gets a billion dollars or something. Look, even that stupid Puerto Rican broad gets a shot at it."

Kenneth arrived for work even earlier than usual at Worldco Publications. He sat alone for a while in the employee lounge, a small, drab room with a few cracked plastic chairs and a Vendomat coffee machine. He drank hot, discolored coffee, listened to the tenorless strains of Muzak and watched the clock on the wall. At 10:45 he went upstairs to his desk in Wrong Addresses. The morning mail had already begun filtering through Computer Processing, and three subscription order rejects waited on Kenneth's desk. Kenneth consulted his desktop library of Southern California street indexes and telephone directories. When the problem was more serious than faulty spelling or incorrigible penmanship he dialed the number given on the order form.

"Hello, Mr. Smead? Or is it *Sn*ead? I'm calling from *Real Action Detective Stories* about the subscription you ordered?"

"I don't want one."

"I'm not trying to *sell* you a subscription, sir. I'm trying to help you receive the subscription you already ordered—"

"My *wife* ordered the damn thing and *I* don't want it!" And then the dial tone recommenced.

Kenneth had already reprocessed a small stack of cards by the time the rest of departmental personnel began to arrive, and more rejects were being brought to his desk every minute. He glanced up reflexively when he heard the snap of heels in the aisle. Veronica passed his desk and winked significantly. "Good morning, Ken." Veronica glistened in the bright fluorescent office: nylons, sleek skirt, lip gloss. She sat just down the aisle from Kenneth, adjusted herself in her chair, then in her compact. She tilted the circular mirror until her eyes flicked teasingly at Kenneth. Veronica's cordiality had been a matter of public record for almost a year now, ever since the afternoon Kenneth returned from lunch to discover he had left his savings passbook on his desk.

By eleven o'clock the remaining employees were at their desks, composing reports on one another's activities. Kenneth's telephone rang.

"Mr. Millar, I have a *personal* call for you," the receptionist said. "I've explained to your friend that the company prefers that its employees not accept *personal* calls at their desk. I hope you will keep the conversation as brief as possible."

"—Hello, Kenny?"

Kenneth hunched and whispered into the receiver. "I don't want you calling me here—"

"Who was that lady I just spoke with? Icy. *Brrr*."

"What do you want?"

"Just some stuff from the store. Beer, especially. Cigarettes, potato chips, sweet rolls for breakfast—are you taking all this down?"

"Listen, Kenny. I like you. I really do. And I'd like to help you. But first you've got to stop believing that life is something dainty and pristine, like Mother's chinaware." The ghost sat in his customary place on the sofa. The blinds in the room were growing dark. He switched on the lamp over the television, selected an apple from the hand-painted porcelain bowl and gripped it like a screwball. "You want to know your problem, pal?" His sharp white teeth took the apple. Juice spattered his upper lip and dribbled from the corners of his mouth. "You think you're too good for the real world. You're afraid to get dirty. So what if this broad Veronica's only after our money? Let's live a little. You saw *Zorba the Greek*." He wiped his mouth with the back of his hand. A white shred of apple remained on the verge of his lower lip. "Romance is just an idea somebody cooked up in order to sell more mouthwash. Me, I prefer a good time. You've just *got* to get out more, pal. You're not an old woman. Mother was an old woman, and that's why she's been dead for fifteen years." The ghost leaned back on the sofa, lifted his feet onto the glass-topped coffee table and tossed his half-eaten apple in the general direction of the fireplace. The apple bounced soundly off the ersatz brick façade and, landing on a burgundy patch of Persian carpet, rolled over twice. "Anyway, that's how I feel. It's just pretty hard to believe that a forty-two-year-old man has never been outside the city he was born in, has never touched a drop of booze, has never done *anything* his mother warned him against since he was age *one,* has never even been—"

"Shut up!" Kenneth flung his newspaper to the floor and started up from the art nouveau side chair, Karpen and Brothers, Chicago and New York, circa 1900, listed as item number 76 in the Orange County Auction Yearbook.

The ghost deliberated, sucked something loose from his teeth. "Kissed," he concluded, and flicked Kenneth a sharp glance.

Kenneth stooped and retrieved the apple. The exposed meat of the apple had already turned brown in spots.

"While you're up, could you get me a beer?"

Kenneth dropped the apple in the kitchen trash and returned to the living room with a damp sponge, dabbed at moist stains on the exorbitant carpet.

"Maybe I'm talking to myself. Maybe I just like to hear myself talk."

Kenneth got up from the floor. "The beer is in the refrigerator, if you'd care to look for yourself."

"Oh, great, *great*. Now you're even starting to *talk* like an old broad."

Kenneth rinsed the sponge in the sink for ten or fifteen minutes, wringing it mercilessly. His ears were flushed and hot, his eyes stung. He heard the refrigerator door open behind him. Cans clattered dully as one was yanked free from the plastic spine.

"Scrub those dishes, Kenny, old pal. And keep practicing. You're gonna make somebody a terrific grandmother."

When Kenneth awoke the next morning it was twenty past ten. He jumped out of bed and grabbed the alarm clock. The alarm lever had been shut off. Kenneth had his trousers hiked halfway up his legs when he realized there wasn't time. Even if he caught the 10:45 he would still be more than a half hour late. He lay back in bed and pulled the gloomy coverlet up to his chin. He felt abysmal, sluggish. His brain and limbs felt hollow, as if he had suffered a slow blood leak during the night. He lay and watched the white stippled ceiling, and after a few minutes noticed the silence in the house. The silence was like an immense, solid object, a statue in the park. He got up and went into the bathroom, kitchen, living room. The house was empty. He lay down on the sofa. The carpet was littered with crushed aluminum beer cans, beef jerky and candy wrappers, and a heavy spray of yellow potato chips, like the fallout from some detonated mini-mart. An empty beer can was stuck to the surface of the Renaissance revival side table. Kenneth gripped the can and yanked it free, uprooting a ring of rosewood and varnish. He turned on the television, nibbled stale chips from the depleted bag.

"It must be a real thrill being on the country's number one prime-time show."

"Oh yes, Mike, of course it is. And Lucinda—that's the character I play—has always liked to think of herself as Number One."

Kenneth could not sleep that night. He was thinking that when Mother died he must have been twenty-seven. The ceremony was informal and closed-casket, preparatory to cremation. Kenneth sat in the front row with Aunt Agnes. The coffin was polished and imposing, like a baby grand piano. Numerous relatives were in attendance, reminiscent of Mother's album of faded snapshots. After the eulogy, strange men shook Kenneth's hand and introduced themselves as Mother's uncles, cousins and business associates. "Let's see . . . if I'm your mother's cousin, then that makes me your . . . *not* your uncle. Your *second* cousin?" A few old women in spotty furs inquired about the estate, but the will proved ironclad. Aunt Agnes received the business, Kenneth the house and the savings account. Kenneth also inherited, as a sort of gratuity, a firm memory of Mother. Mother was not really gone. She was not reducible to dust. She would be with Kenneth always, in the back of his mind, sealed and suspended in an impervious block of clear Lucite, like a scorpion in a paperweight. Kenneth rolled over onto his side, then onto his other side. The weight of the vision made him feel claustrophobic. He got up and padded softly into the kitchen, put the water on to boil. He was pouring hot chocolate when he heard the front door open.

"And here we are!" the ghost said.

A woman giggled tentatively. "Oh my. This is just *too* precious!"

"Come right on in, honey. Watch yourself, there—"

"Oops." Something fragile crashed succinctly, with the *pock* of a ruptured light bulb. "Oh, I'm so *sorry*. Here, let me—"

"Don't worry about it. All this junk belonged to my mother. I don't personally give a goddamn about crystal stemware."

"Your *mother's*. I feel so terrible!"

"Shut up and come here a second."

Then they were silent. Something warm breathed expansively through the house. Even in the kitchen Kenneth could feel the slow, deep vital pulse, like that of a hibernal animal. Kenneth shut off the stove and ducked behind the refrigerator.

He heard footsteps in the hall. Someone's elbow cracked against the wall.

"Ow!"

"Careful, honey. This is the bedroom."

"Oh my. Don't tell me you *sleep* on that? It looks like a museum piece."

"So do you, baby."

"I never had any idea the Ken Millar *I* worked with was such a silver-tongued devil."

The switch snapped in the hall, the light went out in the kitchen. The hush resumed, the slow pulse quickened.

Is that really me? Kenneth wondered, alert behind the frost-free Maytag. Drunk, with a woman in the house? He heard a quick breath, a mutter. Something rustled.

A weightless sensation lifted in Kenneth's chest. The refrigerator clicked and hummed. He peered into the hallway, the steady shadows. They must be in the bedroom. He thought he discerned them, a dark, formless movement, protected even from refracted moonlight by the blackout curtains Mother had saved since the war.

Mutters, a small cry, staggered breathing.

Then, "What's wrong?" A whisper, the woman's.

"Nothing. What are you stopping for? Give me a minute." The urgent sounds were replaced by brisk, short whispers, like dialogue overheard at a clandestine business conference.

"What's the matter? Should I do something else?"

"No, that's not it."

"What's the matter with you, then?"

"I don't know."

"I'm sorry if I'm not exciting enough for you."

"That's not it, honey. Don't be like that."

In the kitchen the mug of cocoa slipped through Kenneth's fingers.

"What was that?"

"Nothing. Come back to bed."

"Is somebody else in this house? Are you some kind of weirdo or something? Is that it?"

"Listen to me, Veronica—"

"I don't *feel* like listening. I'm getting out of here. All the men in this town are crazy!"

Fast footsteps in the hall. The chain rasped, the bolt snapped and the door slammed.

The ghost came into the dim hallway, turning his shirttail into his unbuckled trousers.

Kenneth emerged from behind the Maytag, sidestepped a Rorschach of cocoa and shattered ceramic chips and followed the ghost into the living room.

The ghost cinched his belt. "So what are you looking at?"

"A real man," Kenneth said.

"I had a little too much to drink. So what? It's her loss."

"Whatever you say, Zorba."

"Don't start in on me, pal. I sure as hell got a lot further than you ever did. At least *I* knew what I was looking for. Where you going?"

Kenneth opened the desk drawer, reached behind the walnut case. He removed a gun from the drawer.

"Oh, suddenly we're a real tough guy, huh? Not afraid of guns anymore, is that it?"

Kenneth lifted the gun with both hands, the way he had seen done on television programs. His teeth and hands clenched. The gun was soft in his hands, like clay.

"Christ, stupid. You have to release the safety first. Don't you remember the guy at the gun shop said—"

Kenneth pulled again. The gun made a feeble, hollow click, like a penny dropped into a pail.

"I really didn't think you had it in you. I never believed you'd pull the trigger. Good thing I hedge my bets."

Kenneth lowered his unsteady hands. The gun slipped through his fingers and thudded onto the floor.

The ghost reached into his pocket. "You'll need these." He rattled something in his loose fist, stooped, placed the bullets on the carpet one at a time. "One, two, three, four, five, six. There, now let's try it again. Ready, set? Go."

Kenneth got down on his knees. His hands trembled wildly; his face felt swollen and hot. The objects loomed enormously on the carpet, as if viewed through a magnifying glass. He reached for a gleaming bullet. The bullet squirted out from between his fingers. He reached for the gun. The gun remained on the thin carpet.

"Now let's see how *you* like it," the ghost said. "Being stuck in the house all day without even a television to keep you company."

Kenneth stood in the middle of the living room. He was warm in the white light of the overhead lamp. He stared at a tiny blemish on the wall behind the sofa, a tiny ridge of impasto which contradicted the otherwise smooth surface of paint. An entire world existed in that tiny blemish. Wild, forlorn, alien, crepuscular, a planet of rock and stone and cold, colorless sunlight. Kenneth knew he would be very happy there.

"I'm telling you, pal. Things couldn't be better." The ghost sat on the sofa, drew a long breath from a Camel filterless, spat a sliver of tobacco. "Ever since Veronica and I made up she likes me better than ever. It's not only my money, either." He knocked an ash into the tall rock-cut crystal vase. Deep in the vase sparks smoldered among accumulated butts and black, twisted matches. "She's really crazy about me. You hear me? Pal? Where are you?"

"Right here," Kenneth said.

The ghost peered. "Step out of the light so I can see you."

A fine layer of gray ash settled over the black horsehair upholstery, Persian carpet and Renaissance revival side table.

A few months after the honeymoon Ken Millar sat in his brand-new Naugahyde Barcalounger. On one wall hung a crushed-velvet Elvis portrait, on another a seascape purchased from Starving Artists, Inc. The wall-to-wall shag carpet was described in the Ward's brochure as "cream-of-pearl pile." The television was on.

Veronica sat on the new paisley Hideabed sofa. "This is nice," she said absently, and turned the page of her *Vogue*.

Ken was watching *Today's FBI*. He had seen this one before.

Ultimately the psychotic terrorist would be shot in the head as he ran for the helicopter.

"What do you think, Ken? Wouldn't it complement my eyes?" Veronica held up the magazine. The slick color page glared like an Indian signal from a hilltop.

"Beautiful. Now, if you don't mind, I'm trying to watch this."

"I'm sorry if I disturbed you."

Ken lit a cigarette.

"I sure wouldn't want to interrupt that damn television. It's the only thing in the world that seems to matter to you."

"Why don't you go out and buy something. Just give me a break, will you?"

"Dr. Silverstein says I spend money to compensate. Dr. Silverstein says I need to get out more. He says he can tell I'm the sort of woman that loves to dance."

"Screw Dr. Silverstein." This was the best part. The helicopter was beating down onto the parking lot of the Safeway, swirling old newspapers around. Mike Connors consulted his walkie-talkie.

"I might as well. It couldn't be any worse than what I've *been* getting."

The psychotic emerged from the store. He gripped the gorgeous young prom queen by her long blond hair, gesturing severely with a Magnum.

"What was that?" Veronica asked.

"Sh!"

"Don't *shush* me! I asked what was that noise?"

Something rattled in the kitchen. The King William silver flatware.

"I told you before. These old houses have queer drafts."

"These old houses are spooky, you mean. That settles it. We're moving to Van Nuys so I can be closer to my sister."

The muzzle of the Magnum was wedged into the prom

queen's ear. Her hair fluttered and tangled in the wind from the helicopter. The psychotic angrily shouted his demands over the noise of the rotors. If his demands weren't met, the girl was going to get it.

What if this isn't a rerun? Ken thought. Or what if the producers have substituted an alternative denouement, and in this version the psychotic escapes with his loot to Cuba, Argentina or even Paris, France? Perhaps this time it will be that oh-so-perfect prom queen's brain that litters the asphalt. Ken reached for his can of Bud.

"Damn," he said.

"Oh, *really,* Ken. All over our new carpet. What's the matter with you lately? Can't you hold on to *anything?*"

THE *FLASH!* KID

Rudy McDermott's siege of the termite nest was inspired by the funny word "attrition," introduced to him by his birthday book, *We Were There at the Hundred Years War*. He shoveled a moat circumscribing the infested oak log and filled it generously with Pennzoil looted from Father's outboard. The termites, busy inside their moldering apartments, exhibited no immediate concern, and Rudy dashed home for lunch. He returned a half hour later to find the insects constructing a bridge across the moat with accumulating drowned corpses, swarming headlong into the muck with a sort of conscientious frenzy. Rudy struck a match and ignited the moat. The ring of fire flashed and heat rushed his face. The fried insects smelled like burned popcorn. Greasy black smoke lifted into the bright mountain sky, flames dwindled into the scorched earth. Rudy replenished the moat and lay back against a warm flinty hill, watching the discombobulated insects struggle and squirm in the ashy sludge. He flicked small stones at them as they carted their sizzling brethren into deep, buzzing tombs. Rudy reignited the moat and ran home for an ice cream and a brief chat with Father.

Father was out back on the raised sun deck with Mom. *Bushwah!* Father roared, and flung his newspaper over the railing. A few loose white sheets skimmed down the surface of the hill like manta rays. What's *this* I read? My tax deductible religious contributions go to providing flak jackets for Sister Maria Theresa's guerrilla forces in Uruguay! And who's Sister Maria fighting for? Subversives, that's who! And who do subversives hate most of all? Successful men like *me,* that's who!

For godsake, Mom groaned, prone on her lawn chair and bikinied, brown and glistening with oil like a very old salad. If there's one thing you sound stupid about it's politics.

Father grumbled, his face flushed. A black vein pulsed ominously in his forehead. He poured another icy margarita, sprinkled it with salt.

Termites, huh? Father said later, solaced by now with his fishing rod. He reeled in line from a spool that twitched and tumbled on the deck, and Rudy watched raptly over his dribbling ice cream. My old pal Bob Probosky and I knew all about termites. Or at least I did, yessir. When I was your age I busted open a termite nest, that's what I did. Bob was chicken, scared he'd get stung. Not me, though. I reached in and yanked out that mama termite with my bare hands, diced her for bait. She caught trout like a goddamn Gatling gun—yessir, she did! But did I let that fag Probosky have any? Nosir, I didn't! Sure I got stung. But I knew what I had to do and I did it—and *I* reaped the reward. The world's a jungle, boy. Only the toughest survive. You have to act fast if you want to make your mark on the world. You have to be tough if you want to become a successful man like your Father—

For godsake, Mom said, and reached for her sunglasses. If there's one thing you sound stupider about than politics it's *got* to be your crummy childhood.

* * *

With a sledgehammer Rudy returned and demolished the nest, pried loose sheaves of rotted wood. The mama termite was enormous, Rudy startled. Gravid and glistening, as long and thick as Father's forearm, the queen's convoluted envelope fitted snugly inside the log like the meat of some gigantic walnut. Reach in and yank it out? He would need a bucket. Rudy improvised, swung the hammer again. Pus and slime spattered his arms and face. The stench was terrible, and he wiped the sour taste from his lips. He ran away crying and crashed through bushes and a small stream. The crowd of trees stood around making shadows; birds chirped in the leaves. Rudy forced himself not to shiver, obligated by Father's nostalgic courage. He returned solemnly to the ruined nest. Termites swarmed away from the exploded queen, dragging bits of her flesh. Rudy unscrewed the lid of a jelly jar, crouched, shut his eyes. He scooped blindly at the nest and the jar made a wet *thwuck*ing sound. He screwed back the lid and flung the jar against the flinty hill, where it thudded soundly. Rudy's hands were sticky; he wiped them on the ground. The ground was dry and crusty and broke apart in shards. Rudy threw the flinty dirt over the ruined nest, cut more dirt loose with his bowie knife. Something metallic clanged and the knife bucked against his hand. He scraped the dirt cautiously. Metal screeched. Gradually Rudy cleared a patch of gunmetal black. The black was remarkably smooth, like the surface of an eyeball. A sense of great heaviness surfaced in his mind when he touched the buried object. Like déjà vu, abstract but firm. Patiently he uncovered the statue's entire surface. Two feet long, tubular, black and smooth and unblemished, without any markings or delineations whatever, as seamless as the skin of an egg. He struck it sharply with his knife, and the knife's point cracked. His fingers were drawn again and again across the smooth surface, as if here were condensed the enigmatic stuff of the universe. He clenched his teeth. Overhead the moon hooked vague clouds, and Rudy wondered, Who to tell? Who, indeed?

Sure, we'll take a look at it, Father agreed. Someday, someday soon. But not today, not right this minute. Right this minute there was fishing to do, imported beer to drink, Mom to bicker with inanely. That afternoon Mom drove to Tahoe and returned by dinner, her freshly dyed hair piled high atop her dry red face, accompanied by a strange noisy couple. The man was in the stock market, the woman in the Book-of-the-Month Club. The woman hugged Rudy viciously. The man said ha ha ha, what's that, young buck? A termite *how* big? I saw that movie. Jon Agar saves the world, doesn't he?

The image of the submerged, neglected statue infiltrated Rudy's dreams. They were deep black dreams without faces, a quicksand effluvium which filled his mind like molten ore, as if his identity and the identity of the statue were being inverted. The dreams encased Rudy in darkness; he felt warm, secure; his body was a vessel, hard and unimpressionable, like something fired in a kiln, like the heart of a planet, like the fine black powder he discovered inside the abandoned jelly jar the following morning. The fine kinetic powder jingled sibilantly as he swirled it around the inside of the glass, keening, eerie, celestial, like purported music of the spheres.

The first person Rudy lured to the statue took it away from him. A young surveyor had been prowling the woods for several days, unshaven, muttering, scratching himself, toting a small intricate telescope and clipboard. Rudy's approach was determinedly casual. He was learning that a child's enthusiasm is inversely proportional to the scale of adult priorities. Hey, mister. Want to see something weird? Hey, mister. It's right over here. Maybe somebody lost it. Hey, mister. Maybe there's even a reward.

Okay, okay, the young man conceded finally. Show me something weird. But then promise you'll go home, all right? Could you do that for me? Promise?

*   *   *

Mmmmmmmmmmmmmmmm. Interesting . . . The surveyor touched the statue briefly, as if testing a hot iron. Cautiously he laid his palm flat against the frictionless surface, whistled slowly through his teeth. So heavy, he said, and clenched his jaws.

As the surveyor stared, Rudy's sanctioned enthusiasm burst free. He babbled hectically of his discovery: the doomed termites, the Pennzoil, Father's nostalgic fish bait, Mom's new hairstyle, the gravid queen, the immanent dreams and the fine black powder.

The surveyor grumbled, scratched his oily hair, scrawled something on his clipboard and proceeded to the fishing lodge.

Hey, mister—can I come? Rudy asked, was not refused.

Rudy pressed his face against the glass-paneled phone booth, breathing mist against the glass and pretending he was an enormous fish in a bowl.

Andy? the surveyor said. This is Steve. Yeah, the connection's terrible. I'm up at Caple's Lake. . . . What? Dunnigan, Steve Dunnigan. No, I don't have a sister. We were in Dr. Tennyson's seminar together, remember? Okay, okay—just forget it. I've found something up here you'll want to take a look at—

Here, Dunnigan said, shutting the glass booth behind him. Buy yourself some baseball cards.

Rudy accepted the quarter cordially, slipped it into his pocket, went to the lodge and bought a quarter-pound bag of beef jerky with one of the twenties from his genuine cowhide wallet. He sat on the front steps and chewed as he watched Dunnigan hurry bags and equipment from his cabin into a battered red Toyota. When Dunnigan drove off, the Toyota's flimsy clutch rattled like a marble in a soup can.

Rudy went home to dinner, rapidly consumed two steaks, a potato, no broccoli, three slices of hot cherry pie and a frozen Snicker's bar. Upstairs in his loft he was only mildly queasy, and watched the portable television underneath his bedcovers.

He fell asleep and resumed the dreams again, awoke in a cold sweat, his stomach protuberant and growling. He slipped downstairs and managed a pair of ice cream sandwiches, returned to bed and the dreams again. It was as if his mind were being fed on a very short loop. Eggs for breakfast, four or five scrambled. Mom was pleased, offered encouragement. Another sandwich? Cookies? More milk, Rudy? Eat, *eat*! Marie and the girls are always talking about your skinny arms. . . . Father said, Good for you, boy! Build those muscles—you don't want to be a skinny little wimp all your life, do you? You've got to be tough, you've got to take care of yourself in this world, boy. You think I'm not tough? Go on, then; try me. Hit me in the stomach. Go ahead, hit me. Harder. *Harder,* now! Show some muscle, boy. I've swatted gnats harder than that!

Dunnigan returned in the afternoon with a circumspect goateed man. They conferred beside the sunken statue, consulted pocket-size devices and departed in a jeep. Dunnigan returned again the following morning with more men, equipment, jeeps. Rudy visited the site daily, saw crowbars snap like Popsicle sticks, pneumatic hammers grind to a halt, strong men with ringed underarms herniate in chorus, puny forklifts roar as cables snapped everywhere. Helicopters beat over the secluded lakefront property, CB radios spluttered and squawked in the crisp mountain air. Still, the object did not budge. It would not budge. It was stubborn, heroic and invulnerable, Rudy thought. Just like Superman.

Father and Mom budged quite readily, however, packed Rudy up with the other belongings and relocated to the relative sanctity of their San Francisco mansion, where Rudy explored the daily papers with casual regularity. The initial notice appeared in the back pages of the *Chronicle,* amid advertisements for lingerie and quick-weight-loss clinics. The blurb included

Rudy's name, Dunnigan's, date and location of find, difficulties encountered. A mere journalistic kernel, yet fecund, perseverant, it rooted and advanced to page two as Life Buried in Strange Object! and blossomed ultimately in front-page headlines:

LIFE BURIED IN STRANGE OBJECT!
Child Unearths Cosmic Treasure

Father and Mom began introducing Rudy to their friends as "the little archaeologist in the family" before posting him off to bed when another reporter eventually infiltrated the party. The phone rang constantly, and Mom had the number changed. Reporters and cameramen populated the front porch, lunatics verged on the perimeters. The streets resounded with cymbals and tambourines. Bullhorns proclaimed the sovereignty of Jesuschristalmighty. *The Flying Saucer Gazette* accused Rudy of conspiring with sentient vegetable protein on Betelgeuse. Satanists dropped by evenings for coffee and, rebuked, splattered sheep's blood on the lawn, driveway and deluxe Mercedes convertible. A flurry of Dianetic brochures arrived daily with the harried postman. Red journalism complemented topical hysteria. Cosmic Statue Predicts Earthquakes!!! Jeanne Dixon Communicates with Telepathic Statue in Esperanto!!! Cosmic Boon to Acne Sufferers??? Rudy chatted happily with the interchangeable lunatics and newsmen until his family's tolerance was "overextended," Father's press release declared. All he can tell you, Mom shouted one day, yanking Rudy back inside, is that he found the damn thing, he gave it away and then he came right back home! Crestfallen, Rudy was denied permission to pose for the covers of *Jack and Jill Monthly* and *Isaac Asimov's Science Fiction Magazine*. For the rest of the summer Rudy was relegated to the video entertainment console of his isolated bedroom.

Dunnigan, along with the "cosmic treasure," was appropriated by U.C. Regents Berkeley. A visiting lectureship compensated the former while an elaborate wing of the Physical Research Center secluded the latter. Dunnigan appeared frequently on network news programs and the *Tonight* show, with Johnny Carson. Frankly, Johnny, we're baffled, he conceded. We can't penetrate the object's shell, but ultrasound has detected embedded proteins, minerals, rudimentary enzymes— materials implicit in the genesis of life. As I told you over dinner, the statue's shell is so dense that the molecules are virtually impacted together. Conceivably billions of years old, it's perhaps the by-product—or so contend the latest theories—of some titanic implosion, the devastating force of which would be unconscionable even in our nuclear-conscious age. At this point Dunnigan granted the unconscionable audience a winsome, ingratiating smile, like a Nobel laureate confronted by some giddy coed, and Johnny suggested they play tennis together real soon.

Rudy switched off the television. It was late. He couldn't sleep. The resumption of grammar school foreclosed upon the vanished summer like some formidable mortgage. Rudy awoke the next morning in an empty house. Dad in Rio, Mom in bed. The lunch, prepared by the maid, was folded inside a double bag on the kitchen counter. Rudy scanned the *Chronicle's* comics page and devoured an eight-ounce box of Rice Puffies. Public concern over the statue had receded in the wake of renewed Middle East skirmishes. Rudy went to the bathroom, vomited anxiously, brushed his teeth, removed a frozen Snicker's bar from the freezer and chewed as he departed for the bus stop. Father had won the debate years ago concerning Rudy's education. He's going to public, not be a sissy. Just like me.

* * *

On the street corner Kent Crapps and Marty Femester were passing an untidy cigarette back and forth, inexpertly rolled from Bugle tobacco and parting at the seam. Rudy sat on the curb and handled his lunch bag to tatters.

Hey. If it ain't the rich kid. Hey, Crapps. Ain't that the poor little rich kid?

Sure is, Crapps said. It looks like *two* rich kids, if you ask me. Hey, fat boy. You better stop eating so much. You're liable to *explode*!

Rudy sat forlornly as he heard their approach. The wrecked cigarette bounced off his knee and he brushed at sparks.

Hey, maybe the fat boy's hungry. You think so, Crapps? You think he might like a marshmallow? There's a marshmallow, there in the gutter. It's a little muddy—but maybe the fat boy's *real* hungry.

Rudy hunkered submissively, anticipating his customary ridicule.

Hey, fat boy. Look what we fixed you to eat—

As the imperative mud-filled hand clamped Rudy's mouth, something unfamiliar activated abruptly in his mind. Something alert, canny, uncompromising.

Help help help quit it no no help help blech! Marty struggled weakly, like a small damaged sparrow. There, Rudy thought, his arm not strong so much as intent. *You* eat the mud this time. At a discreet distance Kent Crapps bounded up and down and shrieked for the police. Rudy wasn't even angry. He just wanted them to know he could take care of himself from now on. He had new responsibilities, through his discovery of the statue a sort of implied integrity. The weight of the buried statue filled the deep part of his mind. Nothing can hurt you, the deep voice confirmed, resounding in the immensity of remembered dreams that whirled, unalterable and patient, impervious and eternal.

Young men have responsibilities I don't care who started it

you can't carry on like hoodlums what if everybody behaved like that I'm doing this for your own good, the principal pronounced, and down came their pants. The secretary pulled shut the office door. Rudy neither whined nor protested at his turn. He felt supremely confident, and listened to the deep dreamy monotone of the buried voice. Returning to class he met wary eyes and whispers. He ate a magnanimous lunch alone in the cafeteria and cached burps to be released later, in class, in improvisatory bleats.

Grade school was a breeze.

Ha ha ha, everybody laughed, orbiting him in the schoolyard. Occasionally Rudy grabbed the scrawniest of them—a homely, wheezing asthmatic—and twisted his limbs one at a time. He convinced the asthmatic to confess explicit sex crimes with his mother, his father, his dog. Everybody laughed and even the asthmatic grinned plaintively. You're a riot, Rudy. You are—you're the funniest guy I know. You oughta be a comedian. Rudy never once suspected himself of bullying. He was merely amusing his friends. He viewed popularity as a social obligation, like the ballot. When the bell rang, the timid orbiting boys dispersed readily to their classes and Rudy, in his own time, lumbered along behind, thirteen years old and one hundred ninety-seven pounds, and nobody told him what to do anymore. Not even his parents.

Rudy! Rudy, stop that! You *heard* me, young man! Let *go* of your mother's arm—and I mean *right this minute*. Father bellowed punily.

Damn, Rudy thought, and released Mom's red, perfumed arm. Damn if anybody sends *me* to military school, and flung the academy brochure in the trash. I'm not a failure. I will succeed. I am tough, too, and will make my mark on the world. Just watch.

Father and Mom departed for the Riviera, and left Rudy under the aegis of a flinching, reluctant maid. Just fine with me, Rudy thought. I don't need anybody. I'm happy to be me, just like they recommend on television talk shows. He deposited himself at the kitchen table and trooped through a stack of grilled cheese sandwiches as if through so many Saltines.

Rudy dropped out of school at sixteen. Father leased him a two-bedroom apartment in the financial district and promptly departed with Mom to Rio where, it was rumored, they developed a successful liaison with two blond, liquid women Mom had met in Toronto the year before. Rudy, meanwhile, ate. Mountains of toast, vistas of jelly and syrup, acres of Rice Puffies and Sugar Dongs and Candy Cakes and Twinky Pies. Crushed plastic cereal toys littered the floors of his apartment. A mobile landmark, Rudy strolled immensely through the neighborhood, easily visible from high office buildings, helicopters, incoming passenger planes. He visited Taco Heaven, Mrs. Mary's Candy House, Happy Jack's Ice Cream Palace, and returned home munching candy apples, barbecued sides of beef, Big Macs. He squeezed blithely through crowds of slim, fashionable secretaries, and never glanced twice at their slit skirts, high heels and polished nails. Desire never pestered Rudy; his pubic hair remained downy, innocent. The family doctor proposed hormonal supplementation. Adamant, Rudy refused. He was not sick. He was inconceivably healthy. His life was purposeful, coherent and determined: he ate, he slept, he waited.

Steve Dunnigan appeared at Rudy's door one summer afternoon. Rudy was uncertain of the year. The seasons had flitted by like moths. Rudy shifted his weight away from the door and Dunnigan sidled into the cluttered apartment. Dunnigan wore a faded Grateful Dead T-shirt, stained Levi's, tattered Keds. My, how you've grown, he said. Rudy slumped into a beanbag chair, and the straining plastic envelope burst with a pop, spewing brown varnished beans everywhere. Rudy sagged unconcernedly as the chair depleted, listening to the vaguely familiar man through his stuffy brain.

I came to warn you, Dunnigan said.

Rudy yawned. Dunnigan scratched his head, and white dandruff spilled onto the floor.

Have you heard about IRM, Rudy?

No, Rudy croaked, and massaged his Adam's apple circumspectly.

Innate Releaser Mechanism. Genetic knowledge, knowledge coded into the DNA. Instinct, really. But an instinct, a mechanism, which must be triggered by a behavioral cue, understand? Mother bird does a little dance, perhaps, and activates the fledgling's migratory program. Then the fledgling departs for Tehachapi, Capistrano, Guam.

Rudy reached for the crushed Ritz Cracker box, rattled crumbs into his mouth.

The cue was tactile, Rudy.

Rudy tore open the box, licked more yellow crumbs from waxed paper.

A few years ago, undergraduates at U.C. Research came into contact with the statue. Today these students are withdrawn, antisocial, disrespectful of authority, obese and under heavy sedation at U.C. Medical. The doctors and scientists have agreed on a tentative diagnosis. The prognosis is catastrophe . . . Rudy, are you listening?

Rudy picked up the telephone and dialed Chicken Delite. Three buckets of center breast, he thought, and a gallon of coleslaw. The line was busy.

The statues are containers, Rudy, distributing life's essential ingredients throughout the universe. But the molecules of the container must be fused, the container launched. Think of a simple atomic reaction. A solitary atom is split, and the devastation is well publicized. Your body is composed of how many trillions of atoms, Rudy?

Rudy put down the phone; his head lolled against the wall. A few last beans dribbled from the exhausted plastic envelope.

Cosmic evolution—just think about it, Rudy. Life is forged from calamity, catastrophe, annihilation. The ultimate purpose of life—mere perseverance. And the law of evolution? Survival of the fittest—

Father, Rudy said. Hypnagogic, he stared at the ceiling.

Rudy, wake up!

Rudy started upright. Chicken Delite? he asked.

Would you like to see the statue again, Rudy? Would you like that?

Yes, Rudy thought. Yes yes. He raised himself courageously to his feet. The varnished beans seethed on the floor.

There's food in my car. Hungry, Rudy? Come on, Rudy, come on. . . . Dunnigan led Rudy out the door, rolled open the side of his van.

Rudy clambered inside, smelling pizza. Three cardboard containers streaked with oil. He opened the top box. The pizza was still warm, the cheese stiff and congealed. He divided the slices and transferred them, slice by slice, into his mouth. The van's door slammed shut; bolts were thrown. Rudy chewed pepperoni, mozzarella, briny anchovies.

The van's engine erupted, along with a nervous spasm in Rudy's stomach.

The van moved out. An air vent communicated with the driver's seat.

Everything will be fine, Rudy. They dig out a tiny chunk of your brain—no bigger than a sausage. You'll be happy, then.

People will like you; you'll like people. We'll start you on an exercise regimen, a diet. Hell, with your money, you can just take your pick of the ladies. You won't be lonely anymore. You'll be just like everybody else.

But I'm *not* like everybody else, Rudy reassured himself, and placed his palm against his stomach. Something percolated deep inside; his bowels contracted. He tried to hold it in. Father would get very mad. Father hated when Rudy smelled up the car, and rolled open all the electric windows.

Just you wait and see, Rudy. We'll command top dollar from the university, once I inform them of your condition. Let me handle everything. Did I tell you they fired me from my position? I used to know Johnny Carson and his wife personally. Now what's my doctorate worth? All-night pizza deliveries to junkies, high school parties, perverts. But I've learned. This time they'll deal on *my* conditions. This time I'll demand *tenure*—

The pressure mounted in Rudy's stomach. He cried out.

What's that? Watch your temper, Rudy. I don't want you to end up like the others at U.C. Med. Arm straps and Thorazine—very uncomfortable. And more than anything, Rudy, I want *you* to be comfortable. The fridge at our motel is packed with Candy Cakes, Twinky Pies, Rice Puffies and plenty of that white soul food—mayonnaise and Wonder bread.

Rudy returned the final slice of pizza to the container, closed the lid. He had lost his appetite.

—Did I mention the color TV?

Rudy lay flat on his back, gripping his stomach with both hands. Just when the pain grew intolerable, the deep voice interposed. Life is light. Life is calamity, catastrophe, annihilation. You are life, Rudy. Annihilate. Annihilate color TV, Rice Puffies, U.C. Medical, Innate Releaser Mechanisms, the financial district, military school, the homely asthmatic, the monotone principal, marshmallows, Johnny Carson, icy margaritas, Sister Maria Theresa, Uruguay, Father and Mom. Will they see me in Rio? Rudy wondered. Just before they feel the impact of your cosmic prestige, the voice answered. Rudy chuckled contentedly. His colon fluttered.

Will they be proud? What will they think when they see me?

What the termites thought when the hammer came down. Life is light.

Every muscle in Rudy's body contracted at once. And then suddenly, just before the flash, Rudy realized he would finally make his mark on the world.

GREETINGS
FROM EARTH

Dear Diary,

Well here I have gone and done it, and have decided to keep a diary at this point in my lifestyle because I think the many "out of body" experiences I have been experiencing lately will be of much interest to many different people. Which is not to mention my second reason for keeping this diary, which is that my husband Roger Simpson never pays any attention to my feelings not even one iota, of which this (my diary) is a direct result I think. Sometimes I get so mad at Roger I can't see straight I'm so mad sometimes. Right now Mr. Genius is hammering in the basement on our family room, only he's been hammering on this supposed family room for two years now and I don't see much of a family room. All I see is one big disaster area filled with wood and rusty nails and Bosco, Roger's stupid dog he never walks, has peed and crapped on practically everything. I don't know what most people imagine when they imagine a supposed family room, but big yellow puddles of dog pee is not the first thing that comes to my mind, that's for sure.

"Out of body" experiences by the way are highly interesting

moments which relate to ourselves all the time, of which you are not even aware sometimes since they sneak up on you for instance. At first you feel a sleepy sensation in your toes. Then you see a soft white light and feel very peaceful all of a sudden, as if you did not have a care in the world. Then you hear this faraway music which sounds sort of like Mantovani only better. Then you feel lighter than air and before you know it you are experiencing your "out of body" experience at that very moment! Maybe you are lying in bed reading a good article in the T.V. Guide or maybe sitting on the living room sofa. Maybe you are washing the dishes or maybe vacuuming the rug. Only now you are a disembodied essence standing apart from your physical vessel and looking at it, almost like looking at yourself in a mirror, only now you are free to wander the world in your highly spiritual state and you feel better about yourself than you ever have had previously before in history.

Being in a disembodied essence situation has many highly interesting advantages one can often enjoy. First of all you are on a much higher intellectual plane than ever before, i.e. you're a lot smarter. You're even smarter than Roger "Einstein" Simpson, your stupid husband. Your stupid husband and your stupid house drive you crazy now, since housework and marital duties all seem terribly demeaning to your spiritual essence, and you would prefer to go out to a good movie or even dancing. Maybe you put on some nice clothes and go for a walk, or maybe you go across the street to the Kona Lanes Bowling Alley which has a nice bar and pretty good oar derves for Happy Hour, not that you care much for these material things since being in a disembodied essence situation means you are never hungry and never thirsty and you never have to go to the bathroom.

Roger of course would never believe you are a disembodied essence in a million years probably, since he has told you a million times already he does not think you are a very metaphysical person, which of course is now a big joke on stupid Roger.

Roger thinks a person cannot be highly spiritual unless they read dozens of crazy books all the time like Roger does and try to understand all the metaphysical problems which bother his mind every day of the week. Sometimes these problems keep Roger awake all night and so he goes downstairs to work on our family room, where he says eventually we will have a color teevee and maybe even a pool table. The main philosophical problems facing mankind today Roger says is the mind-body problem and the decay of the earth's ozone layer problem, which two problems Roger says are totally connected to each other all the time. Roger tried for many years to solve these problems and get a Ph.D. at U.C. Irvine, but unfortunately his professors told him he was a "nut-basket" and would not help him one iota in any way, shape or form. Sometimes I tell Roger maybe he should try to get some sleep and stop worrying so much about problems which don't make him very happy or put any bread on the table, but then Roger says I am just like all his old professors and that I cannot understand anything which is not grossly materialistic. Roger says I have what Roger calls a "conventional moral outlook" which makes it impossible for me to see the major issues facing our planet today. People like Galileo, Christopher Columbus and Melvyn Dumar will always have to fight back against people with "conventional moral out-looks" Roger says if our society is to make any decent progress anywhere.

Sometimes I don't think Roger is very metaphysical at all but maybe that he is just emotionally disturbed or something. Or maybe he has one of those seventeen-foot worms eating his brain like I read in the National Star News one time. The man in the National Star News story was a big shot atomic scientist, which just goes to show that even having some brainiac I.Q. doesn't always protect a person from having a worm eat up his brain. But honestly, even if Roger was completely disturbed or something I don't know anyone who would believe me since everybody, my family included, seems to think Roger is a real genius and all and that I have made quite a "catch" in getting him "to the altar" so to speak.

Anyway, I have written enough for one day and so I will stop.

Here for example are the sorts of books Roger reads every day of the week.

Immanuel Kant, The Metaphysics of Morals and The Critique of Pure Reason.

Hegel, The Phenomenology of Spirit.

Wayne K. Shabullah, Know Your Egoic Ray. (Roger by the way says Wayne Shabullah has likewise received much trouble from colleges with "conventional moral outlooks." Roger says Shabullah is the only other person in America besides Roger who has noticed that egoic rays are often misdirected by satellite interference, which means many people are often accidentally aiming their egoic power at their own self-image factor or libido-release mechanisms, which thereby weakens people rather than their opponents in the social battle struggle for proper genetic improvement of our species. Or something like that. Personaly though what I think Roger and Wayne K. Shabullah have in common is that neither of them has both oars in the water, if you will pardon my expression.)

John Locke, An Enquiry Concerning Human Understanding.

Wayne K. Dwyer, Pulling Your Own Strings. (This one I have read a little of, as well as seeing Dr. Dwyer on The Merv Griffin Show, whose book actually makes a lot of good hard common sense unlike Roger's other books.)

I'm afraid though none of these books has done Roger's brain any good at all since his ideas just keep getting weirder and weirder. Today for example Roger tried to tell me that his mind-body problem is a lot like the family room he's building in the basement. Roger says the idea of the family room he has in his brain is perfect, but making this idea perfect in reality is another story entirely. I try to tell Roger that nobody in the world really cares if our family room is perfect or not, particularly since we don't have any children or any friends who still visit our crazy household. Frankly Roger I tell him I think you're just putting a lot of pressure on yourself which you don't need right now, particularly at this point in your life. But of course Roger isn't listening to a word I say, since he is staring at my television program instead which is The Merv Griffin Show, with Merv's special guests today Don Rickles and Gloria Loring. Roger says television is just the sort of problem he is talking about, since nobody on television is real at all but instead is just invented by the worldwide global corporation conspiracy in order to enslave the spirits of mankind. The worldwide global conspiracy wants people to watch television all day long so they cannot see the world around them is being secretly bought up by a group of Taiwanese businessmen, whose next step is to transform the world into a giant petrochemical storehouse which will provide life-giving vitamins and sustenance to invading life-forms from the sixteenth dimension. These invading life-forms (and the Taiwanese businessmen) are seeing to it that Earth is filled with pollutants in order to transform the way men's minds work. Pollutants and petrochemicals create mental imbalances in our cerebral mechanisms, Roger says, because the mind is not a free place but like the family room depends upon its own material existence to survive in the world all the time. That is why once Roger has made the family room just like the one in his mind he will prove to himself and all free-thinking individuals everywhere that mankind can stand against the worldwide global conspiracy no matter how much they fight us, which of course by the time Roger has finished telling me this I have missed practically all of Merv Griffin.

Then of course Roger goes downstairs and starts hammering again, and I could probably have more peace and quiet in an insane asylum probably. Personaly I think Merv Griffin is maybe not a big genius like Roger, but still I think he is a very nice man with a nice sense of humor, and I like him because you can tell he is not the sort of man who goes home and gives his poor wife a lot of grief about how she may not be the proper intelligence quotient for him and all. I like to watch Merv because after work I am very tired and need to unwind, and at least he is not another noisy cop show or another western show. Thank God especially he's not another Bonanza. Bonanza's on just about every station on cable about ten times a day. I hate Bonanza.

I am getting to the opinion that my life would make an interesting movie, being that my adventures in the world of spirit could teach many interesting things that should be shown to the world. I have decided to write my experiences into a screenplay, and have decided the best person to play my part in the screenplay would be Jessica Lange, who's movie Frances I have seen now twice already and understand it very well, boy do I. In it (the Frances movie) Jessica Lange portrays a very beautiful and intelligent woman who gets put into a mental asylum by her mother even though she's not the one that's crazy but actually it's her mother that's crazy.

The first scene should take place in the home where Jessica Lange lives with her crazy husband Roger. The house is filled with books and papers and dirty dishes everywhere, because Jessica has been at work all day making money to put food on the table, and Roger is sitting on the sofa wearing his crummy green and yellow Balboa High School jacket which he never lets Jessica wash, not that washing clothes is the big thrill for Jessica Roger seems to think it is. Jessica Lange's mother is sitting with

Roger in the kitchen eating the rest of the pot-roast Jessica was going to warm up for dinner. Jessica Lange's mother should be played by the same woman who played her mother in Frances, being they are both the highly critical sorts of persons who never say good things to a person but only highly critical bad things. When Jessica opens the front door she is exhausted from working all day and carrying two bags of groceries three blocks from the store, because of course she and Roger can't afford a car as she is the only person in their household with a job and all.

ROGER: Being a highly intellectual person myself I think everybody in the world should worry about things like the mind-body problem and the world global corporation conspiracy, because as very intelligent people like Kant and Hegel say all the time, blah blah blah blah blah blah blah.

JESSICA LANGE'S MOTHER: Roger, this is very interesting and I sure enjoy listening to your brilliant mind in action, especially since you are probably the smartest man in the world, probably even a genius or something. Jessica Lange doesn't have any idea how lucky she is being married to a man with such a high intelligence quotient, since she herself has never been very intelligent at all, and didn't even finish high school due to pregnancy—

At this point I think Jessica really blows her top. She has had a lousy day at work and then had to do the grocery shopping and buy a new Lady Bug lady's shaver at Sears, and now the kitchen is filled with dirty dishes and big bags of garbage because her husband Roger has never picked up a dirty dish or a garbage bag in his entire life let alone wash one. Normally Jessica is a very spiritual sort of person but that doesn't mean she has to

take any nonsense, not even from Roger. She throws her groceries on the ground and says

> Just shut up Mom you stupid idiot. Just because I don't sit
> home all day reading books doesn't mean I'm stupid. Per-
> sonaly I would much rather have some passion and excite-
> ment in my life, and I don't just mean sex (not that I'm
> doing so well around here in *that* department) but I mean
> passion and excitement in a very spiritual sense too. I
> would like to be able to afford a decent vacation every once
> in a blue moon though, or even a cute little silver sports
> car—maybe even a convertible, and if that makes me too
> materialistic for an Einstein such as yourself, Roger, you
> can just go and fly a kite. There's nothing wrong with hav-
> ing a few nice things that make you happy and it doesn't
> mean you can't be spiritual at the same time.

As you can see, Jessica really lets them have it. She is too strong
to let anybody treat her like some stupid cow. Every time her
husband Roger starts talking about his crazy ideas, she will
scream at him, "Earth to Roger! Earth to Roger! Come in,
Roger!" and the entire audience will laugh because Roger will
look like one really stupid jerk. Even though she is a very spiritual person who has many "out of body" experiences, Jessica
knows how to behave reasonably to people and keep her feet
on the ground when she has to.

Being a disembodied essence is important for many different
reasons, some of them being that you don't need anything or
anybody to make you happy, not even money and not even a
man. A lot of the time I watch my physical vessel going through
its daily routine and I can't believe how stupid I use to be. Every
day my physical vessel gets up at the crack of dawn and takes

the bus to Taylor Morgan in Anaheim where it types up invoices for public lavatory appliances. Then it goes to the store and comes home. Then it cleans and cleans, without its husband even coming upstairs for one second to give it a kiss or a hug. Then it eats Cheese Puffs and watches television. Then maybe it takes a Valium and eats some Nugget-sized Reese's Peanut Butter Cups, which come in a large assortment bag and must have about a jillion calories apiece in them. Then maybe finally it lies down and after a while it falls asleep. I feel very sad sitting at the vanity table and watching it toss and turn without anybody to hold it or tell it it's one bit special. I know you are not the happiest person in the world, Helen, I want to tell her. You were raised without any proper father to speak of, except for your mother's stupid boyfriends, most of which were stupid jerks. You are not what they call attractive by any means, and you are also heavy around the middle. You can't even finish the T.V. Guide crossword puzzle which you were working on before you fell asleep, and everybody knows that the T.V. Guide crossword puzzle is the easiest crossword puzzle in the entire world. You had a baby when you were in high school and had to give it up for adoption because your stupid mother made you, which means the only positive thing you ever did in your entire lifetime (i.e. giving birth to another human being) was just a waste. You have always given your life away to other people, and now you hardly have any life left at all. Even when you become peaceful and spiritual it is only in your mind, and so your poor physical vessel doesn't even know what being a disembodied spirit feels like, or how many advantages it has over normal material existence all the time.

My physical vessel doesn't even hear a word I'm thinking about, even though it has woken up and reached for the Reese's Peanut Butter Cups again. This makes me feel very sad and depressed, and so after a while I dress up in my blue dress and even wear my nice high heels. I go out for a walk to the Kona

Lanes bar where Armando the bartender tells me I look pretty, which even though I know Armando is just lying to me to be polite makes me feel good anyway, since some men know a lady likes to hear a nice compliment about her appearance every once in a blue moon and not just a lot of mumbo-jumbo about the seventeenth dimension and all.

Sometimes I go away for a few days. Sometimes I even get a room at the Kon Tiki Motel and put it all on Roger's Visa card. I spend the whole night watching television without having to listen to Roger's crazy hammer all night through. Sometimes I order room service, and sometimes I go to a first run movie. I wonder why it has taken so many years of my life to find happiness, and if there are any problems in life I will ever solve. Sometimes when I think about how difficult life is or how sad my physical vessel must be at home in its lonely bed I feel very sad, and sometimes I even feel a little sorry for Roger. Maybe somewhere in Roger's nutty brain he feels sad sometimes too, and all the big problems he wants to solve are somehow related to finding a way not to be sad anymore.

Whenever I come home again there is my physical vessel getting along perfectly well without me, going from one dull routine job to another just like a robot. While my physical vessel sprays the greasy gray spots on the refrigerator with Formula 409 I sit down at the kitchen table and try to figure why I bother coming back to all of this at all, and I am stumped. On the kitchen table there is a box of Clairol hair coloring which my physical vessel bought for itself while I was away. My physical vessel is wringing the sponge in the sink and humming "God Rest Ye Merry Gentlemen" even though this isn't even close to Christmas, but is actually only September.

Finally I go downstairs where Roger's hammering. The entire basement is one holy mess, with dog hairs and pee and crushed Cherry Coke cans everywhere. Bosco starts whining and wiggling his butt like he thinks I'm going to hit him for peeing everywhere, but I understand why he does it since Roger never lets him out in the backyard even for a minute. I tell Bosco to go away though, because Roger never brushes him and whenever I pet Bosco I get dog hairs all over my clothes and face, not that my clothes are so special or anything.

Roger is hammering thousands of nails into all of the wooden wall supports. When I come in he says, "I'm experimenting with nail-frequency. Nail-frequency means the spacing and design of nails in order to discover the most efficient panel attachment effectiveness ratio. The Parthenon was built both to last *and* look good, you know."

The nails are shiny and in many different patterns, and by this time I am thinking Roger should probably be put in a big boat and pushed into the Pacific Ocean. The nails are shaped in double lines, curlicues, waves, circles and semicircles. I want to tell Roger that his family room looks a lot like Glen Campbell, but then I decide not to bother since Roger never gets any of my jokes at all, not even my good ones. Roger picks up a copy of 1001 Home Ideas from the workbench and shows me the cover. "I've decided once I've finished our family room I'll build one of these." He points with the hammer. "A window box for the bathroom."

I roll up the bag of Gravy Train which is on the stairs and put it on the radiator, and then I sit down on the stairs. "First of all Roger I want you to listen to me very carefully because I won't be telling you any of this again. I am not really your wife Helen at all, but instead I am her disembodied essence which has decided to leave its physical vessel forever in order to wander the world on its personal quest. I don't know what my personal quest is exactly, but it's probably to find out who I am since nobody, not even my mother, ever seemed very happy with me, which certainly never gave me a very good self-image factor."

Roger puts down his hammer, which must be for about the

first time in a million years probably. Then he opens another can of Cherry Coke. "Spirit is not such a great place to be all the time," he says. "Spirit has always gotten all the good press though, so naturally people are often confused. Actually the spirit can't be happy unless it has a nice home in the material world. The material world, and I think most people will agree with me on this, is a very nice place to be most of the time." He shows me his can. "The material world has Cherry Coke."

"I don't like Cherry Coke," I tell him. "I like Tab, because I am trying to cut down on my calories."

"The material world has shopping plazas, Chrysler Le-Barons, Hostess Ho Hos, Mitsubishi, Saran Wrap, Johnny Walker Black Label and Sears."

"I can still go to Sears," I say. "Being a disembodied essence doesn't mean you still can't go to Sears."

"You can't buy anything."

"Yes you can."

"You can't drink Tab. You can't eat Quarter Pounders. You can't you know what."

I can't believe how stupid Roger is sometimes. "Mere physical gratification is not the most important thing in the world, Roger. And as far as you know what, I couldn't do much worse in that department, and that's for sure."

"I should take you out more. I should take you to a movie."

"You can take my physical vessel to a movie, Roger. I'm getting out of here."

"I should take you to dinner. Maybe even dancing. I really hate dancing, but maybe I should."

"You can take my physical vessel dancing, Roger. It's upstairs now watching *WKRP in Cincinnati* and eating Cheese Puffs. I'm sure it would appreciate a night out on the town."

Roger reaches for his hammer. Then he places a nail against the wall and squints at it, as if he is aiming a rifle. "We'll do a movie this week. And next week we'll talk about dancing."

I get up from the stairs and brush the dog hairs off my legs. "Goodbye forever, Roger. I don't bear you any bad feelings, and I hope you find peace with your own inner-self like I have done. I hope you solve the mind-body problem, and that you exercise and eat better and stop drinking so much soda. And someday I hope you sweep up all this dog hair. This basement is a mess."

"Okay, honey." Roger isn't even looking at me. He seems to be thinking about something important. Then he starts hitting the nails again with his stupid hammer.

That's about all I can take. I walk upstairs where my physical vessel is wearing the blue flannel housecoat it bought for itself last week at K Mart. I don't look back, and leave that crazy house forever.

Life is a very funny thing I guess, which is an expression you hear often.

Roger and my physical vessel seem to be getting along better than ever without me since Roger has decided to go back to college again, even though he is almost forty, because he has gotten a teaching fellowship so he can do his part to educate the youth of America about today's big social problems, in which Roger is an expert of course.

Now that Roger is back in school he has forgotten all about his crazy family room, and every day after work my physical vessel sits and watches Merv Griffin without anybody to bother it while Roger is at the library finding more books to bring home. Yesterday I stopped by to see how my physical vessel was doing, and it sat on the sofa staring at the television and eating Cheese Puffs for almost two hours without moving, just getting older and fatter.

But now back to my spiritual quest, of which my screenplay is drawing to a close already. The ending will be very positive and upbeat so the people watching the movie will feel good and not feel like they wasted their hard-earned money. Jessica Lange's spiritual essence gets a good paying job as a computer-programmer and rents a nice apartment in Beverly Hills after selling her first ever screenplay to the movies. Her boyfriend is named Dirk Stevens who she has met at a big Hollywood bash, and he is a real lady's man who goes out with all sorts of different women, but once he starts going out with Jessica she "lays down the law" and he decides to give up all his other lady friends for her, and after they are married he tells his friends he never thought he'd settle down in his entire life, but that was of course before he met Jessica who is a very special sort of woman who won't take any nonsense from men. Jessica takes night classes at UCLA and eventually gets her Ph.D. in creative writing, at which all her professors say she is a natural, and one professor is so impressed that he has an affair with Jessica and falls in love with her, but Jessica doesn't think much about it because Dirk is the only man she can ever truly love. Her ex-husband Roger, though, lives alone in his big house with his books, and he's never happy because he realizes no woman in the world will ever treat him as good as Jessica used to, and he drinks and drinks and drinks every day until eventually he becomes an alcoholic and dies.

Well that's about the end of my personal tale I guess, and now that I am free of the boring nightmare of my physical life I thank my lucky stars all the time. Every day I feel like jumping for joy, or going out to dinner for a really good steak, because spiritual love of myself has taught me how to enjoy all of life and not just some tiny part I happen to be stuck in. Sometimes late at night for example I even get on the RTD bus and travel for hours and hours without even having to pay any extra money, and many of the drivers know me by sight already I am sure. We go to Santa Monica, Encino and even Orange County, where I have never been before. I am very beautiful these days, because true beauty is knowing yourself as a spiritual being and not letting anybody fill you with a lot of negative feelings about yourself, which is about all my stupid life with Roger ever did. Now that I am filled with love and beauty I feel very content and warm in my little seat in back of the bus. Sometimes I feel so peaceful it is like I am not even there at all, and there is only the city outside with all the streetlights and office lights on, and my face shining very clearly in the window. I finally feel in my heart of hearts I am free of that nutroll Roger for good, as well as that crazy house, Bosco's dog hairs and working and cleaning seven days a week just to get nowhere fast. Anytime I feel like it I can go dancing. I am free to travel to many foreign countries and make many new and unusual friends. I can spend weekends at Club Med which I read about in the Sunday Travel Section. Inside I am just like Jessica, dancing with Armando out on Harbor Boulevard like a crazy person and letting everybody in the world watch, and what do I care. I take rafts down the Colorado River, visit darkest Africa and help feed starving babies in poor countries. I travel through space like a beautiful angel and walk on the icy moon. Outside the streets are dark and empty, and the bus is roaring underneath me, and it feels like there's nobody else alive in the entire world.

Sometimes I can travel secretly like this for hours and hours without anybody ever seeing.

DAZZLE

Dazzle was a dog with bushy red hair, fleas and an extraordinarily good attention span—especially for a dog. He was particularly fond of pastry, philosophies of language and Third World political theory. It was Dazzle's express opinion that unless somebody started paying the Third World a little concerted attention, serious consequences faced all mankind. Philosophies of language, on the other hand, were just a hobby, and when it came to pastry Dazzle preferred Sarah Lee Strawberry Cheesecake. There was more dog than dogness about Dazzle. Generally Dazzle knew how to keep his mouth shut, and strenuously avoided calling any attention to himself.

"The little doggy go woof," said Jennifer Davenport, the youngest member of Dazzle's patron family, the Davenports. Jennifer was six years old. Whenever anybody visited they said how beautiful Jennifer was. Dazzle thought Jennifer was just okay. "Woof, doggy. Be a good goddy—oops, I said doog goddy, I mean—" Jennifer looked theatrically around at her family, who had positioned themselves conscientiously around the living room television, but nobody looked back.

Doggies don't go woof, Dazzle thought, suffering Jennifer's cold hand on his nose. The *Canis familiaris* utters a guttural diphthong, much like the Mandarin Chinese diphthong, only less enunciated. Now why don't you leave me alone and go watch a little TV. Jennifer was already tempted. The television radiated warm noise and a flickering colorless haze that illuminated the faces of Father, Mother, Billy and Brad like nuclear isotopes. Mother was the Big One who fed Dazzle. Billy was the Little One who took him for the best walks.

Dogs don't like people, Dazzle thought. Dogs like dogs. Dazzle liked Homer, a resolute and well-groomed dalmatian who often roamed the park during Dazzle's afternoon walks, and Dingus, the hideous Lhasa apso who snorted at Dazzle through the slatted pine fence of Dazzle's backyard. "Life's a game, Dingus," Dazzle would say, contentedly pawing his rawhide bone and gazing up at the blue, translucent sky.

"Life's a game, and you learn to play it by the rules, or else you learn to make everybody else play by your rules. You can either be the ruler or the ruled, and that's the crux, isn't it, old pal? That's the decision we've all got to make. Me, I'd rather live by the rules I'm dealt. I'm no high achiever, Dingus. I like my life. I eat well and get plenty of exercise, and I've pretty much got this whole damn yard to myself most days. Of course, I'm what you'd have to call an exceptional dog, but being exceptional's one of those things that takes a lot of effort, let me tell you. Being exceptional takes nothing but lots of hard work, work, work. Being exceptional just means lots of pain and suffering, pal, believe you me. Look at Kerouac. Look at Martin Luther King. They were exceptional, and where'd being exceptional get them? I'll tell you where it got them. It got them nowhere. It got them nowhere at all."

Dingus snuffled against the pine fence. "Dog smells," he

said. "Food and water. Food and water and dog smells." Dingus snorted and snuffled again, and eventually lay down in the warm dirt and fell asleep. In his dreams of quick rabbits, Dingus kicked. "Rabbits," he muttered in his sleep. "Quick rabbits."

Some days, though, Dazzle was so depressed he couldn't even get out of bed to go to the bathroom. He lay on his desultory, twisted blanket beside the water heater in the basement and awaited the occasional click of the thermostat and the rush of the gas fire which indicated Mother was washing dishes or doing laundry. Dazzle never knew what it was exactly. He just felt a sort of vague and indefinable anxiety, a certain fundamental sadness at the inconclusiveness of things. It was the way he felt when he saw a dead cat in the road. Dazzle hated cats, but when he saw them squashed and senseless in the spattered street he didn't hate them at all anymore. He sniffed at them; they didn't even smell like cat. They smelled like hot asphalt, transmission fluid and gasoline. Sometimes Dazzle just lay on his blanket for hours, contemplating the meaninglessness of dead cats. When the postman pushed mail through the grate he might try to emit a halfhearted growl, but usually he didn't bother. Eventually he would hear Billy's bike clattering onto the dirt driveway, and force himself shaggily to his feet, shaking off his loose, dandruffy hairs. Dazzle simply didn't have any clear idea what was bothering him, but did his best to keep up a good false front. He didn't want people to think he was just feeling sorry for himself.

"It's a good life," he told Homer in the park. Billy was sitting on the softball bleachers with his friends and absently handling Dazzle's disenfranchised leash. "Of course, it's a routine, we all know that. A dog's life, as they say. Dog days in a dog's life, and all that. But you take away routine and what have you got? Have you read the papers lately? Do you know what the world population figures are, going into the next century? Check it out, pal; check it out. And do you know what our President's official policy is on overpopulation? Well, hold still just a second and I'll tell you. Our President thinks any increase in population only creates a larger, wealthier consumer market. That's what our President thinks. The more overpopulated the world gets, the more Volvos we'll sell. The more canned spinach. The more Levi's. The world's going to hell in a handcart, Homer. Let me tell you. So routine, well, maybe it's a bit boring at times. But it's better than no routine at all—and you know what no routine at all means, don't you, Homer? It means chaos, entropy, deindividuation, madness and death. How's that sound to you, Homer? Does that sound better than one square meal a day, and a warm blanket to sleep on? Does it, Homer? You tell me. Because maybe, just maybe *I've* had it wrong all these years."

"Relax and eat a bone," Homer said, imperiously panting, gazing off dreamily at a big black bird on a wire. "Gnaw a bone and dig the yard." Homer was a sage and sensible dog, Dazzle thought. But he was also, like every other dog Dazzle had ever met in his entire life, extraordinarily stupid. Even Dazzle's brave and obvious exercises in false bravado were lost on stupid dogs like Homer and Dingus. It was a very lonely world, Dazzle thought, this world of dogs.

Nights Dazzle suffered long knotty bouts of insomnia which arose in him as charged, eccentric monologues filled with delusions of grandeur and then, just as impossibly, plunged him into the depths of irony, self-mockery and suicidal despair. "The best lives are simple lives," Dazzle tried firmly to convince himself, unable to sit still even for a minute. He heard the mice in the garbage, the beetles on the walls. He got up and turned and turned again on his frazzled blanket. Then, of course, the irrepressible antitheses arose too. "Simple lives are filled with loneliness, vacancy and self-deception." For days he would go without eating, just gazing emptily at the liquefying Gravy Train in his big red bowl. Flies settled in it; then, at night, the mice came. It didn't really matter, he thought. Sometimes when he urinated on the newspapers, a few tiny drops of blood dripped out. His stomach twitched and growled; he experienced long energetic periods of flatulence. Some days he couldn't even bear the thought of facing the world's other dogs.

The family veterinarian, Hsiang the Merciless, prescribed antibiotics. This is life's real horror, Dazzle thought, prone on the ice-cold Formica table, closing his eyes and abiding the flea spray's aerosol hiss. Streams of black fleas spilled across the thin tissue sanitary sheet. We live and we die by the hundreds and thousands, Dazzle thought. And in order to live we visit our doctor. Dr. Hsiang's gloved hands prodded and violated Dazzle in every conceivable way, and in many inconceivable ones. Dazzle shivered with terror, surrounded by the cold, antiseptic office, the menacing banks of glittering stainless-steel blades and instruments. This is the horror of life, he thought. This is life's trial, and then we die.

When Billy hid the antibiotic pills in tiny edible lumps of Dazzle's Alpo, Dazzle would carefully disengage and deposit them behind the hot water boiler where nobody, to his knowledge, ever cleaned. He had heard too much about the debilitating effect of antibiotics on the body's immune system, and anyway, he knew his grief was not merely physiochemical. It was philosophical, ethical and spiritual. It was a logical problem he would have to deal with. Intellectually, he knew he was on firm ground. Maybe life wasn't filled with all the excitement and challenge he might have desired, but, he reflected, you can't always change life. You can't always change history, Kenneth Burke once said, but you can change your attitude toward history. Dazzle had a bad attitude, for which he could only hold himself responsible. Fundamentally, Dazzle considered himself an existential humanist. This meant he didn't believe in God, but he did believe in guilt.

"Good dog. Nice dog. Dazzle is a nice dog," the psychiatrist said, cradling Dazzle's freshly laundered blanket in his arms as if it were a baby. The psychiatrist was balding and slightly pock-marked; he wore thick wire-rimmed glasses. "He looked a little ludicrous, if you want to know the truth," Dazzle told Dingus later. The psychiatrist's name was Dr. Bernstein, and Dr. Bernstein told Mr. Davenport that Dazzle suffered from acute feelings of insecurity initiated by a birth trauma and castration. ("I think it was castration," Dazzle said. "You want to talk about trauma, let's forget birth altogether. Let's talk about getting your balls chopped off. Bastards." Dingus snuffled miserably.) "Nice dog. Good dog," Dr. Bernstein said, burying his silly face in the blanket and sniffing audibly at it as if he, and not Dazzle, were the dog. Then he smiled. "Dazzle smells nice. Dazzle's blanket smells nice." Once each week Dazzle lay on the tiny hearth rug beside the electric fire, peering up at the visibly disturbed and often unsettling Dr. Bernstein. Dr. Bernstein pranced about, made barking and growling noises and offered Dazzle a red rubber chew toy which Dazzle merely contemplated lying there before him like a mantra or something by Wittgenstein. "I think it's true what they say about psychiatrists," Dazzle said later. "They're all crazy. They're all fucking nutty as fruit bats." As Dazzle said this, Dingus lay down in the dirt and began licking himself noisily.

Veterinarians, canine shrinks, other dogs, Big and Little Ones. Things seemed to be getting worse and worse rather than better and better, at least as far as Dazzle's state of mind was concerned. The Family even began to regard Dazzle with a sort of diffracted familiarity. "Hi, Dazzle," they said, without bending to pet him. "How you doing, boy?" They looked genuinely concerned, but they also looked like they didn't really want to get too involved. Dazzle didn't know what to say. Every evening he watched them assemble around the glowing television and sometimes, out of the corners of their eyes, they watched him watching them. He sat and listened unemotionally to the news. The entire world was rapidly being transformed into a gigantic petrochemical dump, Dazzle thought. We are all being steadily infiltrated by carcinogens, toxins, radiation and some sort of irrepressible sadness which is probably the only underlying meaning anyway. Jennifer never snuck Dazzle into her room anymore so he could sleep on the big bed. By now, though, Dazzle had learned to prefer the garage.

Then one cold afternoon, while Dazzle was sitting in the backyard talking to Dingus, he noticed the gate was open. The latch had not engaged; and the wind was beating it gently against its creaking hinges. Dingus noticed it first, and began snuffling and darting back and forth against his own fence, insensibly sensing the sudden miracle of Dazzle's. "Cats!" Dingus cried. "Piss everywhere! Kill all the cats!" Dazzle watched his frenetic neighbor with a cool and cynical distemper. The bravest dogs in the world are the dogs who bark behind fences, Dazzle thought philosophically, and got up and went to the gate which, with a tiny pull from his paw, swung widely open and revealed the rolling hills of the Simon Hills tract estates covered with their uniform houses. With a sinking feeling in his chest, Dazzle stepped outside into the unfenced world.

For days and days he wandered aimlessly, urinating weakly on trees, lampposts and hydrants with a distracted, almost surreptitious expression, as if he were secretly determined to eliminate all the world's traces of other dogs. His legs carried him steadily and rhythmically in no direction at all, and for a while he preferred this sort of primal, nomadic state of disaffected consciousness. "It's not the rhythm of the primitive we've lost," Dazzle said out loud sadly, to nobody in particular. "It's the rhythm of history itself." Other dogs often appeared and sniffed at Dazzle, and with impatient formality, Dazzle sniffed back. "Don't eat our food or piss on our posts," the dogs said. "Don't fuck our bitches." Dazzle disregarded the blind caution of their first warning, contemplated the ironic sadness of their second. One night, while he tried to sleep in an alley, he was even approached by a bitch in heat. She was filthy and bone-hungry, and stank terribly. He looked up drowsily as she sniffed at him. "Sorry, dear," he said, watching her lumber off in her manic, erotic daze. We just bang around the world like that, Dazzle thought. We travel around the world banging into things.

Out here in the unfenced world, Dazzle's dream life gathered strange energy and momentum. They were muted, vegetable dreams, filled with formless bodies and soundless words, and when Dazzle awoke he found himself inexplicably contemplating the migration of birds, the constellations of his youth. He remembered as a pup lying out on the backyard's green grass with his chew toys and identifying them: Orion, Taurus, Hydra, the Pleiades. His sharp canine eyes could discern the rings of Saturn, the moons of Jupiter. Space was filled with awesome distances and complications. It went on forever and ever. Quasars, pulsars, stars, galaxies, vast convoluted nebulas like memories, shattered planets and exploding stars. As Dazzle grew older and older all this universal wonder seemed to shrink and encapsulate him like a glove. He forgot his own wonderment, or at least considered it frivolous. "I'm no adventurer," he used to tell the equally youthful Dingus. "I'm a house pet. I know how to keep my four paws planted right here on old terra firma." Recalling now his own heartless and cynical affectations, Dazzle started to cry. He didn't understand this inexpressible sadness, and wished it would end and leave him in peace. He wanted to be happy in his yard again. He wanted his bland regular meals and his blanket. He wanted that hard, musty world in which he knew the locations of things. He desired the simple dreams before language began, and regretted his own smug complicity in the world's systematic disavowal of imagination.

Needless to say, however, Dazzle didn't find much imagination out in the unfenced world either. Instead he found rampant street crime, bulleting cars and buses, underfunded public schools, political corruption, sad songs, homeless families, bad meat and tall office buildings. "Sometimes there's just nothing you can say," Dazzle told himself, chewing morosely at a slice of stale bread he had pilfered from some addled pigeons. "Sometimes there aren't any explanations. Or if there are explanations, they don't make you feel any better." He slept in parks, alleyways, underneath parked automobiles, sensing his own true home diminishing in the world and reeling further and further away, like stars and nebulas and other planets in a universe of constant motion. All the stars in the world are hurtling further and further apart, Dazzle thought. Dissolution, heterogeneity and death. Even the Davenports were fading from the map of Dazzle's mind. Soon, Dazzle thought, the map will only contain direction and gravity and heat. It will lack a central landmark. There will just be the world, and me in it. It was hard for Dazzle to believe he could feel any more forlorn and helpless than he had when he was living with the Davenports, but now his sadness had become actually inarticulate. He couldn't even compose sentences about how he felt; he couldn't alleviate the weight of his misery with metaphors or figurative language of any sort. His monotonous legs carried him deeper into the world of noise and lights and cities. Sometimes he encountered stray coyotes, or even wild wolves who had gotten lost for years in the big cities and were now almost completely insane. They talked out loud to themselves and yelped pitifully at the least sudden sounds. They suffered from skin diseases, vitamin deficiencies and a wild, unexaggerated fear of all mankind. Howl at the moon, Dazzle told them. The moon's a bitch.

* * *

Dazzle was sleeping in an overturned trash can on a neglected
and undeveloped Encino lot when he met Edwina. Edwina was
a nice dog, though a little lean, who suffered from chronic in-
digestion and a severe overdependency on father figures. "Feed
me," she said. "Beat me. Hurt me. Love me." She bowed her
head as she approached Dazzle's trash can, sniffing suspiciously
at Dazzle's unalpha-like yawn. "Sit down and rest," Dazzle
said, shifting a little to one side. Edwina sniffed more inti-
mately. "Forget it," Dazzle said. "Go to sleep," and Edwina
did. This was the closest Dazzle had ever come in his life to a
real relationship, and as such he blithely accepted much which,
intellectually, he often considered impossible or irrational. For
while most of the time Edwina was disturbingly submissive, at
other times, entirely without warning or apparent provocation,
she would take vicious and sudden bites out of Dazzle's rump
or tail. "Jesus Christ," Dazzle would say. Edwina was like a
beheaded or defaced street sign. There was very little understanding Edwina, which actually reassured Dazzle in a strange
way, for Dazzle was a dog who for many years had felt he could
understand just about anything, particularly dumb dogs.

Edwina didn't know anything, and relied on Dazzle to find
food, evade dog catchers and traffic and some nights even to get
to sleep. "Everything's going to be okay," Dazzle comforted
her, gazing out at the starless, smoggy sky. "You just relax and
go to sleep." Edwina was a hopeless case and even more
screwed-up than Dazzle, and that was why Dazzle suspected,
at times, that he just might love her. He paid her close attention. "You're not going to eat that, are you?" he might ask, or
"Try taking a little bath in the pond in the park. You'll feel
better." Whenever Edwina was in heat, she would bring home
the mangiest, most smelly and disreputable dogs she could find
and fuck them in the bushes behind Dazzle's trash can. Afterward the spent and irritable dogs would often try to pick fights

with Dazzle, or bully him into giving away some of the food he kept wrapped up in newspapers inside his trash can. "One of these days, Edwina, you're going to get fucked by the wrong sort of character," Dazzle warned her after another very long night. "You know what that means, don't you? Rabies. Yeah, you heard me. Frothing at the mouth. These enormous lesions develop all along your spine and inside your brain. You'll be one fucking crazy bitch, Edwina. I mean, I'm just thinking about your health; I think I'm old enough to say quite frankly I've outgrown pride and all those other silly provocations to marital conflict. But I do wonder sometimes, Edwina, I really do. Where do you find these guys, anyway? I mean, do you actually go *looking* for lowlifes, or is it just that lowlifes are irresistibly attracted to you?" Sometimes Edwina made Dazzle feel extraordinarily weary and discomposed, and despondently he would root through his remembered past trying to unearth some forgotten scrap of nostalgia. He tried to formulate romantic images of himself back then, the lone roamer seeking truth in the world, learning about himself and his fellow dogs. But the romantic images rarely held together for more than a few moments at a time. When push came to shove, Dazzle had to admit it was much warmer sleeping in the trash can when Edwina was there.

Even though Dazzle had tried to explain contraception to Edwina about a million times, she never once paid him a moment's notice, and in May during her second month of term Dazzle decided they should head north, into the high and unpaved country where Edwina's litter could at least expect a few simple years of the reflective life before they were meaninglessly smashed beyond recognition by some errant and uncomprehending bus. "Sometimes it's not the lived life that matters at all," Dazzle told them. They were blind and sucking and crawling all over one another, still marked by bits of unlicked blood and placenta. Edwina lay deflated and insensible in the bole of a large tree which Dazzle had padded with leaves and a few scraps of charred blanket he had discovered near an abandoned campsite. They were living in Big Sur overlooking the rough Pacific, the gnarled and wind-shaped elms and shore. "The lived life's just a big con too," Dazzle told them. "Events, possessions, sights, sounds, travel, achievement—oh, and what's the famous one—oh yeah, *experience*. It's all a big cultural snow job, if you ask me. It's primitive accumulation, the myth of the entrepreneur. There aren't any entrepreneurs anymore, kids. There's just ITT, Mobil and General Dynamics—and you know what they all thrive on, don't you? War, slaughtered and commodified animals like us, economic and political repression. Us unincorporated just have to do our best to carve out our own little alternative pockets of living. That's why the family's so important. I guess what I'm trying to say about all this nonsense is simply try and be happy with your life and don't worry too much about *experiencing* it. Let's all relax and enjoy ourselves a little. Let's all find a nice long pause together, okay, and not be in such a damn rush to get anywhere or do anything." The squirming pups just squealed and sucked. Sometimes during those first few days Dazzle felt he was the one who had just been born.

If there was such a thing as happiness, Dazzle thought he had found it. The role of patriarch fitted him quite snugly, and he realized that even if he could not find any sort of subjective comfort himself he could at least meticulously envelop Edwina and her pups in comfort's illusion, that long, slow dream of culture Dazzle had always examined but never successfully comprehended before. It was Edwina's last litter, and since she didn't desire to get fucked that much anymore they were able to construct a relatively stable family environment. The pups grew with sudden and frightening alacrity, and there always seemed to be one or two of them pulling at Dazzle's tail or pawing at Dazzle's face. Dazzle hardly slept at all anymore, and generally he preferred this dulled, unquenched fuzziness of brain and perception. It's best to keep the old brain a little blurred, a little battered, Dazzle decided. He had cleared out a small cave underneath an outcrop of black igneous rock on a mountainside. As the pups grew, he trained them to maintain a system of revolving security watches around their home, and drilled them in defensive techniques and maneuvers.

"A man?" he asked them.

"Hide," they said.

"Wolf?"

"Submit."

"Bear?"

"Run."

"Inexpressible sadness?"

"Run."

"Restless, unhappy dreams?"

"Dream again."

Often in the middle of Dazzle's patient drills, while the addled and hyper pups were growing distracted by buzzing flies and high birds, Edwina snuck up behind Dazzle and took a quick, nasty bite out of his ass.

"Jesus Christ," Dazzle said.

There was a smooth diurnal rhythm to life now, Dazzle thought. You could feel the safe beat of the entire world in your blood, your heart, your dreams. Half-asleep at the mouth of their cave, he liked to listen to Edwina and the pups snoring and contemplate the stars outside again. Pisces, Cassiopeia, Ursa Major and of course the craters and mountains of a vast and irreproachable moon. This is where the cycle ends, he thought, if a cycle it is. It's that convergence of the stars and the blood, the moon and the heart. It's not the world of men. It's not the Davenports' smelly garage. It's not Dingus urinating on everything. It's not clinical depression, or obsessive, convoluted thinking. It's not even barking at the mailman.

There were still days when Dazzle would slip off into the nearest town and check out the newspapers. Islamic fundamentalism, AIDS, the international debt crisis, yuppie liberals, adamant right-wing perjurers. It's not to disavow the world that I've left it, Dazzle thought, and made his mark on the *Examiner*'s Op Ed page. It's to live in the world I've always before disavowed. If he moved quickly, he could pull a nice steak from the grocery's refrigerated cabinet and sneak quietly out the back door like some innocuous delivery boy.

Periodically, though, Edwina grew ill and somewhat disaffected, lying alone for days at a time gazing insensibly at the blue sky beyond their tidy and self-sufficient cave. "Melancholy," Dazzle wondered. "Sad reflections. Lost love. Dead friends." But Edwina never told him what was on her mind; she just growled distantly at him. She never even bit him anymore, and eventually Dazzle realized she was suffering from physical rather than merely philosophical distress. The whites of her eyes grew sallow and bloodshot. Her breath was bad, and she suffered frequent discharges of diarrhea. Small rashes formed occasionally on her back and stomach, and eventually Dazzle diagnosed a low-grade infection, perhaps septicemia, or a common form of acute gastroenteritis. Dazzle recalled the library of antibiotics he had so smugly discarded behind the water heater in the Davenports' garage. You can't go back and change some things, he thought. He liked that world better, the simple one of medicine.

Early on a Monday morning Dazzle descended to the town with Flaubert, the laconic and reserved pup who, like his brothers and sisters, was really a pup no longer. Flaubert was developing assurance and a quick stride. There was something wild about Flaubert which Dazzle didn't understand, something which Flaubert had either inherited from his mother or his uncivil upbringing. It wasn't just his eyes, for he carried a certain alertness in the very poise of his musculature. "The world's crisis is a crisis of representation," Dazzle explained as they descended the mountain. "We're always representing our lives one way or another. We never live them. We never even live them *as* representations, which is an idea I've been giving a lot of thought to recently."

Alpine was a minimal town which contained a small grocery, a pharmacist's, an abandoned movie theater, a Woolworth's, which had been recently converted into a Bill's Jumbo Discount House, and approximately six hundred people. "There's a hidden continuity between signs and things, thoughts and world. Our fears of discontinuity are a fiction, actually, but one which we must be maintaining for some reason. Our anxieties about the world, things, other people, that world which doesn't conform to our dreams of it. We're letting those anxieties determine our world. Instead we should try to determine the world for ourselves." Coolly, Flaubert loped along like a wolf; he didn't say anything. Dazzle thought Flaubert was starting to look a little bit like Warren Oates in *The Wild Bunch*. "They're anxieties because we can't admit the validity of our own dreams," Dazzle said aimlessly. "That's what the world keeps telling us, you see, and that's what makes us so goddamn miserable. We believe what we're told, even when we're told to believe in everything but ourselves. I'm not trying to sound like some adolescent solipsist or anything, Flaubert. I'm not saying we should deny the world or anything. I'm just saying, let's give our dreams half a chance too. Let's maintain some faith not only in the world but in our dreams of it."

They had come to a stop across the street from the Mercury

Pharmacy, where the pharmacist, a tall man named Bill who wore a white jacket and patent leather shoes, was outside on the front curb training his guard dog, a large mean-looking Doberman whom the pharmacist referred to as Dutch, but who referred to himself in his most secret thoughts as Jasmine. The pharmacist pulled sternly at the Doberman's gleaming stainless-steel choke collar; at the same time he showed the captive dog a handful of chicken biscuits. "Sit," the pharmacist demanded impatiently, and gave the collar another sudden pull. "Sit, Dutch."

"Chicken biscuit," the Doberman said. "Chicken biscuit biscuit."

"Sit. Sit *down,* Dutch. *Sit!*" the pharmacist said.

"Maybe he doesn't want to sit," Dazzle said out loud, but nobody in the world was listening. "Maybe he just wants his goddamn chicken biscuit. Maybe he just wants to eat his goddamn chicken biscuit and then take a nice long nap."

When Dazzle was just a puppy his favorite television program had been called *Lassie* and had starred an attractive Scottish collie of the same name who saved members of the human family she lived with each week from various life-threatening situations. Lassie dived into raging rivers and burning buildings. She stood up against wild bears and men with guns. Lassie was a brave dog, Dazzle had thought, but an exceptionally foolhardy dog as well. "Save yourself," Dazzle would cry weakly, whimpering a little under his breath at the terrible trials and misfortunes endured by brave dogs everywhere. "Run like hell. Timmy can take care of his damn self."

"Sit," the pharmacist said. It was a warm day, with only a few high white clouds. "Sit *down.*"

The less and less I understand, the simpler everything seems, Dazzle thought, and at his signal, Flaubert took off and broke the pharmacist's grip on the Doberman's collar like a sprinter breathlessly striking the victory ribbon.

"Cats!" Flaubert cried, dashing off down the street. "Cats!" The Doberman, with a brief flickering expression like the lens of a camera, poised and then, with a sudden start, took off after Flaubert. The pharmacist took off after him.

"Sit!" the pharmacist shouted, running and shaking his gleaming choke collar at the bright sky. "Heel! Stop! Sit!"

Without a moment's hesitation, Dazzle loped into the pharmacist's office, found the Prescription Out tray, and snapped up one hundred capsules of 250mg tetracycline and fifty 100mg erythromycin. Then, with a flourish, he ascended again into the high mountains.

WHITE LAMP

Every morning Aunt Doris brought hot Cup-a-Soup to her great-nephew Cecil in a tall Styrofoam cup. Whenever Cecil visited Southern California he slept in his battered red Toyota in the parking lot of Aunt Doris's retirement hotel, and was usually still asleep when Aunt Doris came down to wake him. Sometimes his engine was running, his car heater turned up high; an easy-listening station was usually playing on the scratchy radio, and his entire car smelled of stale cigarettes. "Here's your soup," Aunt Doris told him. "You need a cup of hot soup to warm you up."

When he opened his eyes, they were red and blurry. "What's that?" he asked. He reached automatically for his cigarettes from the dash.

"It's hot soup," Aunt Doris told him. "It's hot soup to warm you up."

Aunt Doris felt guilty she couldn't let Cecil sleep on the floor of her room, but her room was very small, and the epidermis situation was a problem simply too dangerous to contemplate. "First your epidermis gets into the rug and then my cats pick it up," Aunt Doris told him. "Then I pet my cats and it gets all over me. Before you know it, your epidermis is everywhere. It's in the food and in the water, it's in the towels and in the dishes. Did you know that your average American loses six to eight pounds off his epidermis every month? This is a fact. This is a fact which I have very carefully checked into."

Aunt Doris lived in room 224 of the Hotel San Clemente, which advertised itself in its brochures as "retirement living by the sea." Her room contained a clock radio with a broken hour dial, a single bed, a hand-held rechargeable vacuum and a copy of Mary Baker Eddy's *Science and Health with Key to the Scriptures*.

Health was one of Aunt Doris's primary concerns, and she tried to maintain her proper vitamin intake, keep an optimistic attitude about life and exercise regularly by taking the hotel's carpeted stairway rather than its grinding, inconstant elevator. After delivering Cecil's soup she would fix herself a cup of hot Nestlé's Quik and a Carnation Breakfast Square, which together provided more than twice her daily vitamin and iron requirements. In fact, if Aunt Doris were to list her primary concerns on a sheet of white paper (which she was often fond of doing), her list would just about always include health, grooming, rent and utilities. Generally she tended to include "grooming" out of a vague sense of decorum, since she rarely showered, and even then only to swab her body gently with a damp sponge. Water, she believed, drained the body of its fundamental energies and sustenance. Good health and long life required that people industriously preserve the integrity of their own skin.

Every day, however, Aunt Doris made sure to brush her teeth with mineral water and Crest. She still had a perfect set of white teeth, and in eighty-three years had yet to suffer a single cavity. Every month she received Social Security, Medicaid (for her back) and a generous pension check from Jack's Hardware, the former employer of her deceased husband, Darrell Dwayne Mulhall. Every Christmas Jack's Hardware sent her a nice card as well, personally signed by Jack's surviving son, "Pittsie," who, as Aunt Doris dimly recalled, had seemed like a very nice man the afternoon she met him at the racetrack with Darrell Dwayne Mulhall. Sometimes Aunt Doris added that to her list of primary concerns: the past. The past was a lot like the other things on the list, really. Like health, rent and utilities, the past posed certain standard and often unacknowledged obligations. The past had determined Aunt Doris's name, personality and place of residence; the past was not a force so much as a sort of obstinate weight. It never really motivated you toward anything, but merely accumulated like battered cardboard boxes filled with disused but invaluable mementos. Sometimes Aunt Doris felt she would be much happier as an amnesiac, like one of those confused and often beautifully tragic characters on daytime television melodrama; other times she thought she would be much happier without any past at all.

She rarely slept at all anymore. After Ted Koppel, whom she felt herself distantly attracted to, she might watch a movie, or a rerun of one of last Sunday's community service programs. Sometimes she listened to all-talk radio, or read the newspaper, but usually she just sat by the front window in her tiny room and gazed down at central San Clemente, where alternating streetlights presided over the empty, adobe-tessellated streets, humming and clicking like contemplative machines. One night she saw a young man coming up the street, carrying a large television. He was hurrying, and disappeared into the alleyway beneath her window. In the dark and from a distance, he reminded her of her great-nephew Cecil, and she felt a brief pang of remorse. Cecil was Dotty's grandson, though Dotty herself had never actually lived to see him. Dotty had died when she was only nineteen, shortly after the birth of her first child, Agnes, who was Cecil's mother. Whenever Aunt Doris thought of her dead sister Dotty, she hoped Cecil was sleeping safely and comfortably in his untidy car. Tomorrow she would fix him toast, too. Cup-a-Soup and toasted Wonder bread. If she remembered.

Sometimes Aunt Doris couldn't tell if she was dreaming or not. Throughout the night she could hear definite footsteps outside in the corridor, and sometimes she would get up from the bed where she lay sleepless, pull on her robe and go to the door and open it. It might be Carl from across the hall, fumbling with his massive knot of keys. Or it might be Ted, pacing the corridors with his aluminum walker. But sometimes it was people Aunt Doris had known and loved during her life, many of whom were now deceased. Sometimes Aunt Doris saw her father in the corridor, or her mother. She saw Dotty, or her deceased husband, Darrell Dwayne Mulhall. Sometimes she saw familiar but unidentifiable children, who gazed up at her with unspeakable motives. The people from Aunt Doris's past never said anything to her; in fact, Aunt Doris perceived them as if through a thin veil of heat. There was something heavy and oppressive about the corridor's atmosphere at these times, and Aunt Doris would quickly shut the door, afraid it might infiltrate her room. Then she would lie back down on her bed for a while, wondering if she was still dreaming. But it didn't seem like dreaming, because she never felt herself fall asleep or start awake again. It was as if dreaming and life had become somehow continuous, like the past and the present, like youth and old age. Aunt Doris knew she wasn't young anymore. She knew she was very old.

One evening when Cecil was still visiting, Aunt Doris opened her front door and saw Emmett Stanley standing in the hallway. Emmett was carrying a large black plastic flashlight and looking very young for his age. He didn't recognize her at first, though Aunt Doris recognized him right away.

"Sure," he said finally. "Doris. Of course. Doris Kelly." Doris Kelly had been Aunt Doris's maiden name when she was growing up in Fullerton.

Emmett Stanley was the first man who had ever made love to Aunt Doris, and now, by sheer coincidence, he lived in Aunt Doris's own retirement hotel. "I'm looking for the water heater on this floor," Emmett said. He was wearing very baggy coveralls and a torn long-sleeved thermal shirt. "Do you know where the water heater for this floor is?" He swung the flashlight beam up and down the corridor.

Aunt Doris showed him the door to the water heater, which was just two doors down from her own. The lock was broken, so Emmett didn't have to look for his keys.

"You never came back, Emmett," Aunt Doris said. "You told me you'd come back for me, but you never came back."

Emmett leaned into the cramped and musty closet. The flashlight projected the water tank's interior across the corridor walls, and Aunt Doris found herself standing in the enormous shadows of spigots and winding copper tubes. "It looks like the burner's gone," Emmett said. "I'll have to drive into El Toro and get a new burner for it tomorrow."

"Maybe it's because we didn't have a real relationship," Aunt Doris said. Emmett was pushing shut the closet door; it dragged roughly against the carpet. That afternoon at Baskin and Robbins, Aunt Doris had overheard one young man telling another, "Yeah, I'm seeing someone. But it isn't really a relationship."

Emmett Stanley lived in a minimal storeroom in the hotel basement. The door to his room was located behind the matching Maytag washer-dryers. To get to it Aunt Doris had to step across heavy black tubes, coils of ominous red and brown wiring and large, birthlike clumps of blue lint. She made sure she was careful of her back. The storeroom was very dark as you approached and pulled open the perforated plywood door. "I must confess," Aunt Doris said. "I do think about you sometimes, Emmett." She stepped down onto the cold concrete floor. She felt slightly dizzy for a moment as the dark room grew gradually more luminous and coherent around her. The air was heavy with thick, whirling motes.

"That's nice," Emmett said. He was suddenly beside her, and slamming his steel toolbox onto the floor. "Would you like some coffee or some tea?"

Emmett's room underneath the hotel contained two tattered stuffed chairs, a large mattress on the floor, a couple of throw rugs and a stained wooden end table between the chairs, which held a large glass ashtray and a half-finished cigar. One of the stuffed chairs contained Emmett's wife, who was reading the *Times Sunday Home Supplement*. Behind her chair, balanced atop a ledge of concrete, sat a white lamp with a beige shade. The base of the lamp was chipped and dusty; the bulb itself emitted a dusty, nebulous sort of light. In some ways it didn't seem like light at all, really. It was rather like some chemical or nuclear discharge that actually altered the deep cellular matter of things rather than merely illuminated them. Mrs. Stanley, however, seemed to have no trouble reading underneath it; but then, she was also wearing glasses.

"Hi, honey," Emmett said.

His wife looked up. "What?" she shouted. "What?" She was the most extraordinarily old woman Aunt Doris had ever seen, with glowing blue veins in her hands and a wide, translucent forehead. Aunt Doris thought the old woman might collapse at any moment; then only the raw, humanless stuff would remain, like the clumps of lint behind the dryer.

Emmett looked at Aunt Doris again. "Did you say you wanted coffee, or what?"

Emmett took his cigar from the tray and lit it with a burnished steel lighter. It was, Aunt Doris learned later, a retirement gift Emmett had received from the Torrance Retread and Rubber Company nineteen years ago. That would have been 1967, the year Aunt Doris's husband, Darrell Dwayne Mulhall, had died.

Every morning Aunt Doris brought Cecil his Cup-a-Soup and dimly attempted to converse with him. Cecil referred to his job as something that included a lot of "trading and bargaining," and usually the backseat of his car was filled with various surplus goods he had acquired during his unspecific "negotiations."

"That's a nice set of golf clubs," Aunt Doris might say.

"Yeah, I guess," Cecil said without turning to look, gazing dazedly into the Styrofoam's hot noodles and viscid yellow water. His T-shirt was torn, and he scratched himself.

"Where do you sell nice stuff like you get? Where would you sell that nice electric typewriter, just for example?"

"Places I know."

"Where would you sell that nice toaster oven? I'm not trying to be nosy, but I could use a nice toaster oven myself. How much might you ask for that?"

Cecil scratched at his stubbly face. The scratching made a loud noise, like static on a radio. "Five dollars, I guess," he said. "Actually, make that ten."

Aunt Doris took the toaster oven up to her room and gave Cecil ten dollars the next morning with his soup. Now she could fix toast and hot sandwiches for her friends whenever they came to visit. Somehow Aunt Doris felt less empty than before. She gazed out the window with a less aimless abstraction. She even noticed things sometimes. Boys on bicycles, young girls in summer dresses. She tried to remember these things so she would have something to talk about with her friends, Mr. and Mrs. Emmett Stanley. "I saw a girl with beautiful blond hair today," she would tell them. "She had beautiful blond hair all the way down past her backside. When I was little I had long blond hair too, but then one day my mother chopped it all off." Life seemed very peaceful and safe for the first time that Aunt Doris could remember. For many years Aunt Doris had thought that every person she had ever loved in her entire life was dead, so it came as something of a relief to find Emmett again, even if he was married. Aunt Doris looked forward to the late evenings when Emmett would be finished with his handyman chores and she could go visit him.

"Do you feel good about your life?" she might ask him. He sat in his stuffed chair smoking, and Aunt Doris would lower herself awkwardly onto a large stuffed pillow, her veiny legs splayed out in front of her like awkward debts. "I mean, do you think life has been good to you?"

"How do you mean?" Emmett was peeking over his wife's shoulder. Mrs. Stanley always seemed to be reading the same Sunday supplement.

"I mean, have you ever wished you could live your life over again? Have you ever wished you were young, and knew all the right decisions to make? I mean, it doesn't seem like being happy would ever be such a big problem, but frankly I was never happy at all, and my life was just one big mess actually. I mean, after you went to Oregon, I married a man named Darrell Dwayne Mulhall, not because I loved him but because my parents told me it was a good idea, and since I was pretty stupid when I was young, I completely believed them. Darrell Dwayne Mulhall was the most horrible man the world has ever known, which is not a nice way to speak about the dead, I guess, so maybe I should stop."

Usually Emmett would fall asleep in his stuffed chair, the cigar smoldering beside him. Sometimes Aunt Doris would crush out the cigar for him and douse it with a little water from the spigot. Sometimes she covered him with one of the blankets from the bed. She never thought to check if Mrs. Stanley was asleep or not. All she ever checked was to make sure that the white lamp was still on when she left. Without anybody having to tell her, Aunt Doris knew that the white lamp should never be turned off, even for a moment. The storeroom was so impossibly dark that if you turned off the lamp you might never find your way in or out again.

"You must get this cozy room for free since you're the hotel handyman, don't you, Emmett?" she once asked Emmett Stanley.

"Actually, they just give me a good discount," he said. "Only two hundred and fifty dollars per month. But that includes utilities."

Cecil said, "It's a Gillette Foamy hot foam dispenser. It's still unopened in its original packing case. There's still an original warranty on this sucker. You buy something like this in the store it's gonna cost you thirty bucks easy. I'm talking ten, twelve bucks—and that's not including a nickel for my trouble. Okay, make it ten bucks. You can give it to your boyfriend for Christmas or his birthday or something. I'm telling you. I can get you lots of good deals on stuff like this." Cecil placed the box down firmly on the countertop beside his coffee. He was sitting in the Travel Inn, which was located immediately next door to the San Clemente Hotel. The large clock on the wall said 9:45.

"Did you want to order something or are you just going to sit there yakking all night?" Debbie slung the billing pad against her hip pocket; her left hand scratched aimlessly at a starchy gravy stain on her left shoulder. "You sure like to work your mouth," she said.

Cecil gazed speculatively into Debbie's cleavage, as if he

might have spilled some change down there. "I guess I'll just have some more coffee." Cecil lit a cigarette. He rested his left hand on the Gillette Foamy box. The weight and density of the box felt reassuring, like gravity.

People just don't know what's good for them, Cecil thought, three Manhattans later at Goody's bar down the street. Goody's was filled with crew-cut boy Marines, obese women with bad complexions, and interchangeable men in their late fifties with sunburned, wrinkled faces, tattoos and bushy sideburns. If you don't take advantage when opportunity knocks, boy, don't expect opportunity to just keep coming around. Opportunity's not something that comes to you. No sirree, boy. Opportunity's something you take. Otherwise it's gone for good and you might as well retire. You might as well cash in your chips and leave the game to us professionals.

At that moment Cecil looked up into the wide mirror behind the bar and saw Debbie enter through the swinging front door. She was still wearing her waitress uniform. She carried a lit Marlboro in her poised right hand as if it were a VIP pass.

"Hey, beautiful," Cecil said. "Off work and time to play, huh? Why don't you let me buy you a drink?"

"Get lost, creep," Debbie said, and went into the large, smoky adjoining room where her boyfriend was playing eight ball.

It made little or no sense to Cecil. You ate, slept, took impossible mortgages, grew old, died. Maybe if you were lucky you'd live till you were a hundred, sleeping with your mangy cats and pacing restlessly around the same damn hotel every night, up and down the same stairs night after night, hour after hour, up and down. By the time Cecil returned to the parking lot of Aunt Doris's hotel it was almost 2:00 a.m. Across the building's white adobe face many of the grilled windows were still brightly lit, curtains drawn back to reveal indistinguishable old men and women pacing about their rooms, myopically peering down at the parking lot as if even at this late hour they expected company. The place actually stank of old people, Cecil thought. Old people smelled like junk food, pharmacies, stray clothes in a laundromat. He could hear the distant rush of the sea. I'll be damned if this is my last stop, Cecil thought, and forced the back door lock with his Shell card. The Shell card was embossed with the name of its original owner, someone named Harold T. Willoughby. The wide, half-lit foyer was filled with hideous velour furniture. The pale adobe ceiling was water-stained, and someone had overturned a tall plastic and chrome ashtray beside the manager's door, spilling ashes and butts and crumpled gum wrappers everywhere.

The door to the basement was open, and Cecil switched on the light. The lacquered yellow walls were suddenly very bright, and he descended into the laundry room and discovered the large twin Maytags. The door to the storeroom hung loosely open; Cecil turned on his pocket flashlight, swinging the beam around the low, musty room. "Bull's-eye," he said, and took the Sony cassette player, the hand-held rechargeable vacuum, the dusty box of tools and, after a moment's hesitation, the chipped ceramic white lamp, which he could use once he got a new place. Then he decided to drive to Lompoc, where a friend had offered him the accommodation of his living room sofa.

The fog that night along Highway 5 was heavy and enveloping and close. There were times when Cecil could hardly discern the front end of his own car. But even then, when the actual road seemed to disappear and the fog wrapped you up in its own world of the invisible, you still felt as if you were surrounded by a peculiar sort of meaning. Around 4:00 a.m. Cecil pulled over to the side of the road and fell asleep with the engine running and the heater blowing. He didn't dream at all that night.

There were so many questions Aunt Doris still wanted to ask. Did Emmett believe in God, for instance, or predestination?

Had Emmett supported the war in Vietnam? Did he have any children or grandchildren? Aunt Doris had always wanted grandchildren, but she couldn't have babies, or else Darrell Dwayne Mulhall couldn't have babies. (She and Darrell Dwayne Mulhall never really did figure that one out.)

Then one night Aunt Doris descended into the laundry room and discovered only darkness. She switched on the overhead light, which was pale and unsteady. The perforated plywood door was bolted shut with a large brass Yale lock. "Emmett," Aunt Doris said. "Emmett, are you home? Mrs. Stanley? This is your friend Aunt Doris from upstairs. Are you sleeping? Would you like me to come back later?" Aunt Doris stood silently in the empty laundry room for a long time. The darkness was dense and bristling behind the plyboard door. Cloudy, complicit, brushing against things. Or perhaps that was just the motes of dust, or the dead remembered rays of the white lamp.

Whenever she thought about Emmett Stanley she remembered the white light from the lamp. In fact, when she tried to recall any particularities about Emmett himself she drew a complete blank. She couldn't recall his face or the texture of his voice. She couldn't even recall the first time they had made love. It wasn't the sort of event one was supposed to forget, and sometimes Aunt Doris even doubted her own abstract certainty that anything had happened at all. At times like these she lay on her bed and listened to Daisy pawing the cat litter. Then Daisy jumped onto the windowsill and sat there motionlessly for hours, like a white ceramic sculpture of a cat. Aunt Doris tried to recall Emmett Stanley's face, but all she could see was the hard, pulseless white light, not really light at all so much as a sort of atmosphere, something breathed rather than seen. "Sometimes I think I might like to live my whole life over again," Aunt Doris said out loud, to nobody in particular. "Here I am, an old woman already, and I don't ever remember being happy in my entire life. I lived my whole life with Darrell Dwayne Mulhall, and then when Darrell Dwayne Mulhall died

I really didn't have that many options left open to me. There aren't a whole lot of options left open to you when you're sixty-four." Aunt Doris looked around her empty room. Daisy had spattered brown cat food all around her yellow bowl. Tiny brown cat prints tracked the beige tile floor and disappeared into the thinning carpet like a primitive mandala.

After a few weeks Aunt Doris stopped descending to the laundry room at night and decided Emmett Stanley and his wife had simply moved without telling her. Perhaps one of them had died, and the survivor was too stricken with grief to contact other living people. Or perhaps Emmett and his wife had made a suicide pact many years ago, so that if one of them died the other would take his or her own life at the first opportunity. Aunt Doris thought that a suicide pact was a very romantic idea, and firmly decided that if she were ever to fall in love with someone deeply and truly they would have a suicide pact together too.

Time began to radiate rather than flow. Events didn't occur in the world around Aunt Doris so much as strategically assemble, like places on a map around some large city or natural resource. Doors opening and closing up and down the hall. Voices in the street at night. Marines with blaring ghetto blasters descending the long, winding pavement to the beach. Daisy forever digging in her cat box as Aunt Doris lay on her back on the cold bed, listening to the world outside and watching the bright, angular sunlight sliding across her floor. Aunt Doris saw the open can of kidney beans on the sink, but she didn't feel like eating kidney beans. The refrigerator door was open, but the bulb had gone out, so the food remained cold but unlit. She could smell the baking soda and moldering cabbage, the milk as it turned rancid, the sour cheese and fruit. And Daisy pawing at everything, and knocking down the Kitten Chow from the high countertop. It sounded like gravel spraying, and then the gravel shaking in the cat box and the dense odor of Daisy's excrement. It wasn't Aunt Doris's life at all; she finally understood that now. It had always been Darrell Dwayne Mulhall's life, Darrell Dwayne Mulhall's desires, Darrell Dwayne Mulhall's house and car and job and pension. Now that she thought about it, Aunt Doris pretty much hated everything about Darrell Dwayne Mulhall. He was a hard object in the room, while Aunt Doris was just drifting, drifting. Darrell Dwayne Mulhall didn't make a move or a sound. He just sat there with his newspaper, scratching himself and farting all the time, while Emmett Stanley made love with some other young woman on a rattly cot in the back of his parents' trailer. That other young woman hadn't been thinking about anything while it happened. That other young woman had only wondered why she had been afraid, why the cot rattled so loudly, why they bothered. And then Emmett Stanley went away, into the white light, into the long, pulseless drone of history, the history of other people Aunt Doris would never know.

Every day Aunt Doris lay on her cot and waited for the mail to arrive. Lying there with her hand across her heart, Aunt Doris could hear the mailman on the porch, in the foyer, at the boxes. Maybe there was a letter. The mailman's keys clattered against the boxes. The mailboxes closed shut again. The white light was accumulating in the basement storeroom just like electricity, just like time. The white lamp's light was moving up the cement staircase, into the elevator shaft, suffusing the pale walls and ceilings of the foyer, infiltrating everything, every room and every body in the Hotel San Clemente. The white lamp was still on, Aunt Doris realized, and this meant that Emmett Stanley and his wife hadn't moved or died, but must have just returned from some brief vacation. The white lamp was on, and they were reading and repairing irreparable appliances down in their minimal home behind the washing machines. The white lamp was on, and there was a letter in Aunt Doris's box. Aunt Doris closed her eyes. The letter in her mailbox said:

Dear Aunt Doris,

I know it's a shame not to have written you in so many years and now only because I have bad news but that's the way we are I guess, we've never been much of a letter writing family I guess. But your nephew Cecil was arrested last week on Highway 5 for possession of stolen property, and Alex and I are worried that Cecil may have repaid all your kind attentions and accommodations by taking valuable items from you or your friends there at your nice hotel. We hope maybe he hasn't, but here is a list which was provided to us by the Buellton Police Department, whose address is enclosed in case you must contact them in any way. Maybe Cecil is a very confused young man and we hope he will grow out of his bad deeds, but sometimes it's hard to be very positive thinking about somebody like Cecil who we have loved and tried to teach true Christian values to time and time again. Maybe you could visit us this Christmas, and we will send you a bus ticket. It would be nice to see you again, and your new niece Daphne (who isn't new at all really since she is already eleven years old—time sure does fly!) would like to meet you. Here is the list as you will find printed below:

1 Sony portable b/w TV	1 clarinet
1 Sony cassette player	3 cases Pepsi
2 Sw. army knives	1 white lamp
1 Sears cordless phone	1 Sm Cor. word proc.
1 Canon prt. typer	1 pocket calculator
1 partial Ency. Brit.	1 power drill

Well anyway I hope that none of these things really are yours which would make both Alex and I and I am sure Cecil too feel very bad indeed.

Your loving and very apologetic niece,

Agnes

In a minute, Aunt Doris would get out of bed and go down to the mailbox for her letter. In a minute. But first she would close her eyes. She would rest her eyes for just one minute, and then she would go downstairs to the mailbox for her letter.

THE OTHER MAN

"It's a chemical thing," Edward Thomas said, prone on padded leather, cleaning his nails with a twisted paper match. "There's no use telling me whether he was *really* there or not. That's pretty inconsequential. What *is* consequential is that whenever I enter that house I *know* he's been there. He has just fucked my wife, eaten food out of my refrigerator and sat on my toilet. I'm not talking about breach of propriety, you know. I'm talking about a violation that's practically *cellular,* for chrissake. There I am, home from work, placing bread and milk on the bookshelf beside the front door and taking off my coat, and I *know* it happened right there, right there on the living room floor. He mounted her from behind while she jerked her head wildly from side to side. I've never seen her make such a fuss before. I never even thought she *liked* sex that much, if you want to know the truth. And then the noise they're making. This isn't my wife; it's some goddamn truck-stop waitress. There's a moment in which this imagined infidelity actually *invests* me, like a murmur of the stomach, or a pulse of the blood. It's a sort of biological event; my entire system responds. I'm breathing quickly, my temperature rises. It's an anger that pulls at my stomach—an anger not at my wife, you understand, whom I love, but at this vision itself, this glimpse of some ungraspable life. I don't know if I can explain it better than that. I want to reach into my stomach and haul it out, I want to pull the memory of that vision out of the fabric of my cells and tissue. I have seen something real which is not real. I'm willing to accept that, you see. I'm perfectly willing to continue believing that my wife, Rachel, is a faithful woman who loves me, but that doesn't prevent another physiological world from moving in my blood and beating in my breath. It affects me as strongly, you see, as if these things had actually happened. I guess I really don't know how to explain it. I can't sleep any more. I wake up with these awful anxiety attacks, my heart pounding. I've tried aspirin and Valium. I started sleeping with Phil Brady's wife a few weeks ago, just for a sense of vital retribution. I bought a personal computer. Sometimes in the middle of the night I drive to Ventura, Escondido, even Santa Barbara. I can't keep my mind off it. I'm really hoping you can help."

Dr. Tobias's wristwatch chimed twice, and Edward craned his neck around. The patent leather creaked. From this angle, Edward could glimpse only Dr. Tobias's very casual cotton shoes.

"My policy with new patients is to adopt a very cautious attitude the first few weeks," Dr. Tobias said, shaking Edward's hand again before he left. "If you have any trouble, feel free to call, and I'll see you again next Tuesday at one o'clock."

"He's a strict Freudian," Rachel said, offering Carla Sara Lee Danish in its aluminum tray. She licked her fingers. "That means he's going to delve into Edward's subconscious. Edward's going to see him three days each week, this week and next. Then he sees him twice a week for two years. Edward lies on the couch and Dr. Tobias sits behind him. Edward's not supposed to look at him, or else he'll suffer transference."

"Is he good-looking?" Carla sat on the edge of the sofa with her legs crossed. She was wearing a short white skirt which looked good on her.

"Dr. Tobias?"

Carla bit her Danish and said "Mm-hmm," catching a sudden flurry of crumbs with her hand.

"Yes," Rachel said. "I guess so. But I think he's married."

"Yesterday I found a can of his shaving cream. It was in my bathroom, on my sink. Edge Shaving Gel for Sensitive Skin. I never used Edge Shaving Gel in my entire life. I use Gillette Foamy." As usual, Dr. Tobias sat so quietly Edward could only hear him breathing. Sometimes he imagined that as he talked, he was actually trying to reel Dr. Tobias in on the line of his voice. He could feel Dr. Tobias's presence that way—like some weight hidden beneath water. "I could have brought it along and shown it to you, but I didn't see the point, really. I mean, I don't want this all to degenerate into some pointless argument about whether I'm deluding or not. I know ultimately I'm doing nothing else but. It's all one long dream, you know. The other man, my wife, my therapy. I take all that for granted; I'm not what you'd call naive. The can of Edge Shaving Gel is perfectly real; the other man may very well not be. One way or another, I still dream about him. In my dreams, he and I get along famously. He never makes me feel threatened; he always makes me feel as if this whole thing is quite a bit of good luck on both our parts. It's not him that we're trying to figure out anyway, is it, Doctor? It's me, and the world as I've fashioned it. We're drawing a sort of map. This is where Edward's addled brain ducks, turns, pirouettes, swerves. These are the objects he sees in his way. I guess I should've gone looking for one of those existential psychologists—is that what they're called? I mean, a strict Freudian. Really. But that was a sort of existential choice itself, you see, because I believe in the family romance. I really do. Mother, father, daughter, son. Dark dreams of incest, immolation, taboo. Those are the dreams we need, I think; they make a family *work*. Otherwise, what have you got? Happiness, fidelity, more happiness? Everybody being happy happy happy all the time? That would be a little hard to take, wouldn't it? Is that the kind of world you want your children to grow up in?"

Behind him and out of sight, Dr. Tobias lightly, audibly belched.

Sometimes at night Edward even dreamed of the other man. They ascended strange buildings together in escalators and elevators. They were always on their way to some imminent cocktail party to which Edward's wife, Rachel, had also been invited but was not really expected to arrive.

"Eventually they become great buddies," Edward Thomas said, flicking a Tareyton ash in the glass ashtray balanced atop his chest. "They go everywhere together. Movies, fishing, sporting events, RV shows. Neither has ever fully enjoyed the pleasures of male companionship before. There's something regenerative about this as opposed to a mere sexual relationship. Neither feels *drained*. Neither tries to bring the other *down*. There's absolutely no sense of competition between them. This doesn't mean they don't appreciate or enjoy the company of women. Not by a long shot." Edward crushed out the cigarette, turned to replace the ashtray on the table beside his bed. He heard the bedroom door open, brushing against the shag carpet.

"Edward?"

Rachel's face looked in from the dim hallway. The bright bedroom still swirled heavily with smoke like some domestic cabaret.

"Yes, honey?" Edward fished another Tareyton from his shirt pocket.

"Are you all right in here?"

"Just thinking out loud is all."

"Oh." Rachel's eyes flicked about the room a few times. "Dinner's ready," she said finally, and pulled the door slowly shut again.

"I don't understand why you don't go out with somebody else, then. I mean, if he *thinks* you're out balling some guy, you might as well have a good time, right? That's what I say."

"You don't understand, Carla." Rachel put down her menu, looking over her shoulder at the salad bar. "Ed doesn't think I'm *cheating* on him."

"I don't understand, then. I *really* don't understand."

"Ed's *ill*, Carla. I've explained this all to you a hundred times. He has delusions. He *knows* they're delusions. He needs a lot of love and patience right now, and I'm trying to give it to him." Rachel opened her purse and pulled out a long, crumpled Kleenex. "It's not a matter of he doesn't *trust* me. That's what you don't seem to be hearing." Examining it first carefully, Rachel placed the Kleenex against her nose and blew.

"Okay, maybe I don't understand your crazy husband, but I know what I'm hearing, girl." Carla snapped her compact shut and pushed it abruptly into her purse. She took her smoldering cigarette from the glass ashtray. "Your husband says you're screwing some guy. He says, listen to me. Listen to all my crazy stories. Sit up all night, sit around all day, listening to my crazy stories about how you're screwing some guy when you're *not* screwing some guy—"

"Can I take your order?" The waitress held out her order pad and pencil. She looked about seventeen.

"Just a second, baby." Carla leaned earnestly across the table, stage-whispering. "Because now *you've* got to start listening, Rachel. Now *you've* got to start reading the writing on the wall. What do you think you're going to do? Spend the rest of your life wondering what's best for *Edward*?"

"I'll come back," the waitress said.

"No, of course not. Because you know why? You're not stupid, that's why. So what do you do? You've got Ed thinking about Ed, and you've got you thinking about Ed. That makes two people thinking about Ed. And where does that leave you, Rachel? I'll tell you. It leaves you nowhere, it leaves you with nobody. It leaves you nowhere, with nobody, doing nothing. You think *I'm* going to worry about you, girl, if this loopy husband of yours fucks you over? Then you've got another think coming. I'm looking out for me, girl, because I'm like Ed. That's where Ed and I are a lot alike."

Rachel felt slightly disoriented and fuzzy, as if she had been slapped. She had never heard Carla talk to her like this before; her face felt hot and red. She got up and went to the bathroom and examined herself in the mirror; then, briefly, she cried spontaneously for almost a minute, without any reason at all. They ate their side salads and finished their drinks in silence. Afterward, when she offered Carla a ride home, Carla just snapped at her again. "I'll walk," she said, and that was exactly what she did. Rachel couldn't understand why Carla was in such a terrible mood. After all, she thought, *I'm* the one that should be mad. I think I was being awfully patient with her.

But even later, after she had arrived home, she felt more ashamed than angry. The parameters of the entire house seemed to shift as she put down her bag and sat on the living room sofa. It wasn't as if Carla knew anything. After all, how many good relationships had Carla ever had? It's easy to say just think about yourself when you live alone, Rachel thought. When you've never had the courage to maintain any type of commitment with anyone but your own self. Outside, beyond the living room's uncurtained picture window, the sky grew suddenly dark, and Rachel wondered if it might rain. The air had been heavy all afternoon.

The house was very quiet now, and Rachel lay down on her side on the sofa, the remote control gripped loosely by her right hand, *The New Hollywood Squares* playing soundlessly on the television. Rachel wondered idly whatever happened to the old Hollywood Squares. Nothing significant came to her mind for quite a while. She felt more vacant and muted than sad. Then, eventually, motionless before the television's abstract flickering, she wondered what the other man was really like, and whether he made love to her in Edward's fantasies with great passion or calm assurance. Edward had described him to her many times. He wasn't handsome, really; he was quite "normal"-looking, with brown hair and dimly blue eyes. Usually he wore Levi's and shirts with button-down collars. He was boyish and energetic. He wasn't like other men. His suggestions were always relaxed and disinterested, and always made a lot of good common sense. She didn't have to explain to him more than once that she loved her husband, that she would never do anything to hurt him. When he kissed her mouth his hand moved confidently around her waist. He pulled her close. His right leg moved between hers. Gently he lowered her to the floor, his left hand brushing the backs of her legs. "I love you," he said, but it didn't matter, didn't matter what he said. She took a sudden breath when he entered her, training her eyes upon the cut crystal and silver tea set above her in the glass cabinet. "I love you," he said, "I love you, love you," pressing her against the rough carpet. "I love you," he said, but she only loved her husband, she told him, but don't stop anyway, love me anyway, keep loving me even when you hear his feet on the stairs, even when you hear his hand on the door. The entire floor seemed to contract suddenly; the entire world seemed to swirl. And then she was coming in his arms, and the door was opening, and Edward with his briefcase was staring down at them, not surprised but fulfilled, always expecting it, always anticipating the thrill of the moment when she came, breathless, swelling against the rough carpet, crying, You, you, baby, now, in the hard, enduring embrace of this other man.

When Edward arrived home around seven-thirty, the house was empty. He wondered if this was the very silence he had been somehow expecting. There was something familiar about it already as he lay his briefcase on the bookshelf and stepped into the living room. He thought motionlessly for a moment, listening. "I stepped into the house," he said out loud. His voice was gentle, as if he were trying to reassure someone. "I had just gotten home." He stepped into the immaculate living room and saw the Pledge-bright woodwork and furniture, the blinking digital clock on the video recorder. "Suddenly all the voices in my head went quiet. I tried to remember what the other man looked and sounded like, but I couldn't." He stepped into the hallway, the kitchen, the bath. "I went into the kitchen. Everything was clean. Even the dish towels had been recently washed and folded. I felt strangely hypersensitive, predatory, keen. I wouldn't miss a sound, a motion. But there weren't any sounds. There weren't any motions. I went into the bedroom, talking out loud to myself in the empty house, trying to imagine an object of my conversation, but unable to visualize anybody, feeling only the secure silence situated somewhere in the house like an individual presence. I went into the bedroom, the hallway again, the living room. The television, VHS, sofa, bookshelf. I was trying to track the absence of something, I was trying to locate the place where it had ceased to be. It was like a racial memory, like the dream of falling from high trees. I knew everything would be all right in the long run. I knew everything would work out for the best."

* * *

A few weeks later he received Rachel's letter, posted from Fort Lauderdale.

> Dear Ed. I really can't explain. I've tried to think of a way I could explain, but I can't explain. I still think about you all the time. Please don't hate me all the time.
>
> Love, Rachel.

Sometimes it woke him in the middle of the night. Other times, in order to delay going home to an empty house, he ate dinners at restaurants or attended double features at the cinema mall. The only part of the day he actually preferred, however, was his time at work, where he tried to arrive especially early each morning. The janitors were usually still pulling large gray dustbins on trolleys down the polished hallways, or operating roaring, man-size vacuum cleaners with corrugated, squidlike rubber hoses. Eventually, however, he had to return home and face it. He didn't feel frightened so much as deeply excluded. He felt hurt; he felt inarticulately sad. He wanted to be readmitted to that silence, that absence. He wanted to hear the language of that darkness again.

Three times a week he sat on Dr. Tobias's couch and stared at the ceiling's white acoustical tile. He never felt like saying anything; he couldn't think of anything to say. He tried to imagine Rachel on jets, visiting impossible countries, hearing the other man's voice in her head. What did he tell her? Did he convey advice, affection, information? Edward couldn't imagine. It was as if he couldn't even comprehend language anymore. Strangely enough, it was when Edward grew silent and desultory that he somehow elicited the voices of others.

"What did you do today?" Dr. Tobias asked.

"I went to work."

"Did you speak with anybody?"

"My secretary. I made some phone calls."

"Have you made any plans for tonight?"

"I'll probably watch television."

It was as if Edward could comprehend only literal, dry events. After only a few weeks or so his silence even began to infect Dr. Tobias, who would sit alone in his office for hours after Edward's sessions and gaze silently out the window at high converging power lines and the flashing blue and green lights of planes descending over the airport. When he went home, Dr. Tobias's wife would serve him his favorite dishes and sit silently by his side while he stared absently at the evening paper or smoked his pipe and stirred the ashes in the ashtray with his charred and twisted pipe cleaner. Sometimes Mrs. Tobias would go to bed alone, worried by her own vague suppositions, while Dr. Tobias sat awake late into the night, not thinking of anything in particular, listening to Brahms's *Requiem* on the compact disc player and feeling an odd, indefinable melancholia suffusing his blood like a drink of alcohol.

It wasn't until the following winter that Edward began to show signs of "progress." A few days before the winter solstice he arrived and took his customary seat on the sofa. The weather had been unusually chill for Orange County, and some forecasters were even predicting snow. "Sometimes you don't know why," Edward said. Deep underneath the floor the massive industrial heaters started and began to blow the office full of warm, abrasive air. "It's just something you feel, not something you can talk about. It's not chemical, it's not your parents, it's not even the newspaper. It's some sort of invisible condition. It's that part of the world you can't explain." For the remaining hour Edward lay silent on the sofa, only speaking in order to answer a few of Dr. Tobias's cool, aimless questions.

On his way home that evening he was caught in a traffic jam on Irvine Boulevard. The uncustomarily cold weather seemed to elicit a rather sudden, edged anxiety from everyone. Edward looked in at other cars where drivers gripped their wheels angrily or gave sudden fingers in the Pacific's general direction. Sometimes long white limousines glided smoothly past, their engines generating warm, humming vacuums of space as well as sound, their occupants' faces occluded by dark, glimmering windows. At home Edward knew he would be able to relax. He had learned, and was learning, not to let things bother him so much anymore. He still had his home, his job, his health. In the distance there was a crack of sudden thunder, and the entire atmosphere seemed to give a little. It might rain at any moment, and Edward imagined himself at home already, sitting in his living room and watching television, the other man's discarded possessions heaped on the coffee table before him. The Edge Shaving Gel, Trimco nail clippers, flexible black plastic comb. A linty button and some stray change Edward had fished from behind the sofa cushions. A Casa Maria matchbook with an unlabeled phone number printed inside with a blue felt-tipped pen. If he didn't try too hard to make sense of things, Edward knew that things often made sense of themselves.

Edward never saw his face or heard his voice again, and eventually he even stopped speculating about the other man's name.

THE WIND BOX

Sometimes he stood baffled by white sunlight and just watched cars go by. Bright convertibles, battered Fords and Chevrolets, roaring buses, long smooth white limousines with dark windows. The heat seemed to pull at him, like the sunlight flashing off chrome and windshields, like his sense of great quakes and tremblers stirring dreamlessly awake in the deep earth beneath his feet. Obdurate mountains grew down there, massive and subcrustal seas and continents. That was the first thing he noticed about Southern California: the sea of movement embedded in it. For the first few days he slept in his car on Mulholland Drive, but eventually he found a moldering bungalow studio apartment off Vineland Avenue in Burbank, and a large unsprung stuffed chair in an abandoned lot nearby. He purchased a curiously stained mattress from the local Salvation Army and transported it home in a neglected shopping cart. Large, dense men with rough, menacing beards, sun-stained leather jackets and reflecting mirrored sunglasses intensely disregarded him as they kicked their motorcycle ignitions with spurred black boots. Sometimes at night he would sit on his front porch in his tattered green lawn chair and just watch the high, buzzing power lines. He could hear the power lines when he slept; they invested everything, even his dreams, with a cool staticky mist. It was the only coolness he knew that summer.

The heat woke him every morning at 6:00 a.m. He fixed instant coffee, Cocoa Puffs, Potato Stix with ketchup, hearing the blare of televisions converge in the littered courtyard. The screeching of cartoon automobiles, the abrupt explosions of animated cats, a deep-throated, impossibly voiced villain crying again and again, "Destroy the transformers! Destroy the transformers!" He sat at his wobbly table in the muggy kitchenette, gazing out the window at refuse in the courtyard and mangy, addled cats dozing underneath a tireless Ford Falcon. Unraveling truck retreads lay strewn about, fragments of irreparable furniture, unidentifiable hunks of metal, a sun-bleached stray number 12 billiard ball, and everywhere thousands of crushed and decomposing cigarette butts like gravel at the bottom of a tropical fish tank. There were times when it seemed to him the entire world had ended. There were other times when he just wished it would.

Vast rolling geothermal plates slipped and heaved, buildings toppled, freeway off-ramps collapsed. Earthquakes crashed through the valley like benedictions; the planet's thin mantle abrupted and fell, swallowing entire cities. In his dreams everything was destroyed. There was only the hot amber sand again, the primordial Santa Ana winds turning through everything. Sometimes he lay in bed for hours, feeling drained of energy, as if in his dreams of destruction things had actually collapsed inside of him. Later he would sit on his porch glancing through secondhand men's magazines he had purchased at Phil's Paperback Exchange on Ventura Boulevard, the perennial television playing from the neighboring bungalow into the otherwise abandoned courtyard like some unscathed bit of technology after the soft, impactless explosion of a neutron bomb. In the bungalow across from his, a woman with a brittle voice and pale, dry hands would occasionally prize open her kitchen's dusty venetian blinds and gaze at him for a while, her television mindlessly promoting cereals and deodorants to the courtyard's stunned and diarrheic cats.

"What are you doing?" she asked one day. He could glimpse only smoky dust swirling behind her cracked blinds.

"Nothing," he said.

"Are you the man that drives the bus? Do you drive the yellow bus?"

He thought for a moment. "I don't think so," he said.

A chattering pneumatic hammer started up miles away. "I just want you to know, then," she said after a while. "I just want you to know that we all think you're doing a very good job."

"The mind has special powers all its own," Victory told him, sitting with him during her breaks at the Golden Pancake Coffee Shop on Lankershim Boulevard and smoking Tareytons. "I believe that very strongly. I don't think you can ever get to know me really well unless you understand I happen to be a very mind-oriented sort of person. A lot of people aren't mind-oriented sorts of persons at all. A lot of people just think money matters, or having a nice car." She never really looked at him, but rather out the window at the flashing sun. A painting on the coffee shop window depicted a jolly fat chef staggering underneath a platter of enormous pancakes and syrup. "That's why I came to L.A., you see. Because L.A. is the land of the next great superrace. There's a conjunction of planetary currents and influences here which are very powerful. That's why Aimee Semple McPherson came here. That's why Krishnamurti came here."

He drank his coffee and thought about enormous pterodac-
tyls carrying people off in their bloody talons, withering
droughts, vast clouds of hazardous waste settling over the city
like a bird on its nest. And earthquakes. Sudden, impossible,
perfectly enunciated earthquakes. They didn't speak to his
mind, but to his bones. It was like the articles in supermarket
tabloids about mothers psychically contacted by their unborn
children. Unborn children wanted to tell you things. They
wanted to prepare you for their imminent arrival.

Victory lit another Tareyton. "You're a very good listener,"
she told him after a while. "Men are never usually very good
listeners, you know."

Victory's real name was Eleanor Davenport, and her father
was a fundamentalist minister in Austin, Texas. "Being raised
by fundamentalists can be a very wearying experience," Victory
told him. "There's no room for growth when you've got a big
helmet on your head. Ever since I came to California I feel as
if I have won the most important battle of my life, and nobody
can ever tell me how to think or behave ever again. That's why
I changed my name when I came here. To Victory."

Victory had been living in Burbank for two years, sharing a
two-bedroom block-style apartment with a legally blind Tarot
reader who went by the name of Governor Pearl. "She has
taken the name Governor Pearl because it combines traditional
masculine ideas with traditional feminine ideas, thus helping
create entirely new patterns of socially accepted feminine behavior. A person's name is very important since it tells people
who you really are inside. Otherwise you're just like everybody
else. You're just a Mary, or a Jane, or a Bill. Basically I guess
you could say Governor Pearl's a very thoughtful, caring sort
of person who's hardly ever home, but pays half the rent anyway." David never met Governor Pearl, but a few times Victory pointed her out to him as she drove past the diner in her
long white '57 Thunderbird convertible, maneuvering slowly
through the crowded street traffic, her guide dog, Jeff, panting

beside her in the passenger seat. Governor Pearl wore dark sunglasses, and had a long gaunt face with close-cropped hair. "She's not really completely blind," Victory said. "She can still make out general shapes and things."

Usually they spent the night together at his place, lying naked and pale on the sweating mattress, gazing absently at the thin gauze curtains as if expecting, at any moment, some indication of a breeze. Victory loved to talk, and even when she didn't have anything to say she had numerous questions to ask.

"Do you ever think of spiritual things, David?"

"I don't know. I guess so." He could still hear motorcycles echoing in the courtyard, tearing and shaking at things like tremblers beneath the world's floor.

"Like what sort of spiritual things, David? Do you ever wonder about your rightful place in the universe? Do you ever wonder why you were born, and what your purpose in life is? Do you believe there are spiritual beings who have come from millions of years in our future to determine our lives and thoughts, residing underneath our world because they fear our violence and narrow-minded hypocrisy? Or do you believe we all have free will, and that each of us is a God of his or her own private universe, the universe of the self? In our private universes we live forever. Nothing restrains us in the universe of our minds, because that is the real universe, and this one that we think is real is just a prison where we go when we want to punish ourselves. Do you ever think about things like that, David? Is that why you're so quiet all the time? Have you ever read Jung? Or Gurdjieff? Have you ever been to a phrenologist? Do you believe in phrenology?"

Sometimes David grew dizzy and disoriented by Victory's questions. They seemed to multiply in the tiny, hot bungalow like strange misshapen insects with chitinous bodies and jeweled glistening wings. They fluttered and banged against the naked overhead light bulb; they crawled into your clothes and sheets and facial hair. He developed a flickering migraine, and thought as hard as he could. "I don't know," he said finally. "I don't know if I've thought about that stuff or not."

Victory was convinced David should meet her Spiritual Work Group counselor, who owned a house in Sherman Oaks. The house was filled with paperback books on tidy mahogany shelves, energy crystals, pyramid tents and totems, and original Native American religious artifacts stored behind polished, glass-paneled cabinets. "It's like a museum, kind of," Victory said. "It's like a museum of higher thought." She pulled her battered Toyota Corolla up onto the slender curb. "He's giving one of his famous High Energy Workshops today. People come from all over the world to attend them. But he's graciously agreed to meet us both afterward for a short while."

"Intellectual abilities are not something to be taken lightly," Dr. Simonson said, drinking orange pekoe tea from a large ceramic mug. The mug was imprinted with a blazing red and amber mandala. "With knowledge comes great responsibility, and I don't mean responsibility to mere mankind, for we share our universe with creatures of many different species. There are creatures on Rigel-seven, for example, who breathe pure methane. They have evolved many thousands of years beyond our puny race. Because they dispensed with violence long ago, they no longer possess hands or feet. They make love by means of pure meditation. Often lovers are together for thousands of years without ever meeting face-to-face, without ever knowing what each other looks like." They were sitting in the large ornate living room which was crowded with more bookshelves, enormous fetal stone sculptures, and an intricate stereo system with thousands of records filed in varnished oak cabinets. The room felt infinitely heavy, David thought. It felt like massive tectonic plates jostling underneath continents, oceans, gravity.

David thought he felt something shifting in all that buried weight, tearing. He placed his hands under his knees.

"Ideas belong to the entire universe, David. That's all I'm saying." Meanwhile, David tried to envision the ruptured walls of Atlantis, the ocean pouring through and pounding everything to bits. Enormous cyclopean squid pulled away, pumping like hearts. Strange convoluted creatures with bloated symmetrical features. Vast green plains of algae and rocks, dark intricate caverns filled with unglimpsed and impossible life forms. Nobody could hear or see anything down there. You could only feel it, that sudden *beat* of the sea. The superrace, with their nightmarish faces and inflated, brainy skulls, had long anticipated everything, even their own destruction. The world of the mind goes on forever, they thought. And the world of the mind is all that matters.

David felt a sudden, weightless sense of relief rise in his chest as he considered the earth's doomed secrets. Then, after a moment, the plates in the cupboards began to rattle. The large bay windows chattered faintly in their frames like whirring insects. Victory clasped shut her purse.

"Don't worry," Dr. Simonson said. "It's just a little trembler. We get them all the time."

After the destruction of Atlantis the sea looked exactly the same. A few jostling whitecaps, waves. Gulls screeched and wheeled, clouds drifted overhead. On the ocean's surface it was as if nothing had happened.

"Earthquakes are very important psychic occurrences, you know," Dr. Simonson said. "Earthquakes help the world breathe. They adjust the world's psychic energy so everything can flow smoothly again through our eternal minds."

"This is the guest room," Dr. Simonson said. "This is my office. That's an original Dali, a Braque, a Chagall. Great art gives us knowledge of the soul. This is my *Marvel Comics* collection. This is my science fiction room. My girl comes in four times a week and cleans everything, even the windows. Here's where I keep my pinball machines, video games, hot tub. All of these bay windows—I had them recently installed myself. I commissioned a semi-Olympic-size swimming pool for the yard. I'm going to tear down the garage and the guest bathroom and build a tower, which I will fill with my metaphysical library, my Indian and East African religious statues and a massive, a really humongous Dolby sound system. When I play Strauss, it'll sound like a football stadium. It'll sound like the entire place is lifting off into outer space." By this time they were back in the living room and Dr. Simonson was offering them ginseng tea, Chinese almond cookies and Hershey's Chocolate Kisses.

"When I came to L.A. in 1972, I had nothing," Dr. Simonson said. "I was driving a '63 Chevy Nova. It had three bald tires and no brakes. If I wanted to stop, I had to downshift into low, then pull out the emergency brake. I was drinking two quarts of Albertson's whiskey a day. I was going nowhere fast. I was going to hell in a handcart. Then I met a girl on the beach at Venice and told her about my dream. I dreamed of an institute that wasn't an institute. I dreamed of a corporation that wasn't a corporation. I dreamed of a radical organization which wouldn't get into any trouble. I dreamed of a group of people sharing their noblest thoughts and ambitions. I dreamed of all this." He gestured abstractly with his teacup. The bay windows, library, contracted swimming pool. The San Fernando Valley lay spread out in the distance, dully glittering like an enormous transistor component. "Her father was Andrew McLanahan, senior vice president of the Fluor Corporation, and she had a trust fund she wanted to do some good with. She believed in my dream. As a result, my dream became a reality." He poured more tea, gazing absently out the sparkling bay window. The entire valley was bleached with smog, as if everything in the world were fading into whiteness around them, everything except for this room. Everything except for the statues and books and records and shelves. Everything except for Dr. Simonson and the Worldwide Institute of Higher Learning, Ltd.

Some nights he took long walks through Burbank, Van Nuys, Encino, even White Oak, trying to recall his life before L.A. It was all very cold and indistinct, as if it weren't really his life at all but just some movie he had seen years ago on TV. He saw himself sitting in the backyards of strange houses. The houses were owned by men and women named Nancy and Bob, Dawn and Phil, April and James. Sometimes he sat in their cool beige living rooms and awaited their questions. "Do you like it here in Lompoc? Do you miss your friends? Would you like bologna and cheese, or ham salad? Do you like your room? Do you have any hobbies? Do you ever like to read a good book?" Then the men would take him into the garage to see their power drills, shortwave radios, miniature trains. He liked to watch the trains go around and around on the hissing track, and sometimes the men said, "You can stay and watch for a while, but don't touch anything. We'll call you when dinner's ready." And then leave him in the dark garage to watch the trains run around. He was afraid he might touch something by accident. Then the entire plyboard frame, plastic trees and houses, tracks and cars and station houses would all fall crashing senselessly to the concrete floors. He knew he shouldn't touch anything. Maybe he shouldn't even look. Whenever things were broken or missing, they always asked him first. Trevor and Sally, Alex and Mary Ann. They were always looking at him as if they could see broken or stolen valuables reflected in his eyes. That's why he preferred to sit alone in backyards, where there wasn't anything valuable he could damage or destroy. If he sat very quietly, the women wouldn't ask him any questions, or make him any more sandwiches. If he sat very quietly, they might forget he was even there at all, as if he were the brick barbecue, the high tessellated birdbath, the thorny rosebushes bound to thin green bamboo poles. There were Indians he had read about who could sit so still you couldn't see them, even if they were right in front of you. He would hold his hands clasped in his lap, and open them slightly from time to time, careful not to let too much air out. When he clasped his hands together they formed a wind box, and you could hear the wind if you held your ear close. He liked to hear the wind and keep it safe there in his hands, where it wouldn't disturb anyone, or attract any attention. An old woman had taught him the trick in one of the first houses where he had lived. The woman had made liverwurst and cheese sandwiches. Tomato soup. Chex Party Mix. He couldn't remember her face anymore, but he could still remember the liverwurst and cheese sandwiches, tomato soup and Chex Party Mix.

Victory gave him Gibran's *The Prophet.* She gave him Tolkien's *The Fellowship of the Ring.* She gave him numerous paperback novels by Philip K. Dick. The books had broken spines and were thumb-soiled. Their lurid covers depicted robots, embattled spaceships, babies drifting through space. "Philip K. Dick is the greatest American writer of our century," Victory said. "He was the only great writer to understand what a big and amazing place our universe is, as big and amazing as the darkest places of our own minds." Twice each week she brought him to her Spiritual Work Group at Dr. Simonson's house, where he was encouraged to share his latest "ideas."

"Always remember," Dr. Simonson urged them, solemnly igniting sandalwood incense and pouring the inexhaustible ginseng tea, "all ideas are good. No ideas are bad. There are half-formed ideas and undeveloped ideas. There are ideas which you don't understand, or which don't make you comfortable. But remember: We are a collective human enterprise of this Planet Earth, competing in the universe for greater knowledge, more perfect comprehension and truer love. Even as we speak, our thoughts and ideas are being projected into the living rooms of Tau Ceti and the Omar Asteroid Belt. In Tibet, men of vast religious wisdom have ingested hallucinogenics in order to mentally transport themselves here to Sherman Oaks and thus monitor our secret progress through the world of intellect. Would you like to start, David? Since you're our new member, would you like to give us a little information about your intellectual life?"

He wanted to say yes. He wanted to tell them about the destruction of Atlantis and the imminent destruction of L.A. He wanted to tell them about the wind box, the smooth, taut skin between Victory's shoulder blades, the white moon pulling every evening at the deep earth. But all he could say was "I don't know. I don't think so." He couldn't even look them in the eye when he said it. He looked instead at his hands folded in his lap. The wind in the box. The wind didn't move if you held it very carefully. "I guess I can't really think of anything," he said.

Some nights, at home in bed, Victory tried to draw him out.

"You have to learn to share, David. I don't mean this as an insult, but when you don't share your secrets, you're acting like a very selfish individual. What would the world be like, David, if nobody ever shared their feelings with anybody? It would be a pretty cold place, wouldn't it, David? Don't you think it would be a pretty cold world we lived in?"

"I guess so," he said. He thought it might be like Antarctica, covered with ice. You could wear heavy clothes in Antarctica like a disguise. He thought he wouldn't mind living in Antarctica.

"Tell me, David. Tell me how you feel."

"I don't know."

"Of course you know, David. How do you feel? How do you feel about me?"

"I like you, I guess."

"You *like* me? You *guess*?"

He thought for a moment, watching his Marlboro smolder in the glass tray. He picked it up. He shrugged. "I guess I love you. Is that what you mean?"

One evening after work Victory brought home a Feel Wheel in a large cardboard box. It was packaged like a board game, and contained a cloth sheet partitioned like a dartboard. In each varicolored segment was stenciled a different human emotion. Love. Sadness. Hate. Sorrow. Rage. Embarrassment. In the middle of the design, where the bull's-eye would have been, it said, "I need to be left alone." Victory handed him a red plastic checker.

"Now put the red checker on the emotion you feel most," she told him. "Only you can't put it on the center one this time, because, see, I already put my blue one there."

They smoked some marijuana. David felt cool and blurred. The deep earth seemed very close and compact.

"So why do you feel rage, David? Why do you feel so much rage all the time?"

"I don't know."

"What does it feel like, David? How do you feel when you feel rage?"

"It's like steam in a kettle," he said. "It's like water in a garden hose." As he began to talk he grew slightly disoriented. He felt as if he were fading away. As if the ground underneath his feet were slipping, slipping. "Sometimes I even travel down there, you know. I move among plates of stone and basalt, past sunken lakes of oil and natural gas. The stones are etched with skeletons of prehistoric dinosaurs and men. Enormous fish with teeth and tiny atrophied arms." As he talked, he tried to recall the silence which had resided in his bungalow before Victory. He felt as if that silence were being threatened by the pressure gathering along this deep earth's trembling faults and fissures. "Trilobites like intricate snowflakes, enormous plugs of lava, brilliant veins of gold and silver, and then this terrific pressure just building. I can feel it in my neck, my back, my teeth. I get these sinus headaches. I'm afraid to move or touch anything, because I know I have to be careful, I have to be careful with other people's things. And then other times, you know, I *want* to reach out. I *want* to give it a little push." A sudden weightless sensation filled his chest and sinuses like a gasp of helium. He felt slightly panicked, as if he had been discovered in some embarrassing act by strange people who would post him off to other, stranger houses. Then he heard the dishes rattle in the kitchenette. An aluminum pot clattered onto the floor.

"Did you feel that?" Victory asked. She was leaning back, her eyes dilated and stunned as if by one of her own insights.

"It's like a dead ocean down there," David told her. "It's like Atlantis. There are entire planets down there that have been buried for millions of years. Sometimes they just need a little push. Sometimes they just need you to notice they exist."

The next night after one of his longest walks he could feel the muscles taut and alert in the backs of his legs. He stopped at 7-Eleven for orange juice and Kit Kats, and arrived home around 10:00 p.m. to find Dr. Simonson in the kitchen washing an Underdog coffee cup in the cracked sink. Victory was on the floor leaning back against enormous frayed pillows, reading a paperback copy of Jung's *Man and His Symbols*. The third person in the room was a man. He was sitting on the sofa. He was tall and gaunt, with large, thick-rimmed glasses. He held a large gunmetal black box in his lap. He didn't look up when David entered. He seemed to be thinking about something.

The tiny cap fitted neatly over David's head and was attached by coiled wires to the black box.

"Alpha waves record the mind's mental activity," Dr. Simonson told him. "The alpha wave is the dominant strain in intellectual thought. William Burroughs knows about it. Timothy Leary knows about it. The world's greatest advances were not pioneered by scientists but by artists. Galileo, for example, was not an astronomer but a poet of abstract space. Don't be afraid, David. There's really absolutely nothing to be afraid of."

The thin man adjusted dials on the gunmetal box. Then he attached another thin wire to David's wrist with a Velcro band.

"We are all poets of infinite space," Dr. Simonson said, holding his warm teacup between his hands. "We all deserve worlds as beautiful as the worlds we live inside."

Sometimes they sat for hours in David's apartment while the gunmetal black box emitted its endless ribbons of tape. David felt very uninvolved with the entire process, smoking cigarettes and gazing aimlessly through the books and magazines Victory brought him while Dr. Simonson discoursed about civilization.

"Every individual has a certain skill or talent," he said, slicing Gruyère cheese and attaching the fragments to whole wheat crackers. "Every individual has certain responsibilities to mankind as a whole. Some men are strong, or beautiful, or know how to fix an automobile. Some are good at math, or sculpture, or computer programming. But some men have special skills which you don't come across so often. These men are the guiding forces of civilization. Everybody in the world is equally important, David, but these men I'm talking about are *really* important."

Sometimes, gazing at the smoky television screen, David let

his mind descend into the notched and convoluted maze of the deep earth. The dead planets were still there. The patient faces of special people and superadvanced races. They all kept very quiet now that Dr. Simonson was listening. They, too, heard the whirring of Dr. Simonson's machine, and Dr. Simonson's voice conferring with the thin man.

"What were the readings like?"

"I can't tell."

"Did you check them against the seismograph?"

"Well, there's correspondences, I guess. But we haven't had any strong variations. We need a couple of good jolts first."

They were looking for something. Sometimes it seemed as if they were looking for something inside David.

"David?"

"Yes."

"How do you feel?"

"Okay."

"A few days ago, when you were with Victory. How did that happen? What did you do?"

"I don't know." David had made one firm resolution. From now on he wasn't telling anybody anything.

"What did it feel like?"

"It felt like everything moved suddenly. Everything started shaking."

Dr. Simonson's eyes were very black, David thought. After a while Dr. Simonson said, "I mean in your mind, David. What sort of intellectual focus did you have? Did you hear voices? Did anyone tell you what to do? Was it anybody you recognized?"

David thought for a moment. "I don't know," he said. "I don't think so."

"It was very . . . I don't know," Victory said. "It was very spiritual. I guess that's all I can say. I could feel the energy emanating from him and I knew he was a very special sort of person. I knew David could destroy everything if he wanted to, but he's far too benevolent and caring a person to do anything like that without a good reason."

At night it seemed as if nothing unusual had ever happened. There was just him and Victory on the warped mattress, listening to cars in the street, with no real memory of Dr. Simonson other than the strange strategic shapes of mandalas and pyramids and Navajo totems distributed throughout the musty bungalow. When it was very late David would let himself quietly out of the house and resume his restless walks, feeling all the world's pressure gathering underneath his feet. One night as he was letting himself out he found Dr. Simonson sitting on the bungalow porch in the cat-clawed plastic lawn chair. His white penny loafers were propped on the wobbly wooden porch railing, his hands crossed in his lap.

"I'm not really Dr. Simonson, David," Dr. Simonson said, turning to look up at him, the glare of streetlamps reflecting off his glasses and transforming them into expressionless white disks. "Actually, I'm just Dr. Simonson's egoic projection. I'm the man Dr. Simonson always dreamed of being. Calm, self-assured, loving, immensely intelligent." He was wearing pleated white cotton slacks and a loose-fitting beige shirt. "You just go ahead with what you're doing, David. When I'm in this condition, I just like to drift along. You pretend I'm not even here at all. Remember that I'm still asleep in my bed up in Sherman Oaks, okay?"

These were hard desperate days of terrific heat. Temperatures and humidity soared to record levels, and at night David's walks grew longer and more furious, as if he were trying to outdistance himself. Interminable streets with savage, impossible names like primal litanies. Lankershim, Tujunga, Sepulveda, Vanowen. He walked for miles and miles, often conspicuously trailed by Dr. Simonson, who, blocks away, strolled along imperturbably like a white cloud. Sometimes Dr. Simonson drove his immaculately buffed Eldorado in the street beside David, playing Strauss's *Der Rosenkavalier* on his compact disc player, his windows rolled down and his convertible top popped back. Sometimes Dr. Simonson turned down his music and talked with David.

"You probably don't believe this, David, but I have felt great anger and resentment in my life too. I have felt tremendously violent hatred against the world, have desired terrible retributions for the many cruel crimes committed against me. I know I should be more understanding, but sometimes I'm not; sometimes I'm not very understanding at all. Just a week ago, for instance, the Internal Revenue Service froze my corporate accounts. They subpoenaed many of my most loyal students, my secretary, my entire accounting firm. They're trying to declare me a profit-making institution, rather than a nonprofit therapeutic health maintenance community service, which is, of course, what I really am. Sometimes I'd like to let them all have it. Wouldn't you, David? Wouldn't you like to teach them all a lesson they'd never forget? All those goddamn bureaucratic phonies downtown. They're all asking for it, aren't they, David? They're all asking for one killer jolt, and you're the one that could do it. Let them die. Let them all be crushed and die. Then they'd know how it felt, wouldn't they? Then they'd know how it felt to build something you loved and have it all torn down around you by greedy vultures."

The pressure and heat were growing intolerable. David suffered painful sinus congestion, recurring flus, chills and colds, sudden flashing headaches unrelieved by aspirin or Tylenol. Tension accumulated in the earth's secret faults and caverns, the deep earth filling up with resentment, like some cheated lover. It was all perfectly natural, he thought. In earthquakes natural terrestrial rhythms emerge from the earth's heart. Crippled women were known to walk after earthquakes. Blind men saw. Diseases went into spontaneous remission. Some great eternal pulse was always restored by cataclysm. "You could let it happen," Dr. Simonson said. His eyes were damp and watery with allergy, his nose red and chafed by his pocket handkerchief. "You could give the world back its heart, its breath, its voice. It's like cleaning out all the world's hate with vast white rivers of pure energy."

Then one night he destroyed Los Angeles over and over again in his dreams. Deep subcrustal plains slipped and heaved, enormous fractural fissures opened across the entire San Fernando Valley, swallowing streets and housing tracts, ripping out interminable colonic streams of plumbing and electrical wires. Gas and water mains burst, filling the air with glistening sprays and roiling white clouds. Subterranean toxic waste containers burst and sprayed. The San Andreas Fault gave a sudden pull, and then, with a long, slow and almost graceful flourish, the great fragile promontory of Los Angeles snapped and slid into the boiling Pacific like a string of pearls down the grate of a sink.

David awoke feeling a strange lapse in his stomach and then, faintly, what might have been the subsiding aftershocks of an earthquake. He looked around the room, but everything seemed in place. The bungalow was quiet, and the streets outside quiet too. It was almost eight o'clock. Victory had left for work, and the bathroom was still misty from her shower. David lay half-awake in bed for a while. Something seemed very wrong. He picked up the telephone and heard a dial tone. He turned on the television and saw *AM Los Angeles*. After a while he pulled on his light flannel robe and went out to the porch with a cup of instant coffee.

Outside he couldn't tell if the world had ended or not. Perhaps *AM Los Angeles* was on tape delay in some collapsed Hollywood studio while its actual stars and guests struggled hopelessly underneath fallen girders and masonry. The entire courtyard was littered with wrappers and Styrofoam fast-food containers blown in by the night's muggy Santa Ana. The front end of the crippled Buick had been dismantled, baring rusted axles and joints, corroded drums and cracked brake shoes. The horizon was cloudy with either smog or the dust of pulverized buildings. He felt deeply exhausted, as if he had been running great distances in his sleep. Gradually he realized that someone was watching him. A large grasshopper whirred and chattered and landed by his feet. He looked up at the blinded window of the neighboring bungalow.

"Did you feel it?" she asked. "I was awake all night. I was waiting for it, you see."

The grasshopper looked at him with glassy eyes.

"It's God's fist coming down," the woman told him. "That's where earthquakes come from. From God's fist punishing sinners."

David found a neglected cigarette and book of matches in his robe's vest pocket. The cigarette was frayed and slightly cracked along the seam. He lit it anyway. The grasshopper took off again and crashed into a nest of discarded Wonder bread wrappers. After a while, the neighbor's television started up, and someone on a morning talk show called it a three point seven, and someone else on the panel said, "A three point seven? That didn't *feel* like a three point seven, did it? It felt at *least* like a four point *five.* . . ."

David was alone in the house all day, smoking a pack of Marlboros he bought at 7-Eleven, watching daytime movies and reruns of old sitcoms.

"They've arrested Dr. Simonson," Victory told him when she got home, breathless, her uniform stained with yellow egg matter and ketchup. "Tax fraud, David. I have to go up to his house before they've sealed it off and get his papers for him. I can't believe this. I can't believe they're doing all this to a nice man like Dr. Simonson."

The rest of the summer was much like the beginning, leaving David the bungalow to himself. Victory was occupied with work and grand jury proceedings, and then, in early September, Dr. Simonson was admitted to the Betty Ford Drug and Alcohol Rehabilitation Center in Palm Springs, where Victory regularly drove herself and other workshop members to visit him. David found a job pumping gas and tuning automobiles at a local Gulf station, and in the evenings after he returned home he would sit on his porch and breathe the gas fumes from his soiled green uniform. The thin man with the glasses never returned, but the gunmetal black box remained on the plastic coffee table.

A cool sea breeze had begun developing by the time Victory left for Iowa. "Father mailed me a ticket a few weeks ago, and I didn't know if I wanted to go or not until now. I've been thinking a lot about God and family lately, David. I've been thinking maybe it's all right to rebel when you're young and confused, but that later, when you get older, it's time to settle down and raise children so that you can teach them about God's love. If Dr. Simonson or anybody from the workshop calls, tell them you don't know where I went, okay? I hope you're very happy and find God in your heart too, someday, David. I hope what I'm doing doesn't hurt you."

It didn't hurt him. The next few weeks were filled with a high overcast, muggy and clinging air, a certain heaviness and density of limb and brain. There were no more discernible tremors, but only a sort of faint and misty anxiety which infiltrated news features, community council hearings and all-talk radio. Most of central Los Angeles was inadequately constructed. People recalled the St. Francis Dam in the Santa Clara Valley, built with graft and faulty cement by William Mulholland. Los Angeles was just waiting and vulnerable. It would collapse like matchsticks. The Los Angeles "natives," however, refused to be intimidated.

"All-Talk Radio. You're on the air."

"Hello, Linda. This is Danielle in Whittier. I just wanted to say, about all this fright talk about earthquakes? Well, if you live in the Midwest you've got your tornados. And if you live on the East Coast you've got your flash floods and hurricanes. There are electrical storms in Kansas my boyfriend Gary told me about? He saw this enormous ball of electricity rolling down the freeway and it hit another car and the car exploded? Well, I'm just saying, earthquakes aren't so bad, after all. I mean, they're here and everything, so what can we do, right? Oh, and Linda?"

"Yes, Danielle?"

"Do you really think old Teflon pans could be dangerous for frying foods? My sister Betty gave me her old set, and it *looks* perfectly fine and all. I'm just worried about the kids."

He never saw Victory again, or Dr. Simonson, who was released from the Betty Ford clinic in October and, after an elaborate court trial which lasted nearly two years, acquitted of conspiracy and fraud. After paying a substantial fee to the IRS he reportedly moved to the Bay Area where he organized the expansion of his Free Spiritual Outgrowth Clinics into Arizona, Hawaii and, eventually, even South Korea. Sometimes, in his walks through the Valley, David noticed clinics springing up in disused shopping and medical-dental centers. Lovely blond girls in overalls gave him pamphlets as he passed. He never really looked at these women, though. He preferred to look at the beautiful women driving by in their cool, expressionless convertibles.

Three summers later he was hitchhiking home from work on Ventura Boulevard when Governor Pearl pulled up and offered him a ride in her white Thunderbird. "I enjoy driving at night," she said, turning to look over both shoulders. Without sunglasses, her right eye appeared lifeless and dim, her left eye overlarge and milky with glaucoma. As she pulled slowly away from the curb a passing car honked and veered. In the backseat her guide dog lay unharnessed and senselessly asleep.

"I love to drive in L.A.," Governor Pearl said, and offered him a Coors from a white Styrofoam icebox, Winstons, the electric cigarette lighter. Her right eye, trained on the road, tilted her head to one side. "There's probably some chips or something in there too," she said, gesturing at the large brown 7-Eleven bag cluttered with wrappers, unopened toilet paper and a discarded Big Gulp container filled with dissolving Orange Slush.

They took the Ventura Freeway to Santa Monica, then the winding and exorbitant Sunset Boulevard back into Hollywood, Silver Lake, Chinatown. "It's so big," Governor Pearl said. "And filled with so many interesting people. Is that a stop sign ahead?" They slowed to a stop. It was a DON'T DRIVE DRUNK billboard. They got back on the freeway and drove until dawn, drinking Coors and smoking marijuana. Around 7:00 a.m. they stopped for Egg McMuffins before dropping David off at his home.

After that night, David completely forgot about the deep earth, Dr. Simonson, Victory, the wind box, his many concerned foster mothers and foster fathers. It felt like going away. It felt like awakening to a new life in a new house with strange people in it and just going away from all of them, because it was never a place you belonged anyway. The world was very peaceful after you went away. Everything was new and fresh and clean. Everybody breathed easier, thought more clearly and lived longer, healthier lives.

In the warm regenerate spring he abandoned everything and moved to the Pacific Northwest, where it rained for him nearly every day.

CLOSER TO YOU

In the sunny mornings you chase the orange cat across the green grass. Underneath your feet the shelter, filled with the moon, the rain and the stars and the wind. And the orange cat lands on the fence, its orange tail twisting. Its dead sparrow on the crumbling brick barbecue. Big weeds from the barbecue, and the rusting iron gate, and brown hollow snails all around. The dead sparrow says when you touch it. The yard says, the underground shelter says   The underground shelter filled with everything that is not you. And the dead sparrow says to your fingertips, your tongue and your mouth, and then mother on the back porch shouting the No! The No stella! And you are no longer stella, and the dead sparrow falls to the green grass, its words still feathery and wet on your thick tongue. The No! in the air and the orange cat on the red fence, its orange tail twisting. And you think the No! at the cat, and with your mouth you say   With your mouth you say   The cat's orange tail twisting. And the dead sparrow on the green grass.

*   *   *

Breakfast time and you are stella again, every morning surrounded by the world that is not stella. House, sun, moon, table, cocoa puffs, liquefying margarine, sprays of black bitter crumbs, mother, marcie, tablecloth and dad. The grandma on the stuffed chair, with her food tray and cracked plates. And mother holds the big spoon. The grandma says Aaaah. Aaaah, with gerber peaches on her chin, and mother says Here you go, alice. Be a good girl, and dad says There she goes. Now she's started. Dad doesn't like breakfast and sits on the sofa, wearing his blue robe with the torn blue pockets. And says I thought I detected a minute there. I thought I detected an actual minute of peace and quiet in this goddamn house, and the grandma says Aaaah. Aaaah. So mother gets the medicine and you drink your juice. Orange juice in mother's glass. And the marcie clacks her new pink shoes together, requiring more toast. The marcie wears red paint on her face today, just like mother, and the voice on the radio says Better. Brighter. More Beautiful. The noise of the world on your face. You can touch it with your sticky hands. The noise of the world that is not you, and then you say   And then you say

Dad says Great. Now they're both started. It's like a chorale—one vast great vegetable symphony, and takes his coors out to the sunny back porch.

The grandma's tiny eyes are red and wet, filled with words and memories of words. She says Aaaah. Aaaah, her big veiny tongue extruding from her thin lipless mouth. Her mouth red and glistening, but not like the marcie's mouth, not like mother's.

The gerber peaches are all gone, and now the grandma loves you even more. You and your soggy toast.

And so you give her some.

Every weekday morning mother takes you to the special school for special children. We just hope and hope, mother says. We just hope for the lord's compassion and his love. You hold the seat belt's bright silver buckle in your hands. The silver buckle is a big hard word, and pulls the belt very tight. Mother says the lord words again and again, and you put your hands together to speak the lord words too, feeling them between your fingers. Then you get out of the car at your school filled with special children. Big yellow bumblebees on a big wooden sign, smooth and you like to touch. This is your bright smile, this is your round stomach. Tea, tie, toe, tum, tah, tea mrs. evans says. Her bright red fingertips touch your teeth, your tongue, putting the words there. Tih. *Tih.* With the *t*ip of your *t*eeth, with the *t*ip of your *t*ongue. So you tell her the grandma word and she gives you a green m&m. And she says now with the *tih* sound. Taaah. Taaah. Tooth, tongue, tea, toad, tot, and shows you big pictures in her lap. A big green toad, a cup of hot tea. And you say the grandma word again, and mrs. evans has more m&ms. Red, yellow, black, orange, blue, brown. Because the grandma is a tongue, a tooth, a toad. And all the other special children make grandma sounds too in their big bicycle chairs with their broken eyes and big shiny foreheads, and you're all tea tie toe tum tah tea, and scrub the stiff colored paper with bright crayons. The crayons snap when you break them, just like mouths. You play in the tanbark yard, bang blocks to music, eat graham crackers, and dad picks you up in his car with a coors in his lap. Who's my little dollface, he says. Who's my little cracked brain, my little wordless wonder. Kissing you with his rough face, taking you home to drink more coors on the slanting-sunny back porch. This is your yard. This is your bright sun. This is your green, green grass.

Dad built the underground shelter in the yard because he loves you. In wars words fall and explode. In wars everybody falls wordless to the ground, wordless just like you. Usually wars are on television, but when they become real, dads dig holes in the ground. Big machines come into your yard and eat it. Strange men with hairy arms and beautiful tattoos. But then the war doesn't come and only you are stella, only you and the wordless people on TV. You like to stand on the hard wooden lid. You like to point at the big steel pipe filled with spiderwebs and shrouded, mummified bugs. The hard wooden lid fastened with a big rusty padlock. And then you ask dad   And then you ask him   And dad says I built the goddamn thing so when the thermonuclear war comes and blows us all to hell and back we'll have a warm place to go to the bathroom. Now give dad a kiss and leave him alone. And dad's rough face says kiss. Kiss kiss, it says. How'd I know they'd fucking lay me off? How'd I know I'd blow all our savings on that goddamn water trap and the bastards would lay me off? And pulls his blue robe tighter and cinches his blue flannel belt, just like the seat belt in his rattling car. The same car they drove the grandma home in when the grandma lived in a hospital with the world's other grandmas.

The marcie has her own bed but at bedtime she lies on your bed to play. The marcie plays like mrs. evans and points, reading you the big red book and says This is the spider, the stone, the snake, the sock. And her finger says Point point point. Tomcat, teddy bear, toilet, towel, tripod, toad, and you are watching the goldfish in the round fishbowl. The goldfish mouth moves too, just like the marcie mouth, and you reach for it. The goldfish says   The goldfish says   And you say too

And the marcie says the No! and grabs your hand. *This* is a tripod, *this* is a toad. Now which is the tripod? Which is the toad? And you make your finger say Point point point, and the marcie takes your finger from her mouth and says the No! You want to touch the marcie mouth, the hard round words. You want to take the words in your hand and put them in your pocket with the masticated plastic soldier, the stray pink barbie slipper, the broken crayon. But the marcie says the No! No stella! You're a *bad* girl and *nobody* likes you. Now go to bed now! Now go to bed now!

At night the grandma sleeps in the blue room, strapped to the crooked bed with the car straps, her eyes wide open sometimes. They are very hard clear eyes, eyes eyes, and the moonlight through the curtains talks in her room, but the grandma says nothing. And you say nothing back, wearing your soft pink pajamas. The marcie asleep in your bedroom, mother and dad asleep in theirs. You touch the grandma and she opens her big black mouth. Her thin hand touches you, grabbing. And you listen to the words in the grandma's head, like the words underground in dad's shelter. Spiders and glistening webs across the grandma's window, tiny bugs blurring and buzzing. The grandma sees the bugs too, the moon and the night and you. And the grandma's veiny hand grabs your pajama top tight and you can't get away. And then you whisper   And then you whisper   And when the grandma's eyes close again, you return to your bed and dream of dad's shelter underground, where words echo and resound, hop and crawl. If only you could reach them.

Some days you don't go to school and mother takes you to the doctor and his gleaming silver tools on a clean white cloth. And you say the grandma words and the doctor puts a mirror in your mouth. And mother says She tried to point yesterday. She pointed at the yard and tried to say something. An ess word I'm certain. When einstein was five he couldn't even tie his shoes, and little stella can tie her shoes. Mother shows you your shoelace and pulls, and so you fix it. And the doctor says Cognitive development, aphasia, phonetic, lexical and syntactic, langue and parole. And then mother takes you home to the yard where dad sleeps on the unsprung porch sofa, and then she goes away again.

Underground in the shelter the moonlight's waiting and you walk across the hollow yard and through the hot sun. If you carry the old wood chair you can stand and peer into the rusty metal pipe. You can smell the buried life, rich with words and water and rust. You reach into the pipe with your hand and pull out ropes of dust, collapsed spiders and glistening white insect eggs. Those are the words down there, you can hear them in the pipe. Stone sea sand sister snake sun song soon. And one spider blossoms in your hand and starts to tickle. You hold it in your hand and it scrambles around, this thin tickling word. Sssssss. Sssssss. Some words go up and down, other words go back and forth. The spider is a word. The surf the sand the sea. And you push it through the pipe into grandma's world, where grandma waits in the dark. Spider. Spider spider. That's what you and grandma say together, underground where everything is wet and thick and real. Spider. And then you hear a round word, and under the roses you see it. It is big and fat and green. Ur, it says. Ur. It's wet in your hands when you lift it to the steel pipe. Toad, it says. Toad. A big green toad, a cup of hot tea. Ur. Ur. Falling down the long steel pipe where the other grandma waits for it.

Sometimes the grandma cries at night when you visit, strapped in her small bed, dreaming of the hard wordless night and all the world that is not stella. The grandma dreams with her mouth open, her mouth black and hollow like the steel pipe, her cheeks wet when you kiss them. Like the shelter, the grandma is filled with the world that is not grandma. Words like crumbling concrete blocks and broken red bricks, weeds sprouting and the unsprung sofa and the shelter's hard wooden lid. The grandma has an inside, too, and you touch the *t*ip of the grandma's *t*eeth, the *t*ip of her *t*ongue, and the grandma says Aaaah—the everything word. Aaaah. The moonlight burying itself tonight in the shelter, spilling down the thick steel pipe with the swift-gliding bugs. You reach into the grandma's mouth looking for words there, their hard glittering edges, like plastic toys lost in the overgrown yard. In the underground shelter, swamps and sculpted faces, pockets of fossilized bones and fuel, stones etched with prehistoric brains and skulls. Aaaah, the grandma says, her hands grabbing at you. Aaaah. This is the secret here, she says. The secret sound of words, the secret dream of everything that is not stella. You love the word already as you pull it from the grandma's mouth, the grandma's eyes round and wide and glassy with something which is not moonlight. This is hard. This is real. You place the word on the *t*ip of your *t*ongue, salty on your fingertips. Your throat hurts the word, growling like a dog. "Tor, taw, ter," you say. And the moonlight pulsing in the shelter, and the toad hopping in the dark. "Tord, tawd, toad," you say, and that's it there. That's the word in your mouth now. "Toad." Its salty taste, its scaly skin. "Toad." And the grandma doesn't say anything, just looking at you. Very tired now, very sleepy. "Toad toad toad," you say. And the grandma says Aaaah very softly, very tired. Goes to sleep and her mouth falls open. Then you hear the other word there. Sssss. Sssss. Sea sand spider. Spider. Spider.

You say "Toad" at breakfast and mother gives you french toast with syrup, and you eat the syrup with your tiny spoon, and jam with your toast. "Toad toad toad," and the grandma in her chair with her soggy food, dreaming of other words beneath the yard. "Toad toad, toad toad toad." And mother gives you a big hug, and the marcie gives you a hate face. But dad says It's original sin. My pure little brain case has fallen into the world of already fallen language. Great. More talk, more words. Everybody in the world will be talking someday. Today I think I'll look for a job. I gotta get out of this fucking house.

And mrs. evans says Cognitive aphasia, positive reinforcement, syntactic redevelopment, and makes mother watch as she feeds you more m&ms. "Toad toad toad." And mother says I'm so grateful to the lord, and you open the big picture book and Point point point and everything is "Toad toad toad." And then the other thing in the shelter, the other thing tickling in the grandma's mouth. "Spire," you say. "Spiner. Spider. Toad toad toad." And everybody in the entire world loves you, just like mother.

There's no big rush, little cracked brain, dad says, you in his lap and the television on. There's no real hurry. *That's* all you're hurrying toward. *That's* all language is about. And the television says hostages in lebanon, preschool drug addiction, dioxides, acid rain and nuclear waste.

"Fish," you say. "Fish fish fish. Goldfish. Goldfish daddy." You can still feel the wet squirming word in your hand. You can still see it falling down the long black pipe. And the marcie saying you're in trouble now, boy. You're in trouble now. The round bowl-water empty and opaque with tiny white feces. And next day mother says Where's our family photographs? They were right there on the mantelpiece. And the marcie puts her fists firmly on her hips to tell them, but then you say "Mother. Daddy. Marcie. Grandma. Grandma." All those words you found in the grandma's mouth last night. And nobody hears the marcie say a thing. Now it's the marcie's words that don't really matter.

"Kodak," you tell them finally, just to let them know you understand even big words, too. "Kodacolor. Kodachrome."

But the grandma is never happy when you visit, looking at you with her big black mouth open. Aaaah. All the world's loud words resounding and spinning down there in the grandma's mouth. You try to pet and soothe her. These are the words, you think. These are words right here, and the grandma kicks and grabs, gurgling where your hand is, and so you take your hand back. Grandma grandma. All the darkness inside the grandma grows and grows, whispers and whispers, moves and pushes. Everything's better down there. Down there the grandma can be happy again. Down there the grandma can be grandma again.

You lead her down the hall steps. Doo, doo, doo, doo. One two two four two one two two. The grandma holds the banister because she's afraid. She makes different noises now, wordless noises down in her stomach and thighs and feet. Doo doo doo doo doo. All the shadows hanging from the walls and furniture and curtains, and opening the squeaky picture window, the grandma leaning against you, her body thin and frail and very soft like a giant stuffed giraffe. The grandma all hollow spongy bone. The grandma all sound and word and dream. Outside, the night is filled with stars and the big fat leaning moon, humming there, filling the steel pipe and underground shelter and grandma's black mouth. Aaaah. Aaaah. It is cold, the grandma wants to say. It is hot. It is cold and hot, big and small, boy and girl, happy and sad. Aaaah. Aaaah. Everything, the grandma says. Everything, everywhere.

The grandma doesn't like the steel pipe, the buried shelter, the heavy moonlight down there just waiting for her. You try to help her into the steel pipe. Down there, the other grandma reaches too. Down there the other grandma pulls. But this grandma says Aaaah. Scared but she wants to know. Always the deep earth, always the black night. The grandma is like the orange cat, which clawed and ran away. Grandma grandma. You try to make the soothing sounds mom makes for breakfast. There there Alice. Be a good girl. You like your cereal don't you alice. Aaaah. Aaaah. Into the steel pipe, but both of grandma's arms don't fit. Pull her down, the other grandma says. Pull her down to me. And grandma's big black mouth wide, wide with all the words she'll find down there. Everything words. Aaaah. Aaaah. And the moon all around, and the words down there waiting with the other grandma. Louder and louder the grandma gets. Louder and louder like the moon. Aaaah. And now you try to help her. Help her head into the big steel pipe, but her head doesn't fit. Louder and louder, deeper and deeper, worlds and words. And lights going on in all the backyards, and lights going on in your house, too. Light, light. And the grandma crying for the other grandma, for all the words she can't quite reach when the men come with big steel tools and cut the pipe away, and then pull grandma from it.

Down there. Down there. Toads hop, snakes slither, spiders scramble and crawl. Moonlight talks and dark earth listens. Pih, pih. Paper, pin, pickle, paste, plate, pastry, pigeon, plant. Person. Person. And now the *r* words. Rih. Rih. Everything down there in the dark and the water. And grandma embracing everything too. Vast sunken cities, countries, landscapes and stars. Hissing rivers and steaming forests. Worlds down there, worlds and words. Rih, rih. Rock, robin, rouge, rasp, rattle. Dad's graduation ring. The marcie's transistor radio. And grandma, grandma coming closer. The grandma's arms big and strong and beautiful now, reaching to hold you, reaching to take you home . . .

You wake up.

You sit up in bed. Everything is black.

The marcie kicks in her bed, snorts and rolls over.

Outside moon talks and deep earth listens. Down there. Down there.

In the grandma's room across the hall, the grandma's bed is empty.

Grandma down there.

Grandma caught a cold, mother says at breakfast. Grandma caught a cold and went away.

Then after breakfast you all get in the car together and drive to the cemetery. Round brown slopes and green hedges and tidy, solid tombstones and flowers in little vases. This is grandma's new home, this big green yard. You all stand together under the low cloth awning and watch them lower the grandma into her new, dark room.

"A bad cold," you say, and mother squeezes your hand. "Grandma has a bad cold." And everybody back into dad's car.

Mother snuffles into her handkerchief, and the marcie reads a *Doctor Strange* comic book. The King-size Summer Annual.

"Grandma goes away," you say. And so you all drive home, where the other grandma waits in the darkness.

Maybe she's found what we all hope to find someday, dad says, and now you are all driving into the driveway of your big warm house. The dark clouds breaking apart. Bright blue sky blazing through. And you want to tell dad the secret as he lifts you under one arm and carries you to the front door. Come on, my little sack of potatoes, dad says. Come on, my little fat bag of laundry.

Dad is bigger, but you know the secret.

"Everything," you whisper. "Everything, Daddy."

THE SECRET LIFE
OF HOUSES

Mother was admitted to St. Jude's Hospital in early July for what the doctors called "routine tests." The following morning she underwent surgery for the removal of her left breast and, a week later, was expected to die sometime in the afternoon when Margaret arrived with her schoolbooks and a copy of Mother's *Racing Form*. The thin blond pastor was standing guard outside Mother's door, waiting to take Margaret to the visitors' lounge where, for more than two hours, he spoke to her in hushed reverential tones about the Lord Jesus. "Your mother and I have enjoyed many opportunities to talk personally about the Lord Jesus," he said. "And I think I can say, without fear of contradiction, that she would like you to know that earthly expiration does not mean the end of life but rather the discovery of a heavenly love far greater than you can possibly imagine." The pastor's voice was filled with gigantic glass-paneled cathedrals and vast, beatific white light. Swelling organ notes pulsed in your bones and heart, and the soft, contented faces of very spiritual, loving people in nice suits and summer dresses turned to look up at a beautiful white man in white flowing robes. The visitors' lounge was a chipped gray pastel, and included a pair of wobbly wood-frame chairs, a malfunctioning RCA black-and-white portable television and a few tattered issues of *People* magazine. While the pastor talked, Margaret imagined herself living in the glass cathedral with Jesus, like a tiny mouse. Being much smaller than all the lovely people in their beautiful clothes meant Jesus would love her even more, and she would fix him good healthy meals in the little basement kitchen. Beef broth, salads with blue-cheese dressing, high-fiber cereals and fresh-baked brown breads. Some days Jesus came home very tired, not in any mood to go upstairs and comfort his assorted brethren. At these times Margaret would have to speak very firmly and lovingly to him. "Now I want you to go upstairs right this minute, Jesus, and stop feeling so sorry for yourself. I *know* you're tired, but so are all those nice people who have been waiting upstairs all day to see you, and I'm not going to let you disappoint them. Now get out there and do your best, and know I love you very much or else I wouldn't even bother talking to you like this."

Every day after the first operation when Margaret arrived at the hospital she found Mother asleep in the immaculate white bed. Mother appeared somewhat collapsed and unfamiliar now, like a favorite pillow with the slipcover removed. Her mouth hung open, revealing dull gold and silver fillings. The bright amber diagnostic display hummed darkly beside her bed like a brain. Margaret would sit in the red Leatherex chair beside the bed and read her civic studies book entitled *Voyages to Discovery: Making Friends Around the World* in which a page 37 illustration depicted a primordial woman with large brown breasts hand-sculpting a blue clay bowl. A small brown baby sat naked beside her, ornamented with bright beads. They both seemed very busy and very content. Somewhere beyond the frame of their picture, Margaret imagined, fierce men battled enormous dinosaurs in order to make the world safe for civilization. Primitive men lacked houses, and had to make do with mud huts. Sometimes Margaret examined the pictures of mud huts and tried to imagine what it would be like without the security or real weight of a house around you. The world would seem very shadowy and dim, she thought. The wind would whistle through everything. Parts of your mud hut would be blown away, or eroded by rain. Life would lack depth, weight and dimension. You couldn't hold it in your hands. You couldn't hide among its deepest rooms.

Every evening after visiting hours Margaret would take the bus home to her own very solid house and cook dinner in the toaster oven. She liked to fix Budget Gourmet dinners, because they included vegetables and starch. She prepared large green salads with french dressing and stored them in plastic Tupperware. She also liked tuna melts, toast with jam, frozen pizza. Then she would clean the toaster oven with a damp sponge, wash her dishes in the cracked porcelain sink and fall asleep on the living room couch with the television on. The television marked a clean, warm place in the otherwise silent house. Margaret's favorite show was *Dallas*, but her favorite actor was Peter Graves on old reruns of *Mission: Impossible*. Dense, compact shadows filled the unseen rooms with a hard, dark weight, like the cartons of Mother's old college textbooks in the attic, or the massive and disconnected Whirlpool Frigidaire gathering dust in the garage. Every Saturday she would take Mother's checkbook from the kitchen cabinet and pay the latest bills, writing out the checks in her best penmanship, affixing a tidy postage stamp and adjusting the return statement until the corporate address showed through the envelope's clear plastic window. Then, on early Saturday evenings after her shopping, she would deposit the week's incoming checks from Social Security and Blue Cross in the Home Federal Savings night-deposit box. The night-deposit box had a heavy steel door which Margaret would pull back with both hands; the dark steel vault hissed with shadows, like an enormous seashell. There was something about the vast and bristling darkness that Margaret appreciated, something about it that seemed to connect her with the vaster darknesses of her own house.

Margaret enjoyed being alone in her house at night because it was her house and Mother's house, and in some ways Mother was still there. Often, while the living room television generated its warm noise like a central radiator, Margaret would walk from room to room of the house and take random inventories. The rooms retained a formal simplicity, some fundamental resonance of Mother. Margaret was wary of touching anything, of violating the silent rightness of things. At night the white moonlight fell across the taut coverlet of Mother's bed. The lid of the cracked ersatz-leather jewelry box on the bureau contained an unsprung music box which chimed faintly when you opened it; the box also contained broken costume brooches, unmatched earrings, fractured glass pendants. The chipped plastic bracelets and necklaces had begun to fade and oxidize in places. The enormous television was covered with crumpled white lace doilies, pencil stubs, an open *Racing Form*, in which penciled notations and statistics had begun to fade, and a moldering orange in a painted bowl. The bowl depicted scenes of Florence, where Mother's sister Rita had honeymooned in 1957 just before she died. Mother still had a few faded black-and-white photographs of Rita and her vacationing husband attached to the frame of the vanity mirror. Their features were colorless in the harsh light, like lunar newlyweds vacationing in a sea of dust. Margaret imagined it must be a world without sound, where everything was soft and drained of gravity. Rita died when she was only twenty-four. "She never got a chance to see our house," Mother said. "But I know that if she had seen it, she would have thought it was the best house in the entire world."

On Mother's bathroom sink and counter various vials of pills

were spread about, many of them empty and overturned like
toy soldiers. When you opened the medicine cabinet, its mirrored surface spattered with Crest and Listerine, you saw ant-
acids, aspirins and Tylenols, codeine and bromides. Margaret's
favorite place, however, was Mother's closet. Sometimes she
would open the door and step inside between the two musty
aisles crammed with clothing on hangers. Outdated fat, fluffy
overcoats, beaded flannel robes, moth-eaten gray sweaters and
paisley blouses. A brown and beige Denny's uniform displayed
Mother's name on a plastic nametag: ANN. The name seemed
at once strange and familiar, like a commercial advertisement.
Above the racks of clothing boxes of papers and receipts were
stored. Bulging hatboxes and shoeboxes with cracked joints,
belted with thick red rubber bands, boxes which had formerly
contained blow dryers, standing desk lamps, clock radios. Margaret liked to stand atop a small white ledge and browse among
the boxes, moving them about but always remembering to replace them in their appropriate spot. Receipts, letters, keys in
tiny envelopes, ropes of dust. Often Margaret and Mother had
conducted these late-evening surveys together. "You'll have to
know where everything is," Mother would say. "In case anything ever happens to me. Not that anything will ever happen
to me." She showed Margaret where the fuse box in the basement was, the emergency phone numbers in the kitchen. "Here
are your grandmother's photographs, and Rita's wedding album, and a key to the safe-deposit box." Whenever Mother conducted these impromptu tours of her secret economy she carried
a rum and Coke ahead of her like a flashlight. They would turn
on all the lights and play records loud on the phonograph.
"Here's your Social Security card and your birth certificate.
You know why I'm showing you all this stuff, don't you, baby?
Because when and if I die someday, I don't want your Aunt
Fergie coming over here and taking off with everything. All of
this belongs to you. The day I die your Aunt Fergie will be over

here like a shot. She'll be driving a U-Haul trailer. She'll pull everything out of this house she can carry. She'll take the knobs off the oven. She'll take the toilet paper off the roll in the bathroom. The day I die you watch out for your Aunt Fergie." As Margaret stood alone now in the crowded, dim closet, she could still hear Mother's voice resounding in the close, musty walls, the jumbled boxes and heavy clothing, like the beating of some suppressed heartbeat. It was as if while Margaret's eyes had grown accustomed to the contents of Mother's dark room, her ears had grown accustomed to its voice as well. There was something delicate and infinitely priceless about every object, a certain character and voice which Margaret feared she might accidentally disturb or erase. Alone, Margaret never turned on Mother's bedroom lights; she never played the phonograph. Margaret didn't hear the voice so much as detect it, just as she could detect the weight of halved peaches and syrup in an unlabeled tin can. The voice was Mother's voice and it was not Mother's voice. It was the voice of the house, too. Margaret thought of Mother in the breathing ward, surrounded by unconscious elderly women gazing blankly at the fluorescent ceiling.

Later, with the sounds of the house still resounding in her blood and brain, Margaret would drink coffee and watch the *Tomorrow* show, with Tom Snyder, or perhaps a late movie, thinking about Mother in her white bed. There were times at night when she felt as if everyone in the city were asleep except her and her resonating house. She felt like a monitor, a secret trespasser of sorts. Sometimes she wondered if people passing in the street could detect the phosphorescent glow of her black-and-white television through the venetian blinds; she wondered if anyone knew about her secret life alone in the house.

The nurses began paying Margaret little attentions. Cookies, snacks, preteen paperback novels in which young girls of

Margaret's age solved crimes, met romantic chums in foreign countries and overcame personal embarrassments at school. Sometimes she was awarded secondhand clothing, which she occasionally accepted, and dolls, which she always disdained. One of the nurses even arranged to have a television installed in Mother's ward; usually, though, Margaret preferred to do her homework.

"Are you good in school?" the nurses asked.

"I guess so," Margaret said.

"Do you have a father?"

"He lives in Detroit."

"Do you live with your aunt? Your grandma?"

Margaret thought for a minute. After a while she said, "I live with my aunt. My aunt's name is Rita." Then her eyes would return to her civic studies book. After a few awkward minutes the nurses would depart to other wards, cafeterias, vended cigarettes, and Margaret would feel embarrassed for having told them anything at all, as if she had betrayed the secret life of her house to strangers.

Some afternoons when Margaret arrived at the hospital, there was a flurry of activity around Mother's room. Numerous nurses and orderlies in white uniforms would be going in and out, transporting intricate machines on carts. One of the orderlies held Mother's chart, which was attached to a plyboard and metal clipboard; he told everyone where to go, a stethoscope looped casually around his neck like an ornament. Once Mother herself was hurriedly transported from the room on a gurney by two large black men Margaret had never seen before. Mother lay very quiet with her eyes closed, the white sheet pulled up to her neck, dreaming about the house, the boxes of papers, the safe-deposit key. At these times Margaret would quietly return to the visitors' lounge with the somber, thin-lipped pastor, where she tried to do her homework while he continued describing to her the House of the Lord. The House of the Lord was filled with many rooms and many mansions.

There was a room for Jesus, and a room for Mohammed, and a room for Buddha. There were rooms for Catholics, Protestants and Jews. All these rooms were of equal size and fairly distributed, because all men were equal in the House of the Lord. Every once in a while Margaret would look up at the pastor and try to register a serious moment of eye contact, but once she had done her good deed she let her gaze quickly return to the civic studies book which lay open in her lap.

Margaret's house had two bedrooms and two bathrooms, a living room and a kitchen. The enormous downstairs garage, which Margaret infrequently disturbed, filled with Mother's Ford Galaxie automobile, crates of dishes, and a water-stained rolltop desk Mother had inherited from her stepfather when he died. Dust was everywhere, and a gathering puddle of oil near the tailgate of the Ford. There, deep in the house, Margaret realized, her house opened onto deeper rooms and houses too, just like the House of the Lord. Somewhere deep in those rooms Mother was rolling on her gurney through enormous, echoing cement chambers filled with black and Chicano men who smoked cigarettes while doctors tried to poke and prod her with sharp and complex instruments. Underneath still deeper were even vaster discordant parking garages where automobiles raced and honked and surgeons scrubbed their hands at large concrete sinks.

"Should I call your Aunt Rita?"

The pastor had fallen asleep on the stuffed chair. A tattered three-year-old copy of *People* magazine lay overturned on his lap. He snored.

Margaret looked up at the nurse. The nurse's face flashed with harsh fluorescent light. Margaret didn't recognize her.

"That's okay," Margaret said, and reached for her purse. "I'll take the bus."

*   *   *

All weekend Margaret dreamed of Mother deep underneath the foundation of their house, rolling down long hospital corridors. Mother was very young in these dreams and very beautiful. Mother said, "We live in the house together, Margaret. We need toilet paper, milk and Shredded Wheat."

When Margaret awoke on the living room sofa the house was filled with light. Light from the moon, light from the elevated streetlamps. The entire house glowed with light. It didn't seem like night at all, but rather some weird inversion of it. The house seemed really massive now. Vast underground caverns opened onto still vaster, deeper caverns and passageways. Rooted in the deep earth like a tree, the house articulated with and overgrew other roots, the secret passages of other houses. It's moving toward the hospital, Margaret thought. It's reaching into Mother's room. The house was trying to pull Mother back into the world where Margaret lived. This is my house, Margaret thought. This is where I live. Then, after a while, she fell back into her dreams again, less articulate and threatening now, filled with cool, calm voices. Somewhere she seemed to touch on the periphery of other dreams, and realized, drifting to the surface of her own, that somewhere she converged with the dreams of her own house. The house dreamed fantastic dreams of self-fulfillment, overwhelming pride, spontaneous transformations. The house dreamed it was an ocean liner, a vast white iceberg, a right whale boiling with plankton and animalcula, a duplex shopping center with multiple cinemas. The house heaved up on its concrete legs, ripping at the earth, pulling out long, dwindling complexes of nerve and tissue. The house moved. The house walked.

The following evening when she returned home Margaret tried to phone her Great-uncle Ralph in Volcano but his line was busy. Every few months or so Uncle Ralph would visit and sit drinking all night with Mother in the living room. They talked about all the people in the family that they hated, and when Uncle Ralph left, Mother would admit that she hated Uncle Ralph, too. "He's the tightest man I've ever met," Mother said. "Have you ever seen him *once* bring his own bottle when he visits? You watch next time. He *never* brings his own bottle." Margaret wanted to call and tell Uncle Ralph not to visit this month. She wanted to tell him she and Mother would be away. If Uncle Ralph came and found Mother in the hospital, he might tell someone, and that someone might take Margaret away. That someone might take Margaret away from her house, and then everything would be wrong, nothing would ever be right again. She tried calling Uncle Ralph every five minutes or so, but his line was always busy. She even dialed the operator, and asked if she could interrupt. After a long wait, the operator said, "I'm sorry. The line is not engaged. Would you like me to try another number?" Instead, Margaret took her blanket onto the couch and tried to resist the house's dark undercurrent, the pull of its turning dreams. This is my house, she thought. Mother says this is my house. She thought she heard sounds outside on the front stairs. If they come to take me away, I'll come back. I'll sneak in through the garage window. The noise halted outside; then, after a moment, clumped up the front stairs. It was quiet again. Margaret imagined the head nurse, surrounded by uniformed patrolmen. She was taking pink and white forms out of her big black bag. A pair of enormous handcuffs gleamed in the moonlight.

But if they came she wouldn't let them in. This was her house, she thought steadfastly. Hers and Mother's. "That's the way it'll stay," Mother always said. "If anything happens to me, you'll get the house. Everything goes to you because you're my immediately surviving heir. Like when your grandfather died. That's how inheritance works."

What Mother had often referred to as Grandfather's "estate"

was in the garage, shrouded and damp. In a way, Margaret figured, that made the house partly Grandfather's, too. Margaret
had never met Grandfather, but she had visited his house once.
Grandfather's house was filled with antique furniture, delicate
white china in a glass and mahogany case, assorted bedclothes
and kitchen utensils, and a fox-fur coat with head and arms dangling like weird growths. "He's not really your grandfather,"
Mother said, pushing open the door of the strange apartment
and ushering Margaret inside with a large high-beam flashlight.
"He was basically just your first-rate son of a bitch. He died
right there on that bed." The flashlight's beam drifted across a
sudden white coverlet, as sudden and improbable as a glimpse
of the moon, then slid across a closer wall and into the kitchen.
"Is that a blender?" Mother asked out loud, entering the cold
kitchen with a certain reverence. "That's just what we needed,
isn't it? A blender." The place smelled close and pungent, like
black men on a bus.

It was a few days before Christmas, and when they returned
home they redistributed Grandfather's belongings throughout
their own personal house. "I'm seeing my lawyer in the morning. The bastard died intestate, which means I've got to file
something or other to be declared executor. There's only some
cousins on his second wife's side. They'll probably raise a fuss,
but fuck them, that's what I say. That bastard was my father,
and he didn't even call me once in seventeen years." They fixed
hot toddies in their new blender, then assembled the thinning
aluminum Christmas tree Mother had purchased at Walgreen's
three years before. The tree shed twisted bits of aluminum; sitting underneath the tree and watching Mother pour the hot toddies, Margaret felt as if they were worshiping some archetypal
television antenna. Margaret was awarded a hot toddy as well,
then another. The eggnog was tepid and somewhat scummy.
The alcohol scalded her throat, and she felt herself growing
more distant from the room in which they sat, the long-familiar

anecdotes Mother shared again and again, the voice and weight of Grandfather which was silently assembling in their basement. It wasn't a voice which ever said anything. It was a voice which settled underneath all the other voices and seemed to hold them in place, like the dense colored gravel at the bottom of a tropical fish tank, or the hard gray dirt in their neglected garden. Eventually Mother took the entire matter to court for two years and they inherited the disused Whirlpool, the assorted basement furniture draped in spotty sheets, the living room's stuffed chair, the blender, a toaster oven and four or five thousand dollars in assorted bonds and savings accounts. The fox-fur coat hung in their closet now, its beady glass eyes glinting dully like some secret retribution. Margaret had never met Grandfather, had never even seen his photo. Grandfather was with the assorted furniture in the basement, like a collection of items in some charity thrift store, a certain weight and dimension which altered the weight of Mother's house and voice. Seventeen years of silence and iron disregard. Cartons of stale cigarettes and personalized matches. Retirement memorabilia from Brisbane Brake and Drums. The aroma of black men on the bus. Mother's house was always filled with ghosts.

Then, one Friday evening, Margaret returned home to discover her Great-aunt Fergie in the living room, removing her large, overgrown black wool coat and laying it across the back of Mother's favorite armchair. A battered brown plyboard suitcase, ragged with peeling baggage labels, sat open on the sofa. Aunt Fergie took a drag from her Camel filterless and flicked one long gray ash onto the floor. She stared at Margaret and took one overly appreciative breath. "Well, so you must be my little grand-niece. You must be Margaret." Margaret closed the front door, but did not lock it. Far underneath her feet the great house exhaled a long inaudible sigh.

"I took the bus to Los Angeles and had to transfer. I spent three hours in the Los Angeles Greyhound station. I couldn't wait to see you. I was so sorry to hear about your mother." Aunt Fergie brought a pot of tea and placed it on the living room coffee table. "The hospital called me yesterday and I came right here as soon as I could. They couldn't reach your father or your Uncle Ralph, which is certainly no surprise. Your Uncle Ralph is off boozing somewhere. And your father, well." Aunt Fergie held her teacup under her nose, reflecting on the unraveling coils of steam. Her eyes seemed very far away. She had gray hair with a few stray flecks of black in it, tied up in a bun under a thin, gauzy hat. Her cheekbones were taut and polished with rouge. Margaret felt the entire house growing very cold and lifeless in the presence of Aunt Fergie, as if the electricity had been disconnected, or the fireplace plastered over. "It's such a terrible shame," she said. "Your mother was always so young and full of life." Aunt Fergie's face was expressionless. She put down her drained teacup. "I'll sleep in your mother's room tonight, and we'll go to the hospital together in the afternoon. You still have school, don't you? We could always take you out early in the afternoon. I can write you a note." They sat quietly together on the sofa for a while. The television gazed darkly at them both, registering a murky soundlessness in the dark room. After a while Aunt Fergie crushed out her cigarette in her teacup and her dim, abstract eyes focused on the large RCA console.

"Is that color?" Aunt Fergie asked after a while. "Or is it just black-and-white?"

It wasn't Margaret's house anymore. At night she slept in her cold, voiceless bedroom, gazing abstractedly at the posters of Madonna, Mick Jagger and Prince which decorated her walls. The tiny shelf of preteen paperbacks, the disused dolls and board games on the closet shelf. A large stuffed bear lay beside her on her large pink coverlet like some transient boarder. None of the things seemed at all familiar; everything seemed vaguely impossible and irreproachable, even the shadows which fell across things. The house was cold and silent, and when Margaret slept she dreamed of dark abstract spaces filled with strange people. She remembered her mother in these dreams, but she could not hear her voice. The house was growing very cold and formal, retracting from the dark earth, its great bronchial passages collapsing and decomposing into long, shredded strips of black, inorganic matter.

"It's important to prepare you for the worst, dear," Aunt Fergie said, sitting beside Margaret on the bus and leafing through a Montgomery Ward catalog. "Your mother's lungs have collapsed, and she's only being kept alive by machines. She's been completely unconscious for more than ten days, so there's no way the doctors can assess what sort of damage has affected her brain. She has indications of spinal meningitis. She could die any day." Aunt Fergie turned to the Housewares and Appliances section and grew silent for a while. Outside the bright sun flashed on the pale sidewalks. Every once in a while the bus hit large potholes and the entire bus lurched, Margaret's seat rattling. Aunt Fergie's long gray finger tapped at a Whirlpool photograph which carried a retail price of $499.99.

"It's a lot like what happened to your Great-uncle Havelock in Montreal. He suffered massive, irreversible brain damage." Absently Aunt Fergie gazed out the window at the gray, cloudy Pacific. After a while her gray hand touched Margaret's book. "Don't you feel very sorry for your Great-uncle Havelock?" she asked.

Margaret felt internally displaced, as if even her vital bodily organs were being dispossessed. Every afternoon she returned home from school to find Aunt Fergie conducting secret inventories, peering in kitchen cabinets, fiddling at locked drawers with paper clips. There was something clinical about Aunt Fergie's attentions, as if she were flirting with a lover, or investigating and cataloging the contents of some comatose body with microscopic cameras, like a program on educational television. "This isn't bad," Aunt Fergie said, picking at the frayed antique chair Mother had inherited from Grandfather. "We could always have it reupholstered." Aunt Fergie never permitted more than one house light on at a time. They shared spare, comfortless little meals of macaroni and cheese, canned soups and cheese sandwiches in the darkening kitchen while Aunt Fergie gazed absently at the Authentic Hand-Painted Seascape Mother had acquired three years before with six dense books of Blue Chip Stamps. Aunt Fergie lived in the house now, Margaret realized. Now Aunt Fergie dreamed of the deep earth, the gravid blue sea, the moons of distant planets. Aunt Fergie blinked myopically at the seascape, chewing her tepid macaroni, while Margaret merely examined her fork on her plate. Her schoolbooks lay stacked and unopen on the kitchen counter. Unread and unattended assignments marked their random pages. School seemed a very distant and uneventful place now, echoing with dull, muted voices and strange, unstaring faces. Margaret spent hours there every day, sitting alone at recess and gazing blankly at the pages of her textbooks, trying to find the words she once read there and awaiting the silent evenings she would spend silently breathing in Aunt Fergie's distant and misshapen home.

Sometimes she returned to the house and found unfamiliar men there. An immaculate couple from Century 21 Real Estate, wearing crisp sensible suits. The woman's lips and nails were bright and polished, the man carried a tan briefcase. They both smiled like commercial product spokesmen, and helped Aunt Fergie formulate compliments. "Look at all that cabinet space," they said in the kitchen. "Manageable yard. Two-car garage. Convenient wiring." Vials and prescriptions were gradually cleared from Mother's bureau, and Aunt Fergie's cold creams and plastic tissue dispenser replaced them. The files and shoeboxes had descended from the closet, accumulating and reassembling in tidy stacks on the vanity table. On a Friday Margaret was introduced to a lawyer who said, "I'm going to help your aunt organize your mother's affairs," before Margaret was dispatched to her thin, shadowy room. The lawyer was short and corpulent, and wore a casual Op T-shirt.

One day Margaret found a bulging shoebox filled with letters from Father on her bed. "I'm sure your mother would want you to have them," Aunt Fergie said, brushing the dust from her hands and sleeves. She was wearing black. "I found them in your mother's closet." Margaret knew exactly the place, the place where the box belonged, where it had sat accumulating Father's letters for years and years now. The letters were all uniformly typewritten on white ruled stationery and folded into dense packets which often included fragile and yellowing articles clipped from *The Detroit Sun Times* and *Newsweek*. Sometimes the letters also included photostatic reproductions of box seat tickets to the Detroit Tigers baseball game or even the Ice Follies. Usually the letters said,

Dear Ann,
You must be filled with hate and anger all the time. You have kept my daughter from my love all these years because you in your infinite wisdom believe I am not an "appropriate" role model for her. I pity you all the time for all your hate and rage and for your inability to respect yourself which only makes you hate me more for being happy with who I am. Right now the entire world is poised on the brink of nuclear catastrophe because of people exactly like you, as I hope the enclosed newspaper article

clearly proves. I have decided (very FIRMLY this time) to take immediate legal action, and have even procured the legal expertise of Reginald Dwyer and Associates who say my case is airtight and I should have my daughter back any day now. Then you will be unable to poison her with hate and lies about me or my life, and you will be totally alone and deserve everything that happens to you. You will die filled with your own hate and rage and your daughter won't even love you anymore because by then she will be with her father who only truly loves her and doesn't just use her as a weapon against me. I have enclosed my lawyer's business card just so you can see that I mean very serious business.

Yours sincerely,
Jeremy Andrews

P.S. Legally you can't do anything about it, because my lawyers know exactly what they are doing, and will allow you no alternatives to my personal wishes in this matter.

Usually a brief crumbling newspaper article was enclosed. "Soviets Purchase Japanese Transistors," or "New Trade Agreements with Spain." Two or three brief paragraphs described rudimentary contractual negotiations, names of key participants. Unnamed State Department officials usually declined comment. Father always highlighted these formal disavowals with a yellow Magic Marker.

Margaret sat cross-legged on her bed and looked at the bulging shoebox which remained untouched at her feet. Eventually Aunt Fergie reappeared at her bedroom door, blinking at the dark moonlit room in her dark wool nightgown and carrying a large gold and ivory hairbrush. She didn't have her glasses on; her face seemed very soft and ageless now. "I never disagreed with your mother about how to raise you, but I do disagree with her attitude toward your father. Maybe she doesn't like him, and maybe *I* don't like him. But he is your father, and it's perfectly all right that you should love and get a chance to know him."

After Aunt Fergie closed the bedroom door Margaret sat quietly for a little while. "I always knew where the letters were," she said out loud, to nobody in particular. "I always knew where to find them."

At the hospital the large amber monitors seemed to grow noisier and more eventful as Mother's body grew less and less, as if they were not simply monitoring Mother's life forces but actually translating them into mechanical languages. Margaret couldn't find Mother in the hospital at all anymore, and simply sat beside Aunt Fergie and her knitting, gazing up at the flickering television, straining to hear its dim, humming voices. Aunt Fergie always kept the volume turned way down. "So it won't disturb your mother," she would say, taking up her ceaseless knitting again, blinking behind her thick glasses as if she were sending back telegraphic signals to the fleets of advisers she had already begun mobilizing around the house, like the toy soldiers deployed by boys around beachheads of sidewalk and garden.

The only times Margaret could still find Mother was when she descended into the cool, weightless garage of their trembling house at night like a deep-sea diver. While Aunt Fergie steadily snored in Mother's transgressed bedroom, Margaret would pull shut the kitchen door, careful of her feet on the dark stairs. Watery moonlight spilled weakly through the single basement window, occluded by overgrown ferns and pale cobwebs. Sometimes she had to stand very still for a long time before she felt anything, that deep involuntary tug beneath the earth. The turn of some buried serpent, the darting of some hurried mole or gopher. Then, after a long while, she might hear Mother's voice, distantly at first, tapping underneath the hard, compact earth like a finger. "The bonds are in a safe-deposit box at Crocker Bank in Burlingame," Mother's voice said. "You take the number seven bus to El Camino Real. Then you transfer to the thirty-four. Now, where are the bonds?"

"At Crocker Bank on El Camino Real."

"And how do you get there?"

"I take the number seven. Then I transfer to the thirty-four."

Aunt Fergie disassembled everything. The furniture, the files, Mother, Grandfather, Margaret, Dad. "It's time we faced this situation properly, like mature women," Aunt Fergie said, scouting through Margaret's drawers and closets. "We have to keep a log. We have to get everything organized so that if and when your mother does die, God forbid, everything can get through the courts as quickly as possible. If your mother dies intestate, we have to set up a trust and a trustee." Aunt Fergie moved Margaret's embroidered footstool into Margaret's closet and stood on it. Her hard fingers, adorned with dull gold rings and bracelets, gripped at the upper shelf. On her tiptoes, she reached out one abrupt hand. "There's some bonds of your grandfather's," Aunt Fergie said. "Some rings and jewelry of your grandmother's." Blinking, Aunt Fergie pulled a toaster-size box from the shelf and fumbled at the lid. She stumbled slightly on the wobbly stool, her enormous black coat flapping like enormous black wings, and with a rush like water, domino tiles and Barbie accessories crashed from the box and clattered onto the floor. As solemn as a mourner, Aunt Fergie stepped down, clutching the collapsed box in her arms. The box said Realistic Radio Alarm Clock. AM/FM dials. Digital read-out.

"Now your mother is too smart a woman just to misplace

them," Aunt Fergie said. She wasn't looking at Margaret, who stood at the bedroom door holding her foamy toothbrush, but rather over Margaret's shoulder at the open door of Mother's bedroom. "I've checked with her local bank. They've got to be somewhere in the house. Unless she's got another account somewhere." They stood quietly together in the doorway. Aunt Fergie's chin grew lax and wrinkled. In the house's briefly resumed silence, Margaret heard the old house flickering briefly like a restored pulse. Then, absently gazing, Aunt Fergie pushed past Margaret and into the reassembled shadows and voices of Mother's diminishing room. Late into the night, Margaret heard boxes being reshuffled and banged about, the audible swirling of generations of inherited and relocated dust like cinematic fog in an old black-and-white movie.

Then, alone in her dark bed in her strange and voiceless bedroom, Margaret would open her civic studies text and remove the tiny safe-deposit key taped inside the concluding chapter. The chapter included many photos of the world's children playing together in crowded Bombay, a New York discotheque, a British pub. When Margaret knew for certain her great-aunt was asleep, she would slip quietly into the basement and gently mollify the buried life of her house.

"The surgery hasn't healed," Aunt Fergie said, knitting beside Margaret in the room where Mother's impostor lay. Mother's impostor didn't even remotely resemble Mother anymore. Gradually she was beginning to resemble Aunt Fergie herself, with her pale, slack skin and long teeth, her thinning hair and gaunt, expressionless face. "Arteries near the base of her brain keep opening. Her immune system won't respond, her blood isn't coagulating. They've done all they can do." Aunt Fergie's needles clacked faintly like tiny teeth. "I've managed to contact your father in Detroit. My lawyer and his lawyer see no reason

why the courts won't allow him, under these conditions, to resume custody."

Margaret envisioned Detroit as vast white pavements and reflecting steel skyscrapers. There were no houses there, only Father at his typewriter, corresponding with the world, sifting
through newspapers and magazines. "He's involved in some
kind of project at work," Aunt Fergie said, handing Margaret
the envelope, "so he can't come for you personally. But he's sent
a ticket. We'll start getting your things together and you'll leave
next week." Aunt Fergie left Margaret at the darkening
kitchen table. After a few moments, Margaret heard her own
door opening down the hall, drawers opening and closing. She
reached for the envelope before her on the dim tablecloth littered with crumbs. The envelope contained a Greyhound bus
ticket, San Francisco to Detroit. One-way. Father's letter said,
"I can hardly wait to see you. All the love I have in the world.
Regaining the family we've both lost. Sino-Soviet relations ef-
fectively disenabling the SALT II accord." It was signed, "Your
Loving Father, Jeremy Andrews."

That Friday Margaret took the bus to Crocker Bank in Burlingame and presented her key to a young blond woman. The
woman requested two pieces of identification and, after conferring with a man in glasses and a dark blue suit who sat behind
a MANAGEMENT ACCOUNTS placard, accepted Margaret's Social
Security card and birth certificate. The blond woman took Margaret into a clean, unadorned beige room which contained only
a thin Formica table, like one of the luncheon tables at school.
"I'll give you, say, five minutes? I'll be right outside." When
Margaret was alone, she opened the steel box with her key and
heard something sounding in the back of her mind, as if a key
were being inserted in some other door in some vaster and
deeper room. This is it, she thought. The bonds were bundled
up in yellow six-by-eight-inch envelopes marked URGENT and
FIRST CLASS; the rings were contained by tiny plastic bags, the

flap of each affixed with a staple, like rare coins in a coin shop. When she held the rings and the bonds in her hands they felt firm and obdurate, as incontrovertible as the deep earth, as eternal as the hard formal structures of the house which had once persisted there. Margaret saw the dark and shrouded furniture in the garage, the cold and ticking automobile, the concrete washbasin covered with dust like the chrysalis of some gigantic insect. Everything was growing stronger already; the hard and dreaming foundation of the house fluttered like an eyelid; something deeper twitched. The rings and bonds were a gift, a sacrifice without blood, like investing parts of your allowance in a private savings account. She would surrender them all in the shadows and privacy of the garage; she would regain the home she had lost. This might be it, Margaret thought. Everything's going to be better again. Margaret was almost home.

Within a few weeks, Mother returned home from the hospital's dark, improbable world like an astronaut from outer space.

"A home is always a house, but a house isn't always a home," Mother said as she was lifted on a stretcher and inserted through the back doors of the ambulance. Margaret sat beside her in the long chamber, on a small red seat which unfolded from the side wall. "I'll never forget buying that house just after you were born." Mother's face was regaining a little of its lost color; her hair remained sparse and dry, however; her body thin and haggard. "I was working at Macy's downtown. I never thought I could afford a house of my own. Then Dolger built Daly City. It was what they called a 'planned community,' because it was designed to include everything one could possibly need to live, just like a miniature city. A shopping plaza, restaurants, schools. I wanted you to go to a good school. I didn't want you to attend one of those schools downtown. They don't have any teachers or books, and they're filled with spics and niggers. I don't mean to sound racist or anything, but I had to be at work all day and I wanted you to be safe. I knew you'd be safe here."

Mother was looking out the side window and away from Margaret as they entered the housing tract. The interminable rows of identical houses covered the hills on either side of the ambulance, each house with its own identical palm tree planted in its own identical green lawn. When they arrived in front of the house and the attendants withdrew Mother from the back, the Filipinos who lived next door were all standing arranged around the eldest brother's cherry '56 Chrysler. There were more than a half-dozen of them, and they all stopped talking and stared as Margaret led the attendants to the front stairs. "The yard looks really nice," Mother said. In the sunlight, she looked impossibly old and pale. Curtains were being drawn open up and down the street, and unfamiliar faces appeared at windows. A small boy stood on the sidewalk outside their house and bounced a small red-and-white-striped rubber ball. "Here we go," one of the attendants said. Otherwise everyone was very quiet and solemn, as if this were the anticipated funeral which, scheduled in blue ink, must override any minor inconvenience such as restored health. As all the assembled neighbors stared, Margaret felt as if the most secret parts of her life were being systematically violated. She wanted to return alone to the garage; she wanted to sit alone on the floor and think about nothing for a long time, there underneath the concrete sink where she had sat night after night, the bonds and assorted jewelry in her lap, the flickering spiders spinning and drifting around her in the dark. It all seemed like just a dream now, or some frivolous entertainment on TV. Then, suddenly, it was all over. The attendants deposited Mother in the bedroom and left. "Have a nice day," the talkative one said.

After Margaret brought Mother a rum and Coke, Mother held the glass in her blanketed lap and gazed around the room for a little while. Everything looked very different now. All of the stray newspapers and magazines had been cleared from the floors, and the photographs of Rita and Grandma detached from the cabinet mirror. The broken jewelry box and hand-painted porcelain bowl had been boxed up, along with a few other miscellaneous items of clothing, and stored in the basement. Almost the entire contents of Mother's closet had been removed as well, and the few remaining boxes of papers sat about lidless on chairs and countertops. "This was always our house," Mother said. She had not touched the glass in her lap. "You were raised here. We were the first owners. Even Bill and Julio, they never really lived here. It was always a space just for us." Mother's eyes were moist, her throat hoarse. "I paid for this fucking house. I paid for this fucking house when I didn't have it, when all your father ever sent me in the mail was more fucking misery every day." Mother wiped her eyes with the back of her hand. "Then I get sick for just *two minutes* . . ." Suddenly, Mother began to cry, and Margaret sat beside her on the bed, gazing out the window at dead, disregarded marigolds in the window box. Mother cried silently, taking long sudden gasps of breath every few moments. The air around Margaret seemed to grow moist; she felt Mother's damp hand grasp her arm. "I think I'm going to have Aunt Fergie exterminated," Mother said, and took a long noisy sniff. "I think I'll have it scheduled for next Christmas. We'll treat ourselves to something really special." Mother removed her hand from Margaret's arm and used it to raise her glass.

They sat together in the diminished bedroom, the memory of the room's former litter circulating vaguely in their minds like a private atmosphere. It was the atmosphere of the house's buried rooms and passages, Margaret thought, the hidden secrets of the worlds we've stored inside. Strange desultory clouds were dreamed down there, orbiting buried tarns and murky rivers. This landscape the house dreamed bubbled and transformed itself, like gestating planets, like evolution, like dreams themselves. "Tomorrow I want to take a walk in the yard," Mother said. Gazing out the window at the darkening sky, Margaret tried to remember the yard but couldn't. It seemed as if she hadn't been there for years. The grass was certainly brown and dead by now, the roses and nasturtiums. Margaret wanted to tell Mother that Aunt Fergie's voice invested the house now too. I'm sorry, she wanted to say. It's not my fault. She could hear Aunt Fergie's voice scuttering about downstairs on the cold concrete, scratching at cardboard, sniffing at stray unidentifiable droppings. The previous afternoon Aunt Fergie had taken the Greyhound to Volcano where, Margaret learned later, Uncle Ralph had died of a coronary occlusion and had lain alone and undiscovered for almost two weeks in his bright, airy country house with its white lace draperies and polished hardwood floors.

After a little while, Mother began to snore, and Margaret took the half-full glass from her lap. Now, asleep in the gray moonlight, Mother again resembled that impostor in the hospital. Her slack mouth and doubled chin, her large silver fillings and gold crowns. "I feel so changed," Mother had said that day, that first remarkable afternoon she emerged from her coma. Nurses with strange wary expressions peeked in at the door, and dazed withering patients in loose plaid robes. "My body feels so slow, so different. I don't even feel like the same person anymore."

Margaret left the door partially open, took Mother's glass down the hall and washed it in the kitchen sink. When she shut off the water, the plumbing gave a little tug deep underneath the house, and Margaret wondered when it would all stop, when it would all grow solid and permanent, like a painting on a wall. Turning, reaching, heaving. The house had its own secret dreams and dimensions now, no matter what Margaret or Mother thought about it, its own plans about where it wanted to go and who it wanted to be. Margaret grasped her cold knobby shoulders, felt her own deep eternal body changing too. Buzzing tissues and organs, membranes and arteries, hormones and blood. There was nothing you could do to change or influence some things. Everything lived its own life down there in the basements of houses and bodies.

When Margaret took her schoolbooks into the living room she didn't turn on the lights or the television. She preferred to sit alone in the glistering darkness for a few hours, just listening, and eventually fell asleep on her couch and dreamed the vast dreams of her house.

Scott Bradfield was born in California in 1955. He received his doctorate in American literature from the University of California, Irvine. He presently teaches English at the University of Connecticut at Storrs and is the author of the novel *The History of Luminous Motion*.

VINTAGE
CONTEMPORARIES

VINTAGE
CONTEMPORARIES

VINTAGE
CONTEMPORARIES